THE LAIRD'S WICKED GAME

HIGHLAND SCANDAL: BOOK TWO

JAYNE CASTEL

All characters and situations in this publication are fictitious, and any resemblance to living persons is purely coincidental.

The Laird's Wicked Game by Jayne Castel

Published by Winter Mist Press

ISBN: 978-1-991280-12-1 (paperback)

Edited by Tim Burton
Cover design by Winter Mist Press

'The Isle of Mull' Song in Chapter Two:
https://www.alansim.com/scohtml/sco176.html

Visit Jayne's website: **www.jaynecastel.com**

They could resist anything … except temptation. When a lonely laird hires a widowed lady to look after his sons, an unexpected attraction sparks between them—one that leads to a wicked, and risky, game. Dive into a delicious Highland Historical Romance set on Medieval Isle of Mull.

After Kylie Grant's feckless husband leaves her a penniless widow, she has two choices: return to her family in disgrace or find herself a job. Determined to make herself useful, she chooses the latter and takes up a position at Dounarwyse broch on the Isle of Mull.

Rae Maclean is a powerful chieftain … but an unhappy one. After a passionless marriage, he's sworn never to wed again. However, with his two sons running wild, he needs someone to keep them in check. Hiring the stern but lovely Kylie seems like a wise choice at the time, but from the moment she moves in, he fights a growing desire for her.

And when he discovers that, like him, Kylie has given up on love—but not sex—laird and employee embark on a sensual game: for the next few months, they will enjoy each other's bodies and explore all the things they've both missed out on. But once Yuletide arrives, their relationship will go back to being platonic.

They both agree to the arrangement. What could possibly go wrong?

But what begins as a game of excitement and discovery eventually takes a twist that risks breaking both their hearts.

Full of impossible choices, forbidden love, and steam, Jayne Castel's new series, HIGHLAND SCANDAL, is set on Medieval Isle of Mull and follows three unconventional sisters, and the men who put everything on the line for them.

CONTENT WARNINGS

THE LAIRD'S WICKED GAME is a steamy Historical Romance intended for mature (18+) readers. Here is a list of content that some readers may find triggering:

Attempted rape
Graphic sex
Violence and murder

*To those who have the courage to love with all their heart ... and to Tim,
who gave me his.*

1: A SOUND DECISION

Craignure,
Isle of Mull

Late July, 1318

AS LAIRD OF Dounarwyse broch, and cousin to the Maclean clan-chief, Rae liked to tell himself that he was a man who made sound decisions. He was measured and practical in nature, not impulsive and reckless like most of the men in his family.

But if that were the case, why then had he hired an attractive widow to look after his sons?

"Ye aren't brooding again, are ye?" Jack's voice yanked Rae from his thoughts, and he cut his younger brother a frown.

"No," he replied gruffly. "I'm merely considering whether to tell Lady Grant the position is no longer available."

Jack's dark-auburn brows shot up toward his hairline. "Ye can't do that … the woman is just about to step off the ferry."

Jaw clenching, Rae looked away, his gaze alighting on where the wide flat-bottomed vessel with a single sail was sliding into port.

The brothers were riding south, down the last hill before their destination. A small party of warriors on horseback followed the laird and his brother, leading two saddled garrons behind them. The small fishing port of Craignure spread out below: a collection of cottages mostly crammed along a single street that faced onto a curved white-sand beach where fishermen were hauling in their catch.

A wooden jetty thrust out from the port, where more boats bobbed with the tide, while gulls wheeled overhead, waiting for a chance to swoop and steal some of the glistening mackerel the fishermen had caught.

"Cods," Rae muttered then. "I didn't think this through."

Jack snorted. "What's to consider? Lyle and Ailean need looking after, and a widow has offered ye her services."

"She's a *lady*, Jack … it's not a 'proper' arrangement." His brother made another, rude, sound before Rae cut him a censorious look. "Esme is doing a fine job anyway."

Jack pulled a face. "Yer sons run rings around the lass, and ye know it. Just yesterday, Tara found her in tears."

Rae stiffened. Why hadn't anyone told him? In truth, he'd been distracted of late. Only one month of summer remained. After that, the fog would roll in, and Dounarwyse would likely have to fend off the Ghost Raiders again. "She should have come to me," he said stiffly. "I'd have sorted the lads out."

"Maybe," Jack replied, with a shake of his head. "But the fact remains, ye needed to hire someone who will take no nonsense … and Kylie Grant sounds right for the job."

They rode into Craignure then, slowing their coursers to a walk as they joined the throng of villagers. The port was a thriving one, although the burned-out shells of crofters' shielings on the way in, and new sod roofs on two of the cottages on the waterfront, spoke of the recent trouble. Rae's brow furrowed at the reminder of the two attacks Craignure had weathered over the past year.

However, he also noted another change since his previous visit—one that had nothing to do with reivers. A new tavern had opened up, to compete with the village's older establishment, *The Craignure Inn*, at the opposite end of the waterfront. And as they rode past it, Rae caught sight of two scantily-clad women hanging out of the upstairs windows.

"Good afternoon, lads," one of them called out, thrusting her lush bosom forward. "Looking for some entertainment?"

"Aye," her companion sang out, licking plump lips. "Two fine-looking men like ye are always welcome at *The Barnacle*."

"Thank ye for the offer, lasses … but I'm a happily wedded man," Jack replied with a roguish smile.

The women pouted.

"It's just a silver penny a-piece," the first answered, not easily put off. "For an afternoon of hot, sweaty pleasure!"

Still grinning, Jack glanced at Rae. "Hear that? Ye should come back here later and take them both for that price."

Rae flashed him a scowl in reply, and Jack laughed. "The look on yer face … I swear it could curdle milk." He paused then, his expression turning wicked. "When did ye turn into a prude, brother?"

"Shut yer mouth," Rae growled. He was on edge as it was this afternoon and wasn't taking well to Jack's ribbing. For a long while, the two brothers had been estranged, but nearly four years earlier, they'd reconciled, and Jack now captained his Guard. They usually got on well enough too, except for when Jack pushed things—as he was now.

"Cods, ye are a grumpy bastard these days," Jack said, with a rueful shake of his head. "Who knows … a tumble with those two might improve yer mood."

"Enough," Rae shot back. "And wipe that smirk off yer face before I do."

Behind him, he heard some of his men call out to the women, and shortly after, the musical sound of feminine laughter carried through the morning air.

Rae did his best to ignore it, even as an odd ache rose in his chest. His men seemed able to make light of things, to laugh and be in the moment, but he couldn't. Of late, he'd been easily irritated and often found himself entertaining bitter thoughts.

They rode on, approaching the crowd that had gathered to meet the ferry. Then, swinging down from their horses, they waited for the passengers to disembark. Rae's warriors drew up a few yards back, their gazes curious as they observed the boat.

As he stood there, the pungent smell of smoking herring from the shop a few yards away tickling his nose, Rae did his best to soften his expression.

Jack was right: when Rae's mood was sour, his face was forbidding. Even his wayward sons quietened under his withering stare. His brother had spoken true about something else as well. Lady Grant had traveled from her late husband's broch in northern Argyll to reach him; he couldn't send her away.

No, he'd offered her a position at Dounarwyse, and he'd go through with it, even if his gut told him he was making a mistake.

The ferry was emptying now—men, women, and horses making their way onto the pier.

And there, amongst them, Rae spotted her.

Actually, he saw her sister first. Makenna swept her way up the wooden dock, her cape fluttering behind her. As he recalled from when they'd met at Moy Castle on Mull's southern coast, the lass wore a surcote that had been split at the sides for ease of movement. She carried a longsword and a dirk at her hip, and a bow and quiver of arrows upon her back.

Kylie Grant followed a few steps behind her self-confident sister. The widow wore a blue-grey surcote over a butter-yellow kirtle. Her oak-colored hair was twisted in a tight braid that crowned her head; it was a prim, severe style, although Rae's belly tensed as his gaze lingered upon her.

The woman likely didn't realize it, but that hairstyle, far from making her look like a stern widow, merely highlighted the graceful sweep of her long neck.

One evening at Moy, he'd caught himself staring at that neck, his rod stiffening as he imagined sinking his teeth into her soft pale skin.

Rae checked himself now as his thoughts traveled in the same direction.

The woman had only just stepped off the ferry, and he was having lascivious, depraved thoughts.

This wouldn't do.

In truth, the offers from those lewd lasses at *The Barnacle* had tempted him more than he'd ever admit to Jack. What would it be like to give himself over to lust, to have *two* lovers in his bed?

He started to sweat at the thought.

The only woman he'd ever bedded in his thirty-four years had been his wife, and these days, frustration simmered within him like a pot about to boil over. Jack was wrong—he wasn't a prude. He'd been a painfully shy lad, and a virgin on his wedding night. However, to his disappointment, Donalda had never welcomed his touch, and had only suffered their coupling so her womb would quicken with bairn. If he'd ever tried to bite her neck, she'd have slapped him soundly.

The memory of his passionless marriage brought with it a clutch of familiar guilt, which doused any lusty thoughts, as if someone had just thrown a pail of cold water over him.

And just as well too, for Lady Grant had spied him.

Her full lips curved, and she lifted a hand, waving to him. Next to her, Makenna also saw him and grinned.

"Interesting," Jack murmured. "The widow travels with a female bodyguard, it seems."

Rae snorted before casting his brother a sidelong look. "I told ye Lady Grant's younger sister would accompany her. She serves in her father's Guard at Meggernie."

"She does?"

"Aye … and she doesn't suffer fools either, so I'd keep yer tongue leashed."

2: TOO LATE FOR REGRETS

DRAGGING IN A lungful of salty air, heavy with the scent of smoking herrings and the less savory odor of rotting fish, Kylie's belly fluttered with excitement.

A fresh start. As a childless widow, and at the mature age of thirty winters, she'd thought she wouldn't get such a chance. But then, nearly three months earlier, Rae Maclean had announced he needed someone to take his sons in hand—and Kylie had offered her services.

Following her sister along the dock, and weaving her way through the knots of crab cages and coils of heavy, tarred rope, she tried to ignore the nervousness that accompanied her anticipation. She hoped she'd made the right choice.

Goose ... it's too late for regrets now.

Kylie's offer had been bold, and her behavior had shocked even her at the time. Nonetheless, her choice had also been a practical one. Her late husband had left her destitute. Her only other option was to return to her kin in Perthshire. And although her parents wouldn't blame her for Errol's poor choices, they'd likely pity her, which was worse. And once she was back at Meggernie Castle, she'd also sink back into her old role—the one she'd happily escaped from. Her family was better than most, but she'd always felt overlooked at home—the helpful one everyone else took for granted.

This job would give her a much-needed purpose.

She caught sight of the laird then. Rae Maclean stood at the end of the pier, a sea breeze ruffling his auburn hair. Tall and strong, with broad shoulders, the chieftain of Dounarwyse was impossible to miss.

Kylie's belly fluttered once more—not from excitement or nerves this time though.

Catching her body's traitorous response, she squeezed her hands into fists, throttling it. She'd not start off on the wrong foot by allowing the attraction that had sparked within her toward Maclean at Moy Castle in early summer to distract her.

Remembering her manners, she lifted a hand and waved to him. Then, she hurried after Makenna up the gangway to where Rae and a strikingly handsome man with wavy auburn hair, who bore a strong resemblance to the laird, waited next to him. She guessed that this was Jack Maclean, Captain of the Dounarwyse Guard. During her conversations with the laird at Moy Castle, she'd learned that his brother worked for him. Both men had similar build, bone-structure, and coloring, although the captain held himself with an unconscious arrogance, his mouth curved into a playful smile. In contrast, Rae's expression was almost severe—and a deep groove had furrowed between his eyebrows and either side of his mouth.

He looked like someone with the weight of the world on his shoulders.

It made him seem older than she remembered. She still found him attractive though—distractingly so.

Makenna glanced over her shoulder, her eyes twinkling as she flashed Kylie a grin. "Ready?"

"Aye," Kylie replied, swallowing her sudden nerves and forcing a bright smile in return.

Makenna slowed her stride, allowing Kylie to draw ahead so that she reached the chieftain first. And as she did, Kylie met Rae Maclean's gaze. Despite his austere expression, his fern-green eyes were warm. And then his lips lifted at the corners in a smile.

Her belly went into a steep dive, and her step faltered. Cursing herself, she picked up her skirts, stepped over a coil of rope, and closed the gap between them. *Daft woman*, she chastised herself. *Enough of this foolishness!*

"Greetings, Maclean," she said briskly, halting a few feet distant.

The laird nodded, his expression softening a little more. "Good morning, Lady Grant … it is a pleasure to see ye again."

Ignoring the quickening of her pulse at these words, Kylie gestured to where Makenna had halted next to her. "Ye remember my sister?"

"Of course. I hope ye are well, Makenna." Maclean nodded then to the man next to him. "May I introduce my brother, Jack?"

"Welcome back to Mull," Captain Maclean drawled, flashing them both a grin.

"It's good to be back," Makenna replied with an answering smile. "Although, regretfully, I won't be able to stay long."

Kylie's chest tightened at these words. It made sense that Makenna wouldn't want to linger, yet ever since Errol's death, her younger sister had been her rock. Despite that Makenna was busy at Meggernie Castle, she'd made regular trips to Kylie in Argyll, where she'd been preparing to leave her home of a decade—the broch that her husband's creditors now owned. Makenna had put everything aside to help her, and her company had eased the ache of loneliness.

"Ye are welcome at Dounarwyse for as long as ye wish," Maclean assured Kylie's sister. His gaze then traveled behind the women, to where two burly men trudged up the pier hauling heavy leather satchels. "Have ye brought much with ye?"

"Just these bags," Kylie replied. "My clothes and personal effects … everything else belonged to my husband."

The chieftain nodded. "Well then, my men will carry them back to Dounarwyse for ye," he said, his tone turning more businesslike. He then gestured to the group that waited patiently with the horses a few yards back from the end of the busy pier. "And we have ponies to carry *ye*."

They headed north along a well-traveled road that hugged the isle's eastern coast. A stiff breeze whipped in from the Sound of Mull, ruffling their horses' manes and tugging at their clothing. The sky above was blue and full of scudding white clouds, and the air was sweet with the scent of summer.

The jangling of bridles and creak of leather accompanied the steady thud of hooves as they left Craignure behind.

A short while into the journey, Kylie found herself riding alongside the laird, while Makenna had fallen back next to Jack. The rest of their escort brought up the rear.

For a spell, they traveled without speaking. However, the silence was slightly strained. The laird of Dounarwyse didn't seem to have anything to say to her. Eventually, Kylie cleared her throat. "How have ye been, Maclean?"

"Well enough," he replied, flashing her a shy smile. "And ye?"

"Busy … the time has flown since we last saw each other."

"It certainly has."

Another awkward pause followed before Kylie spoke once more. "It's a bonnie isle, this." She immediately clamped her mouth shut, cursing herself for uttering something so inane. Nerves, as well as an uncomfortable awareness of the man who rode beside her, were making her babble.

However, her comment made his face relax a little. A moment later, Maclean smiled once more, and then—to her surprise—he started to sing.

> "The Isle of Mull is of isles the fairest,
> Of ocean's gems 'tis the first and rarest;
> Green grassy island of sparkling fountains,
> Of waving woods and high tow'ring mountains."

And then the rest of the men accompanying them, Jack Maclean included, joined in. Verse after verse, they sang, extolling the virtues of their beautiful island, the resonant boom of their voices echoing through the warm afternoon air. Kylie's skin prickled as she listened, for there was nothing more stirring than hearing someone's love for their home in song.

"That was lovely," she said when the singing ended, before she flashed him a grin. "And ye have a fine voice indeed."

She shouldn't flatter him, yet couldn't help it. The laird's deep voice had touched her.

Maclean gave an embarrassed laugh, his gaze flicking to her before it slid away. She noted the faint blush that rose to his cheekbones, and his response intrigued her. Was he not used to receiving compliments?

"Aye, well … it's easy to sing about this isle," he replied his tone gruff now, his attention firmly upon his horse's ears. "We *Muilich* have a fierce love for our home … and would lay down our lives to defend it."

Kylie didn't doubt the man. There was a strength to him that was grounded as deep as the mighty mountains of this isle. Rae Maclean came from a line of chieftains who belonged to Mull as much as every clump of heather, blade of grass, and twisted oak that grew here.

Nonetheless, he didn't appear as comfortable with her as he'd been when they'd met at Moy, or as at ease with himself either. His mood was more subdued than she recalled, his gaze often shadowed.

Catching the wayward direction of her thoughts, for she shouldn't be scrutinizing the man so, she pulled herself up. She then cleared her throat. "Have ye had any more troubles with the Ghost Raiders over the summer?"

The laird cast her another sidelong look. "No … but that's only because there isn't much fog for them to shroud themselves in this time of year." His features tightened then, a deep groove etching between his dark-auburn brows. "But rest assured, the bastards will be back as soon as the weather turns."

A chill skated down Kylie's spine at these words. The pirates, who disguised themselves in black hooded cloaks and horned sheep skull masks, had terrified the folk of Mull for nearly three years now. "I take it the clan-chief never apprehended their leader?"

Maclean shook his head, his mouth thinning. "MacBeth disappeared like a wraith. Loch is still searching for him though."

It was now her turn to frown. She didn't like the thought of that villain—or the pirates he led—still being at large. The attack at Moy Castle the past Bealtunn still haunted her sometimes. "Fortunately, I hear Dounarwyse is well defended," she murmured.

"Aye … it has a sturdy curtain wall and a position that's hard to lay siege to." Maclean's focus returned to the path that stretched out before them, his brow still furrowed. "But I must remain vigilant … a laird can never let down his guard. I will defend my broch, and my lands, until my last breath."

Kylie found herself studying his profile. His face was even more forbidding now, and she was sorry she'd brought up the Ghost Raiders.

She tore her attention from him then, focusing on her surroundings instead in an attempt to regain her equilibrium. She admired the rocky coastline and the rolling meadows that swept west to where a high sculpted ridge rose against the horizon, its deep corries highlighted in the sun. "That mountain ridge," she asked, keen to steer their conversation to a more neutral subject. "What's its name?"

"That's Dùn da Ghaoithe … *Fort of the Two Winds*," he replied. "From the top, ye can see the sea in nearly every direction."

"I'd like to see such a view," she admitted.

Maclean's mouth quirked, yet he still didn't look her way. Was she imagining it, or did he avoid her gaze? "Then we shall organize an excursion before summer's end."

"I don't want to be a burden," she answered swiftly, anxiety fluttering up. "I'm sure ye are too busy to—"

"Even a laird must take a break now and then, Lady Grant," he replied with a shake of his head. "We can take my sons with us and make a day of it … neither of them has climbed Dùn da Ghaoithe."

Another pause followed then, while Kylie chided herself for asking him about the mountain. He'd think her pushy now, despite that she'd merely been making conversation.

"Would ye tell me a little of yer sons?" she asked finally, deciding it was best to focus on the reason she was here.

Maclean gave a soft snort. All the same, his gaze remained on the path ahead. "They're both a bit wild. Ailean has reached his sixth summer and Lyle his fourth … but don't let their tender ages fool ye. The pair can be wee devils. Ailean, especially, reminds me of Jack at the same age. Willful." He grimaced then. "I haven't paid them much attention of late … and the lads often do as they please."

Her chest tightened at this admission. In truth, despite her bold offer, she'd had little to do with bairns over the years, having had none of her own. His sons were still of a tender age though. Surely, they couldn't be too much trouble?

"So, ye wish me to teach them their numbers and letters?"

"Aye, if ye are confident enough to do so?"

The challenge in his voice was clear, and her spine stiffened in response. The last thing she wanted was Maclean to think he'd hired someone incompetent. "My father hired a tutor for all his daughters," she replied firmly. "I speak French too and can teach them that tongue … if ye wish?"

The laird shot her an approving look then, and his lips tilted at the corners. "Aye, the quicker ye establish a routine, the better."

3: FIRST IMPRESSIONS

THE OUTLINE OF a stone tower house surrounded by a high curtain wall rose against the pale northern sky. Dounarwyse broch loomed before Kylie, and her pulse quickened in response. Suddenly, the nervousness that had plagued her on the ride north evaporated.

This was it. Her new beginning.

The journey from Craignure had taken longer than she'd anticipated. She and Maclean had lapsed into silence again after a while. Noon had come and gone, and it was now mid-afternoon. They'd left Dùn da Ghaoithe far behind. The land was more arable here. Perched upon a high grassy hill, with a patchwork of farmland and copses of oak and birch stretching west and north, it was clear to see why the Macleans had built a fortress in such a spot. The broch had wide views out across the Sound of Mull. No one sailing the narrow stretch of water between Mull and the mainland would pass Dounarwyse unseen.

They rode up the incline toward the castle, and the laird urged his courser into a brisk trot, drawing ahead of Kylie now.

And as the mighty walls of Dounarwyse reared above them, a noise greeted her.

A roar—men's voices, amplified as they echoed off stone. Tensing in the saddle, she peered ahead at where the chieftain had led the way into the castle across the lowered drawbridge. Rae had just passed under the stone arch, beneath the wicked iron teeth of the portcullis under the guard tower, and disappeared into the yard beyond.

She couldn't see anything as yet, although the noise now assaulted her ears.

The shouting erupted into cheering then, and chanting began.

Kylie's pulse leaped into a canter. What the devil had they just ridden into?

The garron's heavy hooves clip-clopped on cobbles as she rode into the barmkin—a wide courtyard that encircled the broch itself. However, her attention didn't linger on her surroundings. Instead, it traveled to where two men were brawling with bare knuckles, egged on by a crowd of guards.

"Cease this!" The roar of Maclean's voice made Kylie's breathing catch. The man she'd met at Moy, and the one who'd escorted her from Craignure, had been restrained—this one was not. His unleashed temper was blistering.

The raucous cheering cut off as the warriors watching the brawl whipped around to face their laird. Their expressions turned slack with surprise. His arrival had slapped the grins off their faces. The entertainment was over.

However, the two fighting men ignored him. One—tall, lean, and fair-haired, his face twisted with rage—drove a heavy punch into his opponent's belly. The burly man with receding dark hair wheezed like a winded carthorse. A moment later, the two of them were rolling on the ground.

Snarling a curse, Maclean swung down from his courser and stormed toward the pair. The onlookers hurriedly drew back to let him pass.

All the while, the two brawling men still paid him no mind. If anything, the blond warrior grew even more savage. He'd now gripped the dark-haired guard around the neck and was throttling him.

Panic caught Kylie by the throat. *Mother Mary, he means to kill him.*

Another tall figure strode into the fray. Jack Maclean had also dismounted and was making a beeline toward the brawlers. But his elder brother reached them first. The laird grabbed the fair-haired warrior by the collar of his leather vest, yanking him hard. However, the man was still fixated on choking the life out of his opponent—whose face was now going an alarming shade of purple.

Cursing again, Maclean drew back. An instant later, a heavy booted foot collided with the warrior's ribs. And this time, he paid attention. A rasped oath echoed through the barmkin as the man released his chokehold and lurched sideways.

Jack was on the fair-haired warrior then, hauling him roughly to his feet! "Explain yerself, MacDougall!"

The man snarled at his captain, only to find himself in a headlock. He paid Jack little mind though. His attention was on the man he'd been fighting. "I'll end ye, Bryce," he shouted. "I swear it!"

His opponent wasn't listening. Instead, the man rolled onto his side and vomited.

The chieftain stepped close to the man Jack still held fast. He then grabbed a handful of the warrior's long pale hair and yanked his head up so their gazes met.

Once again, Maclean's savagery cowed Kylie a little. Even from a few yards away, she marked the murderous glint in his green eyes. She'd had no idea the man possessed such a temper.

Silence fell in the barmkin. Meanwhile, Kylie's pulse started to thump in her ears.

Where have I ended up?

"Tormod MacDougall," Maclean growled. "Ye had better have an iron-clad reason for trying to throttle one of yer fellow men-at-arms."

The warrior's ice-blue eyes glittered, his handsome face taut with pain. "Macquarie cheated me."

"Liar," Bryce wheezed, pushing himself onto his knees. "Ye are a poor loser ... and off yer head to boot!"

MacDougall spat a curse, only to go rigid when the laird yanked his head back further.

"A game of knucklebones got out of hand last night, Maclean," one of the other men spoke up, his tone subdued. "Tormod's been in a vile temper ever since."

"That turd took five silver pennies that belonged to me," MacDougall growled, fury still vibrating off him. "He's a dog-humping thief!"

"I've no interest in yer petty grievances," Maclean countered. His own voice had lowered to a rasp now, his face set into forbidding lines. "But if I catch ye fighting like a mad dog in my barmkin again, I shall take a horsewhip to ye. Do ye understand?"

Kylie shifted uncomfortably upon her garron's back and cast a sidelong glance at where Makenna had pulled up her pony alongside. Her sister's expression was veiled. It was likely she'd seen many scenes like this one, for she served in the Meggernie Guard. But Kylie hadn't. The hostility that crackled like lightning and the violence shivering in the air made her skin prickle. She now felt a little queasy.

"Answer the laird, Tormod," Jack said, his tone equally dangerous. "Before I choke the words out of ye."

A nerve ticked in MacDougall's cheek, his internal battle plain to see, before he ground out, "Aye, Maclean. I understand."

"Apologies for the ugly scene." Rae flexed his hands by his sides as he approached the two ladies who'd dismounted from their garrons and were waiting for him by the stables. Anger still boiled in his gut in the aftermath, although witnessing Lady Grant's pale, tense face made it settle to a simmer. He then kicked himself.

That wasn't how he'd planned to welcome her to Dounarwyse.

"There's no need to excuse yerself," Makenna replied, with an approving nod. "Behavior like that can't be tolerated."

"No," Rae agreed. "It can't."

His attention flicked back to Lady Grant. She was frowning now. His chest constricted. Cods, she likely thought the Macleans of Dounarwyse were brutes.

He'd been struggling all day though. The journey from Craignure had been awkward, and he'd often been at a loss for what to say to the woman he'd hired.

He hadn't even been able to meet her eye when they talked—but now, she'd seen him lose control.

He really wasn't himself at the moment. Ever since the Ghost Raiders had attacked Lochbuie earlier in the year, he'd been like a cat on a hot bake-stone. Over the past months, his worry about when they'd resume their reiving had grown. The Mackinnons' siege of Dounarwyse three years earlier had left a deep scar on his broch and lands, and they'd only recently rallied. He wanted to shield those under his protection from harm yet feared he couldn't.

Aye, it was bad enough that his lands and those who farmed them were at risk from attack—but arriving home to find one of his men trying to kill another had just pushed him over the edge.

At least the situation had been resolved swiftly, for the moment. Bryce had retreated into the barracks, and Tormod had disappeared into the stables, no doubt to cool off. Meanwhile, Jack was upbraiding his men for abandoning their posts and not stepping in to stop the brawl. "Ye left the walls undefended and the gates wide open!" he roared at the shamefaced guards lined up before him. "Anyone could have ridden in here!"

"Come," Rae said tersely, gesturing to where stable hands approached. It was best the women didn't witness any more of this. Makenna might be used to it, but her sister wouldn't be. "The lads will take care of our mounts, while we go inside."
He paused then, forcing himself to meet Lady Grant's eye. Curse him, he needed to pull himself together.

Ever since greeting her by the dock in Craignure, he'd battled shyness and self-consciousness around the woman.

Every time she focused on him, he felt like a gauche lad. "Ye will be hungry and tired after yer journey. I instructed the cook to have a meal ready for ye in my solar."

"Thank ye," Lady Grant replied, her oak-brown gaze shuttered. "Although, I am keen to meet yer sons."

"Aye … and ye will." He grimaced then. "Brace yerself."

Makenna snorted. "Careful, or ye shall frighten my sister off."

Lady Grant's expression tensed at this, and she cast her sister a quelling look. However, Makenna merely winked at her.

Meanwhile, Rae's gut hardened. He wouldn't be surprised if the lady was already reconsidering her life choices.

They made their way across the barmkin then, skirting around where Jack was still upbraiding his Guard—Rae would speak to his brother about the disorder among their ranks later, in private—and headed toward the steps that led into the broch. And as they climbed, a large shaggy dog bounded out of the tower house through the open door.

Tail wagging, the Highland collie arrowed straight for the laird.

"Oof, Storm!" Rae braced himself as his dog barreled into him. "Careful, or ye'll knock me over."

Storm started to bark then, bouncing in a circle around the three of them, as if he was attempting to round them up like sheep.

"Someone didn't like being left behind," Makenna noted with a laugh.

"I remember this collie from Moy Castle," her sister added.

"Aye, Storm usually goes everywhere with me … but not today."

Embarrassment washed over him then, warmth creeping up his neck. Would Lady Grant think him foolish? Donalda had often been dismissive about his bond with his collie.

Don't be a daft bastard, he told himself, irritation spiking through him. *Why does it matter to ye so much what the lady thinks?*

Shoving aside the insecure thoughts that were starting to vex him, he moved on.

The small party entered the broch with Storm bouncing at Rae's side, tail wagging like a banner, crossing a narrow entrance hall. The heavy oaken door at the far end was open, revealing a large rectangular hall beyond, yet Rae didn't take the women into that space. Instead, they climbed the narrow stone stairs to the floor above, where the chieftain's chambers were located.

His solar, a room where he spent much of his time when he wasn't busy with other matters, was a rectangular chamber with a great, currently unlit, hearth up one end, flanked by two high-backed chairs—and a wooden table at the other. Shelving up against one wall held neatly stacked ledgers, ink pots, and quills. There was also a tidy row of books upon the shelves, his pride and joy, although most of them he'd inherited from his father.

A tapestry depicting Dounarwyse broch surrounded by a glittering sea and bucolic fields hung from the wall opposite the hearth, and a stag's head—a magnificent beast Rae's great grandfather had killed—was mounted above the fireplace.

A familiar hollow sensation settled within Rae's chest then. As much as he loved his solar, he'd spent too much time alone here, of late. Brooding. Worrying. Listening to the sounds of life and gaiety outside the open window but feeling apart from it all.

Halting inside, he watched the two women take in their surroundings. Lady Grant's gaze lingered upon his books before it traveled over to the open window.

Is she comparing my solar to her father's at Meggernie Castle?

These two were daughters of a clan-chief. It didn't usually bother him what others thought of his home—for he'd always been proud of this fortress—but now he worried they'd think his solar cramped and shabby.

Heat washed over him then, and he curled his fingers into fists at his sides. Hades, what was wrong with him? He wasn't used to lacking such confidence within the walls of his own broch.

Silently berating himself for letting such ridiculous insecurities get to him, he motioned to the table. As he'd anticipated, servants had already brought up food. Storm, who'd entered the solar with him, had calmed down and now sat at his side, gaze trained upon the meal. A pot of mutton stew, a basket of fresh oaten bread, and a wheel of cheese awaited the three of them. "Please take a seat," he said, more brusquely than intended, "and I shall pour some wine."

"This is delicious," Makenna enthused as she helped herself to more stew. "Ye are blessed with a good cook."

"We are," Maclean admitted. "Cadha is getting on in years, and her eyesight is starting to fail, but she still always manages to produce a fine meal." He picked up a ewer and glanced over at Kylie. "More wine?"

She nodded, watching as he poured the apple wine into her goblet.

In truth, she wasn't used to being waited on thus by a man—especially the laird himself. At Meggernie Castle, her mother, she, or one of her sisters poured refreshments for guests, and during her marriage, she'd always done so for Errol. The break with the traditional order of things was disquieting.

Perhaps, after his show of temper outdoors earlier, Rae Maclean wished to demonstrate that he did, indeed, have a softer side.

Taking another mouthful of stew, Kylie admitted that, indeed, it was one of the best she'd ever tasted, the gravy rich and velvety, the meat tender and full-flavored. She savored it while sipping from her goblet.

Slowly, she started to relax. The violent scene that had greeted them below had made her question her sanity in coming to live here, but the good food and wine unknotted the tension in her chest, as had the laird's hospitality. This was a pleasant place to have a meal too. The solar's single window sat opposite the table. It was open this afternoon, giving her a view out to sea. The sun glistened gold on the water, turning it molten, and in the distance, outlined against the faint shadow of the mainland, she spied a cog traveling the Sound.

"What a sight," she murmured, eager to talk of pleasant, positive things. "Ye must never tire of it."

She glanced over at Maclean then, meeting his eye.

Feeding Storm the last scrap of his bread, he favored her with a half-smile. "No … I never have."

4: NO REGRETS

THE TWO LADS rolled around on the floor, their squeals and shouts lifting to the rafters.

"Cease this!" the laird shouted, his voice slicing through their play-fighting.

Immediately, the boys obeyed, springing apart as if someone had just emptied a bucket of cold water over them. Entering the room behind Maclean, Kylie abruptly halted.

Meanwhile, a thin, pale lass with wispy blonde hair and a cowed expression stood behind the bairns. "I'm sorry, Maclean," she gasped, wringing her hands together. "I tried to get them to stop … but they wouldn't listen. They—"

"Don't fash yerself, Esme," he cut the lass off, his gaze never leaving the bairns, who now exchanged guilty looks. "The entire broch could hear ye two. It sounded as if two cats were being skinned in here."

The harshness of his tone made Kylie wince. It was as if he were addressing his warriors, rather than his sons.

The taller boy—a handsome lad with a mop of auburn hair, mischievous green eyes, and an impish face—lowered his gaze. "I was just teaching Lyle his place, Da," he muttered.

"Ye aren't the laird of me," the smaller lad retorted, wiping his sleeve at his runny nose. Lyle was of a stockier build than his brother, his hair walnut brown, his eyes blue.

"Aye, I am!" Ailean dug him hard in the side with an elbow.

Lyle let out a squawk before stomping his foot down upon his brother's, and Ailean retaliated by putting his younger brother into a headlock.

"Enough!" Maclean snarled, and the lads sprang apart once more. "Any more squabbling and I'll bash yer heads together." They both flushed red at this, but their father plowed on. "Is this how ye behave in the presence of a lady?"

Both boys looked Kylie's way then, marking her presence for the first time. In return, she nodded to them, not sure whether to smile or school her features into a stern expression. One look at these two and she could see they were trouble; it was clear they ran rings around the hapless lass, Esme, who'd been trying to marshal them.

All the same, Maclean didn't need to roar at them like a bull. She could tell he was exasperated, and likely on edge after the incident in the barmkin, but that was no excuse.

"Lady Grant will be yer duenna from now on," the laird announced then, ignorant of her misgivings.

"Duenna?" Ailean frowned, while his younger brother stared at Kylie with unabashed curiosity.

"Aye, it a bit like a companion … for older bairns," Kylie explained, relieved to be able to move on from scolding.

Back at Moy Castle, Kylie's sisters had teased Maclean that he needed an Iberian 'duenna'—a stern older lady who usually chaperoned lasses—to take his wayward sons in hand. Their mother, who hailed from Iberia, had told them of such women. It was then that Kylie had offered him her services.

"And I've given her permission to take a birch wand to yer arses if ye play up," Maclean added.

Both lads paled at this, and Esme made an anguished noise in the back of her throat, while Kylie stiffened. "I don't think that will be necessary," she assured him.

"Well, if they disrespect ye, let me know," he replied curtly, "and *I* will tan their hides."

Kylie pursed her lips. She had little experience with fathers and sons, for she'd grown up with four sisters and had no bairns of her own, but she couldn't imagine *her* father speaking to any of his children this way.

Maclean had done a fine job during supper of appearing calm and collected; however, the man was clearly still riled, and his sons had unwittingly stoked his temper.

Her breathing grew shallow then. Had she misjudged him? When they'd met at Moy, she'd found him a tolerant, even-tempered man. But she'd only just arrived, and he'd already shattered the illusion. Did she really want to work for him?

Another, awkward, silence settled in the chamber then, before Kylie realized that Lyle was gazing, wide-eyed, at her. "Ye are bonnie," he blurted out.

"Milksop," Ailean sneered at his brother.

"I am not," Lyle answered, pushing his lower lip out. Suddenly, the wee lad looked as if he might burst into tears.

Kylie's chest constricted. The bairn was only four summers old and motherless. Couldn't his brother and father be gentler with him?

"Lady Grant is to be listened to and respected," the laird replied, his tone clipped now. "She will teach ye letters and numbers … and *French*."

Both lads looked nonplussed by this announcement, although Esme's blue eyes went as round as moons.

"I don't want to study," Ailean muttered under his breath. "I want to learn to fight and ride a horse."

"I don't care what ye want." Maclean took a menacing step toward his son then, and Ailean visibly wilted under his father's censure. "By God's rood, ye and Lyle will learn some manners. By Yuletide, ye shall both read, write, and do basic sums. I also expect ye to greet and have an exchange with me in *français*."

Neither of the lads argued with this, although the tears in Lyle's eyes now glistened, and Ailean's jaw had set.

Kylie's belly clenched as her gaze flicked between the bairns and their stone-faced father.

Mother Mary, what have I done?

"Still no regrets about accepting this position?"

Kylie glanced up from where she was hanging the last of her kirtles upon a peg on the wall. In truth, she did, but pride meant she wouldn't admit such to her sister. "Not yet," she replied lightly, even as a queasiness rolled over her. *Liar.*

"Ye don't sound convinced." Makenna, who'd just finished bathing behind a screen in the corner of the chamber, now sat upon the bed they'd share. Her legs were tucked underneath her as she sat in her night-rail, combing out her wet hair.

"That's because it's too early to tell."

"How did meeting his sons go?"

"A little awkward." Hades, that was an understatement. "It will take a while for my charges to warm to me … to trust me." She paused then, swallowing a grimace. "Unfortunately, their father seems exasperated by them."

Makenna's brows raised. "Aye?"

Immediately, Kylie wished she hadn't made such an admission. Her sister's moss-green eyes were now bright with curiosity.

"He's probably still on edge after breaking up that fight earlier," she said, brushing lint off the kirtles now hanging from the wall.

"Aye, although there might be more to it than that," Makenna replied. "He was widowed not too long ago, remember? Perhaps he still grieves." She paused then, eyes narrowing slightly. "Ye two chatted a little on the way up from Craignure. Did he speak of his wife?"

Kylie stilled at this. She hadn't considered that sorrow might be the reason for Maclean's volatile temper. "No … and I wouldn't expect him to." In her experience, love matches were rare. Her parents were still blissfully content, even after nearly four decades together, but most unions amongst the high-born were contracts made to strengthen clan alliances and gain lands.

"I'm surprised he isn't looking for another wife," Makenna replied before giving a jaw-cracking yawn. "A man in his position needs one."

Kylie cut her sister a sharp look. "We shouldn't gossip about Maclean," she said, her tone clipped now. "Such matters are his business, not ours."

Makenna made a rude noise in the back of her throat. "Ye are tetchy this eve, sister … are ye sure ye want to remain at Dounarwyse?"

"Of course … I'm not going to let a grumpy laird and his rowdy sons cow me." Kylie's stomach clenched. Lord, for all her fighting talk, she *was* intimidated. Avoiding her sister's eye, she crossed to the bed then, throwing back the covers, and climbing in. The bed ropes creaked under her weight as she settled herself.

Makenna finished combing out her hair and climbed into bed too. She then lowered the cover over the lantern, plunging the chamber into darkness.

Silence fell between the sisters, and fatigue dragged at Kylie's limbs. She let out a long, deep sigh. It had been an exhausting day.

"Did Maclean give ye a tour of the broch?" Makenna asked finally, wisely changing course.

"Aye … he showed me all three levels of the tower house," Kylie answered, "and then we took a walk around the ramparts together." A little of the tension in her chest unknotted. It was a relief to talk about the things that *had* gone well today. "I also met Tara, the laird's sister-by-marriage."

Jack's flame-haired wife, and their wee daughters, didn't reside in the broch with the laird; instead, their quarters were in the largest of the guard towers.

"And did ye warm to her?"

"Very much so," Kylie replied honestly. "She appeared friendly … and it will be good to have another woman my own age to spend time with when I'm not looking after the laird's bairns."

"So, the first lesson is tomorrow?"

"Aye."

Makenna nudged her with an elbow. "Nervous?"

Kylie snorted, even as her chest tightened. Curse her, why had her sister turned the conversation back to uncomfortable matters? She'd never tutored anyone before, let alone two naughty lads. Until now, she hadn't given the lessons much thought, but after meeting Ailean and Lyle, she dreaded teaching them. "Not at all."

Makenna made an irritated sound in the back of her throat. "Ye don't have to always appear so stoic, ye know? I saw yer face when ye watched the brawl downstairs. I won't think any less of ye, if ye admit ye're scared."

"I'm not!"

Her sister huffed an exasperated sigh. "Christ's bones, ye have such a tough shell."

Heat rolled over Kylie. "And ye don't?"

"We aren't talking about *me*."

Kylie pulled a face, knowing Makenna couldn't see her in the darkness. "Maybe we *should* discuss yer situation, instead," she replied, adopting the 'elder sister' voice she knew vexed Makenna. "I asked ye two days ago if Da had settled a wedding date for ye, but ye pretended not to hear me."

Makenna muttered an oath under her breath. "I should have known ye'd bring that up again."

"And?" Kylie pressed. "Has he?"

"He's sent Bran Mackinnon a missive … inviting him to travel to Meggernie at Bealtunn," her sister finally replied, her tone cooling. "The wedding will take place then."

"That sounds like progress."

"Is it? I'm hoping Mackinnon won't answer him."

Kylie scowled. Sometimes her sister could be vexingly argumentative. "He will respond … and *ye* will become his wife."

Makenna made a stubborn noise in the back of her throat. "On the contrary, when he discovers Da has tricked him, he'll refuse to honor the agreement his father struck."

"No, he won't."

"Well, *I* don't want to wed him," Makenna shot back, her ire rising now. "I'm needed at Meggernie. Ye haven't visited in a long while … ye don't know how bad things have gotten with the Campbells of late."

Kylie heaved a sigh, even as worry curdled her belly. She'd grown up under the shadow of feuding between the two clans, yet hadn't realized the situation had worsened. Nonetheless, she wouldn't let this news distract her. "All the more reason why ye must wed Mackinnon," she said firmly. "They're a powerful clan, and Da needs allies more than ever."

"I thought ye of all people would understand how I feel," Makenna ground out. "Ye *hate* the idea of ever marrying again."

"Hate is a strong word. I never—"

"Yer mouth purses like ye just supped vinegar every time anyone suggests ye take another husband," Makenna cut her off. "Ye wish to choose yer own path, but *I'm* not allowed to."

Kylie glared at her sister in the darkness, forcing herself to swallow her anger as if it were a lump of gristle. Makenna truly tried her patience at times. Seven years separated the sisters, as did much life experience. Kylie had dedicated a decade to a bad marriage while so far Makenna had avoided any such commitment.

Kylie had earned her freedom. Her sister had not.

Her chest started to ache then as ire pulsed under her breastbone. Just once, she'd have liked to let herself go. Other people lost their temper when provoked, but Kylie didn't. Instead, she merely swallowed it, choosing to simmer in silence. And it cost her—every time.

And so, Makenna didn't receive the sharp edge of her tongue, just silent judgment.

"Ye didn't tell me MacDougall has become a problem."

Jack screwed up his face. "He hasn't been … until today."

The brothers stood together in the solar, the fire crackling behind them

"Really?" Rae flashed Jack a skeptical look and handed him a cup of wine before carrying his own to one of the high-backed chairs before the fire. Storm had sat down by the laird's chair and was now scratching. Rae nudged him with his toe, and he halted before leaning into his master.

And when Rae glanced Jack's way once more, he noted the deep groove that had etched between his eyebrows. "Aye, he's gotten a trifle mouthy of late," his brother admitted after a pause, "And I'd noted he could be hot-tempered … but I didn't think he'd try and *throttle* anyone."

Rae scowled. The scene that had greeted them upon their return home had been unacceptable, and he was still stewing over it—among other things.

What a terrible first impression Kylie Grant must have had of Dounarwyse. Certainly, his sons' feral behavior hadn't helped either.

Or yer vile temper.

Shame prickled his skin. No, he hadn't shown the best side of himself when he'd introduced Ailean and Lyle to their tutor. His blood had still been up, after dealing with MacDougall, but that wasn't any excuse. In truth, his sons had embarrassed him, and he'd lashed out.

He wouldn't be surprised if, the next time he saw her, Lady Grant announced she wished to leave.

His breathing grew shallow at the thought. *Cods.* He'd made a mess of things.

Raising his cup to his lips, he took a deep draft, welcoming the burn in the back of his throat. However, it wasn't enough. Right now, he felt like flinging the cup across his solar and watching it bounce against the wall.

It was all getting too much.

"Discipline is vital," he said finally, dragging his attention back to the conversation at hand. Storm nudged him with his nose, and he absently reached down, stroking the Highland collie's thick, wiry coat. "Dounarwyse is only as strong as the men defending it."

Jack nodded, even if faint spots of color rose upon his high cheekbones. He thought Rae was criticizing him, but he wasn't. It was *himself* he was angry with. If there was a problem with discipline within his broch, he had to deal with it.

Considering the situation, he swirled the dregs of his wine absently in his cup. Before them, the fire glowed in the hearth. It was getting late, and despite that it was still summer, the air was cool this eve. "MacDougall's a troublemaker," he said finally before taking another large swallow. "If ye catch him misbehaving again, haul him up to see me."

5: RIVALRY

AN AWKWARD SILENCE stretched out inside the chieftain's solar, one that only served to put Kylie further on edge.

From now on, she was to break her fast each morning with the laird of Dounarwyse and his sons. And since Makenna was a guest, she had joined them this morning as well.

Maclean sat at the head of the table, eating his porridge, while his sons toyed with theirs. Both the lads kept shooting their father nervous glances, but the laird ignored them. His gaze was focused on the opposite wall as he ate, his thoughts clearly elsewhere.

However, Kylie noted the laird's shadowed eyes and tense jaw. There was an air about him that was almost ... sad. Meanwhile, his collie, Storm, sat faithfully at Maclean's side, hopeful that his master might share a morsel with him.

Buttering a wedge of bannock, Kylie met her sister's eye.

Makenna raised a questioning eyebrow, making it clear that she too had marked the tension at the table.

Is every morning like this?

Shifting her attention across to where Ailean now scowled down at his half-eaten porridge as if it had done him an injustice, and then to where Lyle was stirring his as if it were a bucket of grout, spilling it over the sides of his bowl, Kylie let out a soft sigh.

"Is something amiss, Lady Grant?"

Her chin kicked right. To her consternation, she found Maclean's attention fixed upon her. Moments earlier, he'd been worlds away, but now, his gaze was sharply focused.

"No," she replied quickly—too quickly. Heat flushed over her at the lie. "I slept heavily last night and am still a little tired, that is all."

"Was the bed comfortable enough?"

"Aye … very."

Cutting his attention away, the laird picked up a cup of the watered-down ale the servants had brought up with the porridge and bannocks and took a sip. "Good … if ye need anything, let me know."

"I shall … thank ye."

He took another sip of ale. "Ye will take yer lessons with my lads in the lady's solar."

Kylie nodded, even as a sickly sensation washed over her. She had no idea how she was going to approach the laird's wayward sons.

"Ye will find wooden boards and sticks of charcoal waiting for ye on the table," he went on, oblivious to her dread. "As well as an abacus."

"Thank ye."

Another ponderous silence settled in the solar, and Kylie was aware then of two sets of eyes observing her from across the table. Lyle and Ailean were both watching her boldly. She'd need her wits about her this morning.

"Maclean," Makenna spoke up, after swallowing a mouthful of bannock. She then broke off a bit of the large griddle scone and fed it to Storm. The dog wolfed it down in an instant. "It's been too long since I swung a sword. Might I train with the Dounarwyse Guard this morning?"

That got the laird's attention. Likewise, his sons' gazes snapped to Makenna. The lads now stared at her as if she'd just turned into a toad before their eyes.

Kylie clenched her jaw and silently cursed her sister.

She should have known Makenna would make such a request. She lived to fight and had complained on the trip here that she was afraid of getting rusty. Her sister's 'mannish ways' were a bone of contention between them. With her wedding imminent, Kylie felt it was time for Makenna to put down her blades, yet she stubbornly refused.

Kylie cleared her throat, drawing both her sister's and the laird's attention. "This isn't Meggernie, Makenna," she murmured, censure creeping into her voice. "Jack Maclean and his men might not *like* having ye training with them."

This comment made the chieftain's lips tug into a wry half-smile. "On the contrary, my brother appreciates women with a spine." He picked up his cup of ale then and drained it. "Nonetheless, I suggest ye ask his permission first."

Makenna smiled back at him. "Then, I shall."

"Ye fight with the men?" Ailean asked, his young voice high-pitched with incredulity.

"Aye, lad," Makenna replied, her moss-green eyes warm. "Back at Meggernie Castle, I proudly serve in my father's Guard."

"Do ye have a sword?" Lyle asked.

"Aye … a longsword, as well as a dirk and a bow."

"Does yer sword have a name?" The wee lad asked, his tone hushed with awe.

Makenna favored him with a wink. "Of course … it's called 'Arsebiter'."

Both boys burst out into peals of laughter at this, while their father snorted.

"Really?" Amusement laced Rae Maclean's voice. "*That's* its name?"

Makenna nodded, grinning. "And it has pierced many a Campbell hide, I can tell ye."

"Da's broadsword is named 'Honorsteel,'" Ailean announced, his chest puffing out.

"Aye … that's a fine name," Makenna admitted. "Isn't that similar to the Maclean motto?"

"Virtue Mine Honor," Lyle shouted, his apple cheeks flushing.

The enthusiasm of both lads was endearing, yet Kylie wasn't entertained by this scene. Instead, trepidation had now lodged in her gut like a lump of iron. Hades, how would she ever live up to the impression her sister had just made on Maclean's sons?

"Is that my name?"

"Aye … A … I … L … E … A … N," Kylie replied, handing the boy a nub of charcoal. "Now, I want ye to copy it." A wooden board, made of sanded pine, sat between them.

The lad pulled a mutinous face and put the charcoal down. "This is stupid." Beside him, Lyle sniggered.

The two brothers exchanged glances, and Kylie's heart started to thump against the cage of her ribs.

Aye, they'd already decided they wouldn't cooperate. Kylie had spoken to Esme before the lesson, and the maid had regaled her with tales about what terrors the laird's sons were; how they never listened to her and often became rebellious the moment she asked something of them. The relief in the lass's eyes—that they were someone else's problem now—had been palpable. Esme usually worked as the broch's chambermaid and seemed to prefer emptying privies and cleaning out hearths to marshaling the laird's rumbunctious sons.

Kylie didn't blame her. Right now, she too would rather be scrubbing floors than playing cat and mouse with these two. "Why is it stupid?" she asked finally, silently uttering a prayer to the Virgin Mary for patience.

"I don't need to write my name," Ailean replied, his jaw tightening. "I only need to learn how to wield a sword and fight."

"And ride a horse," his brother piped up, eyes shining as his elder brother led the charge.

"Aye," Ailean replied, his manner smug now. "Only monks need to learn their letters."

"Really?"

"Aye."

Kylie drew in a deep breath, silently counting to ten, before an idea came to her. "Yer father writes."

Ailean shrugged. "I don't care."

"Don't ye want to be like him?"

The lad's expression shadowed then, and Kylie swallowed a smile. She had him there. Rae Maclean might be growly with his sons, but they both clearly adored him.

"Well, if ye want to grow up to be as strong and *wise* as yer Da, ye will need to learn yer letters and numbers," she replied triumphantly. She shifted her attention to his brother then. "Do *ye* wish to be like the laird, Lyle?"

The cherub-faced lad's blue eyes glinted. "Aye."

"Well … since yer brother isn't interested in following yer Da's lead, do ye wish to learn how to spell yer name?"

Lyle nodded eagerly.

Another jolt of victory thrilled through Kylie. She'd hit the mark in two areas this morning. The first was the love the lads had for their father, and the second was the competitiveness between them. She'd had little experience with bairns yet followed her instincts now. If she had to use the rivalry between the two boys as a weapon, she would.

"Very well, shall we—"

"Ye asked me first," Ailean burst out, pink spots of indignation rising to his cheeks.

"I did," she replied. "But ye weren't interested, so—"

"I am!"

Kylie inclined her head, careful to keep her expression inscrutable. She had the wee imp. She then gestured to the nub of charcoal Ailean had set down earlier. "Go on then, let's see ye write yer name."

Standing by the window of the lady's solar, enjoying the warm breeze that feathered across her face, Kylie looked on as her charges copied out the alphabet.

Neither lad looked overly happy about the chore. However, their faces were now screwed up in concentration, their fingers clenching around the sticks of charcoal as they wrote. A smile tugged at the edges of her mouth as she watched them. Maybe she could handle these two, after all. After a slow start, the morning had flown, and the rumbling of Kylie's belly warned her that the noon meal was approaching.

Frankly, despite that there was a glimmer of hope now, she was looking forward to the morning's lessons ending. She felt wrung out. Both lads had questioned every instruction she gave, but she'd held fast. She couldn't let them think that their 'duenna' was going to burst into tears and run from the room if they played up.

The rough shouts of men drew her attention then, and she glanced away from her charges, out the window, her gaze traveling down to the barmkin. Captain Maclean was taking his men through drills.

Kylie stiffened.

Makenna was amongst them.

Standing tall—despite that she was actually the shortest of all five MacGregor sisters—the morning sun catching the red highlights in her long braided hair, her sister held a bound blade in her right hand while she listened to Jack's instructions.

Unlike the other warriors, who were all dressed in fighting leathers, Makenna cut an incongruous sight in her finely made kirtle, with its long skirt slit at the sides.

Her only other concession to practicality was that she wasn't wearing a restrictive surcote this morning; instead, she'd donned a tight-fitting leather vest, laced at the front, and wore leather bracers to protect her wrists and forearms.

And, unsurprisingly, most of the guards were gaping at her.

As Kylie looked on, her sister leaped forward and began sparring with an opponent. The rhythmic thud of the bound blades colliding echoed through the yard.

"God's bones." The oath burst out of Kylie before she could stop it. "Why does she need to draw such attention to herself?" The sisters were so different. Whereas Kylie went through life trying to fit in, Makenna went out of her way to stand out. And it didn't matter how many times Kylie viewed her behavior with a jaundiced eye, or murmured a reproach, Makenna did what she liked without a thought to how it might impact others.

Selfish.

Resentment arrowed through her then. Soon, Makenna would depart Dounarwyse, but Kylie would remain; it was *she* who would have to put up with the whispers and smirks.

"What is it?" Ailean cast aside his charcoal nub and leaped up. Lyle swiftly followed, his expression eager.

"Nothing," Kylie muttered, cursing herself for voicing her thoughts aloud. "Return to yer work."

However, the lads both knew it wasn't 'nothing', and so they rushed to the window, squeezing in next to her to look down upon the training men.

And it wasn't long before they realized who was currently sparring.

"Lady Makenna *can* fight!" Lyle exclaimed as he leaned forward, his fingers digging into stone. "Look!"

6: THE STERN VOICE OF REASON

MAKENNA KICKED the legs out from under her opponent, sending him crashing to the ground.

Around her, the guards cheered.

Breathing hard, she straightened up, her gaze flicking to where Captain Maclean stood a few yards away. "Where did ye learn that trick, Lady Makenna?" he asked, folding his arms across his chest.

Makenna flashed him a grin. "Alec Rankin taught me."

His eyebrows shot up to his hairline. "The pirate?"

"None other." Still grinning, she glanced around her then, raising her bound blade in a challenge.

She knew Kylie disapproved of her choices—of the fact she'd learned to fight like a man and now served in their father's Guard—but she didn't care.

Her sister had never tasted the exhilaration that came from winning a fight, and from seeing respect ignite in a man's eyes. "Who's next?"

A heartbeat passed, and then a tall, lean warrior with long flaxen hair pushed himself off the wall where he'd been lounging. And as she looked on, he approached her with an arrogant, loose-limbed stride. "My turn."

Makenna held onto her smile, even as tension rippled through her.

Not him.

She'd been enjoying sparring with the Guard. After a fortnight on the road, accompanying her sister to Mull, restlessness boiled within her. This morning was a chance to flex her muscles and keep her skills honed. And she got to show off a little—something she found hard to resist.

But MacDougall made her uneasy.

She'd watched the ugly scene the day before, had marked that he might well have killed the man he'd been choking if the laird hadn't intervened. She'd also caught him staring at her earlier that morning when she'd taken a walk around the walls. His stare had been carnal, and she hadn't liked it.

And the glint in his eye now made wariness flutter up once more.

Nonetheless, she wasn't a lass who backed down from a fight. And so, she nodded brusquely to MacDougall before stepping back and lifting her sword, readying herself to spar once more.

"Go easy on her, Tormod," the captain murmured, and Makenna clenched her jaw.

Go easy on her? Hadn't she just proved she was a worthy opponent? It looked as if she was going to have to prove herself—again.

They circled each other briefly before MacDougall leaped forward, making the first strike. Makenna was ready for him though, their bound blades thudding as she parried his blow and danced back.

The blond warrior flashed her a smile that revealed strong white teeth. "Ye're fast."

Makenna cocked her head, even as she flexed her fingers on the grip of her blade. "Faster than ye," she taunted.

Something moved in those ice-blue eyes, and once again, nervousness slithered through her belly. *Don't goad this one.*

She'd trained and fought alongside many men since joining her father's Guard and had developed an instinct for sizing up her opponents. There were those men who were all brag and bluster, while others said little yet let their blade do the talking. But MacDougall was different from any man she'd fought—and as their swords met once more, she caught the glint in those unnervingly cold eyes.

Makenna usually enjoyed adding a little flair to fights, giving the onlookers a spectacle, but she cast the temptation aside now. Instead, her gaze never left MacDougall. The man fought with fluid grace, and she sensed his leashed power.

He impressed her. The bastard was better than her. Better than anyone she'd ever fought—even Alec Rankin. The former pirate captain had taught her several 'tricks' earlier in the year, and she used them now. She tried to kick his feet out from under him, to confuse him, and to lure him into making a mistake. Unfortunately, MacDougall anticipated them all.

All the same, she got in a few hits, one across the ribs and another on his hip, before he lunged at her, slicing under Makenna's guard.

The next thing she knew, she was on her back, staring up at his gloating face, the point of his sword at her throat.

"Well fought," he said, with a smirk that made her blood heat. "For a *woman*."

The training had ended for the morning, and the aroma of baking fowl pie that drifted out of the nearby bakehouse made it clear the noon meal wasn't far off.

Makenna was sweaty from sparring with half a dozen of the Guard, her muscles pleasantly sore, as she unwrapped the cloth from her longsword. It was a warm morning, and she stood in the shadow of the granary. It had been a good session, although she'd been relieved that her other opponents had been more straightforward than MacDougall. She'd avoided looking his way ever since their fight.

All the same, she'd felt his gaze upon her.

Sheathing her sword, she glanced around, realizing that she was now alone in the barmkin. The others had already gone inside. She would quickly return to her bedchamber and splash some water on her heated face before joining everyone for the noon meal.

She was about to step away from the granary wall when a male voice, laced with amusement, intruded. "A feisty one, aren't ye?"

Stiffening, Makenna glanced left at where MacDougall had just stepped out of the armory. He moved toward her now, with that same stalking gait that had unnerved her earlier. And, just like before, she held her ground.

The man drew close, nearer than was appropriate, although she refused to give him the satisfaction of seeing her step away. He was tall and she short—so she was forced to lift her chin to hold his eye. "Did ye want something?" she asked coolly.

"Only to congratulate ye on yer skill with a blade."

Makenna's gaze narrowed. "Ye bested *me*, remember?"

"Aye ... but ye fight better than most men." Despite herself, warmth ignited in her chest at this compliment, before he added, "Not better than me though."

Makenna snorted. "Sure of yerself, aren't ye?"

"Aye." His gaze held hers. "I'd be happy to show ye some of my techniques ... if ye wish?"

She stilled.

Was he offering to train her, as Rankin had earlier in the year?

He isn't Rankin though, common sense whispered to her. *Alec won yer sister's heart and proved himself worthy of trust. This man hasn't proved anything to ye ... except his arrogance.*

Her instinct screamed at her not to be drawn in. But there was a part of her that was tempted. She held her own amongst her father's Guard, and the other warriors minded her. But she was aware that as a woman, she had to train harder—had to be better—than any of them. She was constantly looking for an edge that would make her invincible, especially against the hated Campbells, and as much as she loathed to admit it, this warrior had one.

She could learn from him. As long as she exercised caution, what could go wrong?

"Very well," she said after a lengthy pause, shoving aside the warning that still whispered to her. "I'd appreciate that."

"Good." He flashed Makenna a wide smile before winking at her. "Our first lesson is this evening. Meet me on the east terrace after supper."

Pouring himself some more ale, Rae shifted his gaze down the chieftain's table—past his kin—to where his two guests sat.

Of course, Lady Grant wasn't his guest but his sons' tutor. Nonetheless, since she'd only been here a day, he hadn't yet gotten used to seeing the woman at every mealtime. She was wearing a demure golden-brown kirtle and had coiled her hair into two buns, pinned neatly above each ear. It was another prim style, yet he found himself wondering what it would be like to unpin them, to let her silky hair slide through his fingers. How long was her hair anyway? How would it feel, trailing across his naked chest and belly?

Rae blinked, jerking himself out of a reverie that had caused his rod to turn to wood inside his braies. Where did these lecherous thoughts come from? He was sitting in his hall, surrounded by his kin and retainers. He couldn't let himself start fantasizing about the comely widow he'd just hired. It was unseemly—and embarrassing. Maybe Jack had been right, maybe he did need to visit a brothel. It might improve his mood, at least.

The two sisters sat at the opposite end of the table and were fortunately unaware of his turmoil. Instead, they both seemed to be enjoying the fowl pie that Cadha and her assistants had prepared, while the rumble of conversation in the hall rose and fell around them.

"How did yer first day of lessons go, Lyle?" A woman's voice carried across the table. Rae tore his attention from Lady Grant to where his sister-by-marriage, Tara, was smiling at his youngest son across the table. Her youngest, Arabella, perched on her mother's knee—the bairn's chubby fingers clutching at the food upon the trencher before them. "What did ye learn?"

"Lady Grant taught me to write my name," the lad replied, his cheeks bulging with pie.

Beside Lyle, Ailean sniggered.

"Did ye learn any numbers, Ailean?" Jack asked. The elder of his daughters, Grace, who was now entering her third summer, perched on his knee.

Ailean sobered. "Aye."

"How old are ye then?"

"Six summers," he replied proudly.

"And can ye tell me how many months there are in a year?" Jack pressed.

The lad didn't hesitate before replying, "Twelve."

His son's bumptiousness made Rae frown. "And have ye learned any French words?" he asked pointedly.

"Not yet," Lady Grant spoke up from the far end of the table. "That's for tomorrow."

Rae noted that both his lads now wore unenthusiastic expressions.

"It's too sunny to be indoors," Ailean whined, while Lyle adopted a sulky look.

"Aye." Jack glanced Rae's way then. "It's perfect weather for a *riding* lesson."

Both lads perked up at this before following their uncle's gaze, their faces expectant.

"I'm busy," he growled, and their faces fell.

"Surely, ye can spare an afternoon to give the lads a lesson, Rae?" Tara teased gently, her silvery eyes glinting. "They've been wanting one for months now."

Rae took a gulp of ale, even as irritation quickened inside him. He hadn't lied earlier; he had a mountain of work awaiting him in his solar. Tax collection was coming up, and he wanted to make sure he had the correct levies ready for when his clan-chief's bailiff came calling. He wished to get administrative matters out of the way so he could focus on other projects. Currently, he'd hired masons to construct a wall around Dounarwyse village, shielding it from the coast—and from attack. He wished to venture out and view their progress. "It'll have to wait."

"It's just one afternoon," Jack added. "I'll saddle the quietest garron for Ailean."

"Let me get the taxes sorted," Rae muttered, stabbing his eating knife into his pie.

"So, the end of the week?" Jack pushed, winking in the boys' direction.

Rae swallowed a curse. Cods. His brother was like a dog with a bone. He could see he wasn't going to get out of this. "Very well," he ground out. "Friday afternoon."

The lads squealed at this, all smiles now—and Rae's gut tightened, a familiar sense of guilt settling in. He really was a surly bastard. He'd also spent little time with Ailean and Lyle since Donalda's death. They wished for nothing more than to trail after him like puppies, learning at his knee. He remembered how he'd adored his own father, and how much time Baird Maclean had spent preparing his firstborn to take his place.

In truth, he'd lavished attention on both his sons. Jack too had always been made to feel cherished. However, their father's murder, at the hands of Kendric Mackinnon, shattered their lives. It had turned Jack bitter and thrust Rae into lairdship before he was ready.

Aye, he knew he should give his sons the attention they craved, yet he found himself resisting it.

"Did the lads behave themselves today?" he asked Lady Grant then, forcing himself to squarely meet her eye.

"Aye," she replied, favoring him with a polite smile.

Rae frowned. Was she merely telling him what he wanted to hear? He knew Ailean and Lyle could be difficult—and Esme had suffered much under their tyranny before he learned about it. He didn't want her to fall into the same trap. He'd keep a closer on his sons over the coming days.

"We saw Lady Makenna fight," Ailean announced then, waving around his eating knife. "We watched from the solar window."

Beside her sister, Makenna's mouth curved. "Did ye now?"

"When ye should have been studying?" Rae grumbled.

"It was just for a short while," their tutor assured him, a blush rising to her cheeks.

"Aye," Lyle chimed in. "If a lass can fight, why can't we?"

"Ye will learn soon enough," Jack said, grinning.

"Don't encourage them," Rae snapped. Jack didn't make things easy sometimes. He wouldn't have been surprised if his sons preferred their exuberant uncle to their dour father. Jack always had an easy smile and a teasing comment at the ready, and the boys liked his irreverence. It was up to Rae to be the unpopular one.

"*When*, Da?" Ailean asked, leaning toward him, green eyes bright. "When can I practice swordplay?"

"When ye prove to me ye know yer letters and numbers competently," Rae replied with a scowl. "And not before."

7: THE LAIRD'S REPRIMAND

"THIS IS DAFT." The mutinous look on Ailean's face made Kylie's belly sink. "I don't want to learn French."

Holding his gaze firm, Kylie tried to fight the panic welling in her chest. Curse it. After their initial lesson, she'd thought she was making progress, but her charges had lulled her into a false sense of security. It was now Friday morning, and she was a hair's breadth from losing control of them. "Yer father has instructed me to teach ye, Ailean."

"I don't care."

Heart racing now, she switched her focus to Lyle. "Repeat after me: *Je m'appelle Lyle.*"

The wee lad burst into fits of giggles. "Jem pepple Lyle," he sang out. "Jem pepple Lyle."

This caused his elder brother to hoot as well.

"Lads!" she said, her tone sharp now. "Stop it!"

"Jem pepple! Jem pepple!" the bairns chanted together, ignoring her.

At that moment, the door to the lady's solar flew open—with such force that it bounced against the stone wall.

The laird of Dounarwyse filled the doorway.

Kylie's heart kicked like a mule against her ribs, even as hot shame washed over her. Had he been listening in on the other side of the door?

"Do my sons have the manners of goats?" he roared. "How dare ye answer Lady Grant thus!"

High spots of color had risen to his cheeks, and his eyes had gone a dark, murderous green. Both his sons visibly wilted in the face of his anger.

Kylie rose swiftly to her feet, her hands coming up to placate him. "All is well, Maclean, I—"

"I was on the way to my solar and heard a ruckus," he cut her off before turning his wrath upon his sons once more. "Yer mother and I didn't bring ye up to mock others!"

"Sorry, Da," Ailean said weakly. Next to him, Lyle had gone pale and had started to tremble.

"I made it clear ye shall both study French," the laird replied, his voice still harsh. "And I told ye to heed Lady Grant in all things."

"I was just playing," Lyle squeaked, his lip quivering now.

"No, ye were jesting at another's expense … and as punishment, yer brother won't be having a riding lesson this afternoon."

Both boys jolted at this. "Ye promised!" Ailean burst out, his disappointment too great to be borne.

Despite that she wasn't feeling charitable toward either lad at present, Kylie's chest constricted.

She knew how much Ailean had been looking forward to his first proper riding lesson with his father. Both lads had talked of nothing else over the past days.

"I promised *nothing*!" The laird moved farther into the lady's solar, looming over the bairns now. They both sank down in their seats, wilting under the force of his wrath. Lyle made a choking sound then, tears spilling from his blue eyes and trickling down his cheeks. Meanwhile, his elder brother trembled, his face taut with disappointment and anger he was trying hard to leash. "And unless ye learn some manners, ye'll be spending yer afternoons mucking out the stables instead of doing as ye please."

Maclean glanced Kylie's way then, his gaze spearing hers. "If they act up again, come straight to me," he ordered roughly.

Swallowing, she nodded—even as humiliation scalded her. Hades take him, the man was heavy-handed. How did he expect his sons to concentrate on their French lesson now? Teaching the lads was hard enough as it was without his interference.

It appeared such matters didn't concern the laird at all, for a moment later, he turned on his heel and stormed out of the lady's solar, leaving a brittle silence behind him.

Alone with the lads, Kylie didn't speak for a while. Lowering herself back down onto the bench seat, she watched her charges try to compose themselves.

Lyle was sniffing while his elder brother was scrubbing at his cheeks. Their faces were both red, and she imagined her cheeks also burned like embers. The laird's reprimand had scalded them all. In the aftermath, it was tempting to crawl into a corner and hide.

Lord, how she wanted to. In truth, she was tempted to rush out of this solar, head straight up to her bedchamber, and start packing.

But she wouldn't. Not yet, anyway.

Clearing her throat, Kylie stood up once more. "I think we'll finish a little early this morning," she announced. "Go and play for a bit before the noon meal while I tidy up here."

Both lads regarded her warily, as if expecting a rebuke to be added to her words. But none arrived.

They departed from the lady's solar as Kylie deftly packed away the boards and charcoal. She then dusted off her hands—noting that they were shaking slightly.

But she wasn't just humiliated. She was vexed.

Her belly started to ache then. Was this how her new start was to be? She'd spent her marriage putting up with ill-treatment. Would she let this man do the same? She'd only been at Dounarwyse a little over a week, and already she was turning into a mouse.

Deal with this now, she told herself sternly, even as her heart quailed. *Ye can't let Maclean get away with that. If he shames ye like that again, life here will become impossible.*

Nausea rolled over her at the thought of confronting him. She *hated* confrontation. But if she didn't do this now, she never would.

Gathering her courage, she left the chamber and crossed the landing. However, standing before the door to Maclean's solar, her nerve nearly failed.

What if he lost his temper again? What if he dismissed her?

Maybe I should save him the trouble and resign. Indeed, things weren't working out as she'd hoped. Ailean and Lyle didn't respect her—and now she wouldn't be surprised if they thought she was weak. Kylie's pulse quickened. Perhaps she was. She'd certainly overestimated her ability to work as a tutor.

But then she reminded herself that she had no alternative plan for what she'd do if she left Dounarwyse, other than returning to Meggernie.

Mastering herself, she clenched her jaw. *Ye aren't going anywhere! Don't be such a coward!* Then, before she changed her mind, she raised her fist and knocked briskly.

A gruff voice answered, "Aye?"

"Maclean … it's Lady Grant … can I come in?"

A pause followed. "Aye."

Kylie pushed open the door and stepped inside. The laird was seated at the table to her right, a large ledger open before him. Bright sunlight streamed through the open window, bringing out the red in his thick hair and gilding his proud bone structure. He'd rolled up the sleeves of his lèine, and his strong forearms were dusted with auburn hair.

Storm, who'd been asleep by the window, roused himself. Long hairy tail wagging, the collie rushed across the solar, greeting Kylie with a cold, wet nose. Distracted, she ruffled his ears before turning her attention back to the laird.

Putting aside the quill he'd been using, Rae straightened up. "Are my sons still giving ye trouble, Lady Grant?"

"No," she replied, her tone clipped. "I dismissed them from their lessons early."

His brow furrowed. "Why did ye do that?"

"Because, after having ye roar at us, I'd had enough." Her answer, delivered with force, carried across the solar.

He jolted at the fierceness of her reply, his lips parting slightly. "Excuse me?"

Kylie drew herself up, even as her pulse went wild. She couldn't believe she was saying such things. She wasn't impulsive like Mackenna. In all her years wedded to Errol, she'd leashed her temper. Even when she'd learned of his dalliances with local lasses, she'd bitten her tongue. But today, she wouldn't. "If I need yer assistance with Ailean and Lyle, I shall ask for it," she plowed on, her voice rising now. "But ye must *never* burst in on us like that again."

Rae stared back at her. His frown then deepened. "They were misbehaving," he said roughly. "I couldn't let it continue."

"And I was about to deal with the situation," she shot back, even as heat surged up her spine. That was a lie. She'd lost control of the lesson, but she wasn't about to admit such. "But ye undermined me."

Rae shut his mouth, pressing his lips firmly together. He then pushed back his chair and rose to his feet. "That wasn't my intention."

"Maybe not, but the result was the same." Her heart was pounding now, a lifetime of frustration on the verge of gushing forth. The force of it made her tremble.

To her consternation, he moved then, skirting the edge of the table and approaching her. She wished he wouldn't. It was easier to speak her mind when they were standing far apart. His proximity flustered her, even though he'd halted so that over three feet of space lay between them.

Storm, thinking there was a game afoot, gave an excited bark and started to bound in a circle around them, forcing his master to take a step closer still.

"Ye didn't tell me the lads were playing up," Maclean said, his voice surly now.

"That's because I knew ye'd snarl at them." Lord, she wished her voice didn't sound so raw.

"Aye, and they clearly needed—"

"Respect isn't demanded," she cut him off, clenching her hands at her sides. "It's *earned*. Yer sons need time to get used to me. Having ye barge in and tear into them doesn't help things at all."

His brows knitted together at this, even as Storm, frustrated that they weren't playing his game, nudged the laird hard in the back of the knees. Cursing his dog, the laird lurched forward, closing the gap between him and Kylie.

Suddenly, he was looming over her, and she became aware of the heat of his body. The man was a furnace. He smelt delicious too—of cedar and leather. Unbidden, her nostrils flared before panic erupted.

Focus!

"I thought ye were made of sterner stuff, Lady Grant," he rumbled, a challenge in his voice now. He grabbed Storm by the scruff then, stilling his antics. "The lads were running rings around ye, as they did Esme."

Kylie flushed hot. Her pulse now thumped in her ears. How dare he? Drawing herself up and lifting her chin to eyeball him, she stepped in as well. They were now standing so close there was barely a handspan between them, but the fury in her blood pushed aside all embarrassment. She forgot to be afraid of confrontation now. For the first time in her life, she'd truly stand up to a man. "They were testing their limits," she growled. "That's not the same thing."

"Really? Is that what ye call it?" There was scorn in his voice now. "It was bad behavior … and it won't be tolerated."

Their gazes held then, and something inside Kylie gave way. Enough. She couldn't take this anymore. Suddenly, every frustration, every humiliation she'd suffered at Errol's hands rushed in. The wound had barely scabbed over, but Maclean had just ripped it off. She wouldn't go on letting men make her feel small. She couldn't. Even if it cost Kylie her job, she'd put an end to this. "Overbearing bastard," she snarled, poking a finger into the hard wall of his chest. "Is that how ye get what ye want … ye plow over everyone … crush their spirits?"

The laird's auburn brows crashed together once more. "Excuse me?" His voice had chilled.

"Ye heard me. What's the point of hiring someone to tutor yer sons, if ye eavesdrop outside doors and judge all of us harshly? Ye may as well tutor them yerself!"

A flush rose upon his cheekbones, and his fern-green eyes darkened. She'd vexed him, but she didn't care. A strange power thrilled through her veins.

"I was trying to help ye," he replied, his words coming out jerkily now. "But I didn't expect to receive such ingratitude."

"Why would I thank ye for shaming me?" She poked him in the chest again, just to make her point, although this time, he surprised her by catching her hand and holding it fast.

Kylie's breathing hitched. His fingers were warm and strong, and his touch caused a frisson of awareness to ripple up her wrist to her elbow. She blinked then. What was she doing, standing so close to the laird, raging at him, and stabbing her finger into his sternum? Had she utterly lost her wits?

Mortification rushed over Kylie, her flare of courage waning.

"Ye should unleash that adder's tongue on my sons," he bit out, his gaze smoldering now. "Ye'd have them cowering under the table in no time."

She made a choking sound, her heart slamming against her breastbone as her temper flared once more. She couldn't let him get away with that. She had to cling to her courage.

Her lips parted, but she never got the chance to answer him—for Maclean let go of his dog and stepped into her. Then, he lowered his head and covered her mouth with his.

The kiss was hard, fierce, and it stole her breath away.

In an instant, the anger that had flared between them—as volatile as a flame to bone-dry tinder—changed into something else entirely. Something that had smoldered between them ever since they'd met months earlier at Moy Castle.

A heartbeat passed, and then Kylie clutched at his lèine, fisting the material and pulling him hard against her as she kissed him back, wildly.

Their lips parted, their tongues tangling, mouths devouring, and teeth grazing. Heaven help her, he tasted good, and the rasp of his shaven chin against her cheek made hunger quiver like a drawn bowstring inside her.

She'd never been kissed like this, and nor had she ever responded to anyone in this way either.

His embrace was heady, like autumn cider, only even more delicious. And when he sucked her lower lip into his mouth, before giving it a gentle nip, the flesh between her thighs started to ache.

A low groan escaped her, tearing up from the bottom of her throat.

The noise shattered the moment. Chest rising and falling sharply, Maclean drew back, his hands dropping away from where they'd been gripping her shoulders. Likewise, Kylie let go of his lèine. They stepped away from each other then, the ragged sound of their breathing filling the solar.

Kylie's legs started to tremble, mortification stealing over her.

Their gazes met and held, and the startled look in the laird's eyes told her that he was just as shocked by what had happened as she was. One moment, they'd been arguing, the next kissing.

She raised a shaking hand to her bee-stung lips. *Christ's blood, what have ye done?*

Maclean swallowed. "I'm sorry," he said huskily. "I don't know what came over me."

She stared back at him, rendered mute by embarrassment. Her cheeks burned like twin suns as she began to back toward the door.

His green eyes guttered. "Kylie … please, don't go."

She shook her head. He'd never addressed her so familiarly before. The intimacy of it made her already racing pulse hammer against her breastbone. She was suddenly desperate to get away. If she remained, she might do something utterly daft, like throw herself into his arms. His kisses still burned upon her mouth, and she ached for more.

Turning then, she darted for the door, threw it open, rushed out of the solar, and fled up the stairs toward the sanctuary of her bedchamber.

Rae watched Kylie hurry from the solar, the door thudding shut behind her.

For a few moments, he merely stood there, staring at where she'd disappeared. And then, rousing himself, he growled the filthiest curse he knew.

Since when did he behave like a rank knave?

The woman had been angry and upset, for pity's sake, and all he could think about was sticking his tongue down her throat. And the Lord smite him, he'd done it. He'd kissed her lewdly, boldly.

Storm gave a low whine then, and he cut the collie a sidelong look. His dog was behaving himself now and had sat down a few feet away. Storm viewed him reproachfully, as if he'd ruined his fun.

Cursing once more, Rae dragged a hand down his face and crossed to the open window, welcoming the breeze on his heated face. He'd overstepped. Grossly.

If he'd ever handled Donalda like that, she'd have been incensed. Indeed, after the first few years of their marriage, he'd ceased embracing his wife, for she didn't seem to enjoy it. She suffered their coupling as a duty and didn't welcome the intimacy of kissing.

But Kylie hadn't raged at him.

She'd fled the room, but she'd responded to his kiss with a hunger that had turned him dizzy with lust. And he'd heard the groan of pleasure that had escaped her—the moan that had brought him to his senses.

Clenching his hands at his sides, Rae squeezed his eyes shut. *She isn't 'Kylie' to ye*, he reminded himself grimly. *She's 'Lady Grant', a decent widow whom ye have just disrespected.*

No, as delicious as that kiss had been, he couldn't let himself repeat it.

8: THE WAY OF THE WORLD

"YE ARE AS pale as a ghost this eve," Makenna murmured, digging her elbow into Kylie's ribs to make her point. "Is something amiss?"

Glancing up from where she'd been toying with her venison stew, Kylie forced a smile. "Not at all."

Makenna studied her intently, her sharp features tightening. "Liar … ye've been out of sorts for the last couple of days." She leaned in, concern shadowing her moss-green eyes. "Have the laird's sons been causing ye trouble?"

Kylie shook her head. She hadn't breathed a word of that day to her sister—not about Ailean and Lyle's poor behavior, and certainly not about the illicit kiss. Makenna wasn't the sort to judge, but Kylie was so used to locking everything inside that it was easier to keep silent.

Makenna's observation now was correct though. She wasn't herself at present.

After their father's harsh words, the lads behaved meekly. However, their manner with Kylie was painfully stiff. They got little enjoyment from their lessons, and that bothered her. "The lads are behaving themselves … I'm just a little tired." She then pulled a face. "And I've hardly spent any time with ye since we arrived. I'm sorry about that."

"Oh, I've kept myself busy," Makenna replied lightly, tearing herself off a chunk of bread.

Now it was Kylie's turn to observe her younger sister. It was true, she'd been busy with tutoring Rae's sons, but she'd also marked how Makenna trained with the Dounarwyse Guard every morning. And over the past few days, she'd spied her sister pacing the walls in the afternoons.

Kylie's attention traveled past Makenna then, to where a tall, lean man with white-blond hair sat with the other guards at a trestle table. Her sister might not realize it, but Tormod MacDougall spent most of the mealtimes staring at her. Kylie didn't like the hungry glint in his eye now either—as his gaze lingered upon their table.

"Ye aren't still training with MacDougall, are ye?" she asked, lowering her voice lest anyone overhear them. Presently, Tara was teasing Ailean and Lyle while wrestling with Arabella on her knee, and the laird and his brother were deep in conversation. It was safe to speak frankly.

"I am," Makenna replied with a shrug. "Every couple of days … why?"

"Be careful with him."

Makenna gave a dismissive snort. "I can handle myself."

Kylie frowned. Her sister's arrogance could be abrasive at times. "Do ye really need to train with him though?"

Her sister sighed. "I swear he's the best fighter I've ever met." She halted then before giving a rueful shake of her head. "I must return to Meggernie soon … for ye can never trust those Campbells not to stir up trouble." Her expression turned fierce then. "But before I do, MacDougall's teaching me some valuable swordplay techniques." She paused, lifting a hand as if to wave her sister's concerns away. "Don't worry about me. I know how to handle him."

Kylie compressed her lips into a tight line at this. Hades, her sister could be frustratingly blinkered at times, and arrogant too. Studying Makenna's face then, Kylie did her best to understand what drove her. It didn't seem to be enough that she was a respected member of their father's Guard, that she had learned skills most women never would. She strove to be stronger. Better. But to what end? She couldn't take on the Campbells single-handed.

"How will swordplay help ye, when ye are a clan-chief's wife?" she asked after a pause.

Annoyance flashed in her sister's eyes. "Why do ye keep bringing that up?" She paused then, her brow furrowing. "It just makes ye sound bitter."

Ignoring the jibe, Kylie leaned toward her. "Ye will be a wedded woman soon … and ye need to ready yerself."

"Will ye stop banging the same drum?" Makenna growled. "Fear not, I'll soon be fat with bairn and mending my husband's braies … but why shouldn't I *live* in the meantime?"

A brittle silence fell between the sisters, and Kylie's chest tightened. She swallowed a heavy sigh then, leashing her temper. Arguing with Makenna was the last thing she needed—especially since her new start at Dounarwyse was on the verge of being a disaster.

Why did everything have to be such a struggle?

Her attention shifted then to the man sitting at the head of the table.

Rae lounged easily in his carven chair, nodding as Jack explained something. His expression was composed, his eyes slightly narrowed with concentration.

Kylie shouldn't have let her gaze linger upon him, yet she did. It was the first time she'd focused on the laird properly since their kiss in the solar two days earlier. They had barely spoken afterward—only a few stilted greetings and polite responses had passed between them—and Kylie had taken care to avoid being alone with him.

That wasn't difficult though, for Maclean had been busy. He'd been out overseeing the wall he was having built around Dounarwyse village, to protect it from raids. He'd also gone on patrol with the Guard, Storm running at his side. She wondered if his frequent absences from the broch were on her account.

Enough. She had to stop ruminating about this. Over the past days, she'd gone over every word that had passed between them before the kiss, had looked at it from every angle.

And try as she might, she couldn't get him off her mind.

The softness and firmness of his lips, the heat of his mouth, and the masterful stroke of his tongue. Maclean had shocked her, and it was impossible to look at him in the same light.

As if feeling the weight of her stare, the laird glanced away from his brother then—and looked straight at her.

Kylie's heart fluttered, embarrassment flushing across her chest. She had to look away.

But she didn't.

And what she saw there made her breathing catch. She'd thought he'd come to regret kissing her, but the expression on his face now, and the heat in his eyes, told another story.

Like her, he remembered every detail.

Like her, he couldn't forget it.

Heart pounding, Kylie tore her gaze away and dug her spoon forcefully into her stew.

This attraction between them was inconvenient indeed. She wasn't supposed to lust after the man who'd hired her.

Her belly clenched then. He'd kissed her, but she should have pushed him away and upbraided him for his lusty behavior. Instead, she'd embraced him with just as much enthusiasm. Her reaction to his kiss shocked her down to her bones.

And ever since, her belly had been in knots.

When Makenna leaves, I should go with her.

Her breathing grew shallow then, panic bubbling up. But where would she go? Back to Meggernie Castle, to weather her father's disappointment and her mother's concern? They now knew of Errol's debts and her destitution, for she'd finally written to them after they left Moy Castle in early May—and when Makenna had made the trip to Argyll to escort her back to Mull in July, she'd brought word from their father.

Bruce MacGregor would welcome his daughter home.

It was a kind offer, yet she didn't want to live out the rest of her days as a bored widow at Meggernie. Just the thought filled her with dread.

Resentment surged up then, and her chest began to ache. Since the day of her birth, men had controlled her destiny.

If it wasn't her father, it was her husband, and now it was the laird of Dounarwyse. Kylie's gut told her that Rae Maclean wasn't a bad man; however, life under his roof wasn't turning out as she'd hoped. What would it be like to be her own mistress, to be the one who made the rules?

Don't be a goose, she chastised herself then, shoving her bitterness down deep. *Ye can't change the way of the world.*

"Lady Grant … a letter has come for ye." A servant stood in the doorway to the lady's solar, waving a rolled parchment. "A rider just arrived from Moy."

Kylie cast aside the embroidery she'd been working on and rose to her feet. Excitement stirred in her breast then, unraveling a little of the knotted tension. It had been a few months since she'd heard from Liza, and reading her news would be a welcome distraction from her troubles. Telling herself she needed to hold fast was one thing—finding a way to repair her relationship with Maclean and gain his sons' respect was another.

It would be a relief to hear how her sister's new start, as the lady laird of Moy, was going.

Makenna and Tara looked on as she crossed the solar. The women were seated opposite each other before the gently glowing hearth, for it was an unusually cool day for summer and a misty rain fell outside.

Taking the missive with a nod of thanks, Kylie carried it over to where a lantern glowed brightly on a table by the hearth.

She then broke the seal, unfurled the scroll, and began to read. However, after a few moments, her mouth pursed.

"Well?" Makenna asked, her voice tight with impatience. "How is Liza faring?"

Eyes still trained on the missive, Kylie didn't answer immediately. She was too busy trying to throttle her indignation and disappointment. Finally mastering herself, she glanced up. Makenna had put aside the basket of wool she was winding onto a spindle and now leaned forward in her chair, while Tara looked on with curiosity.

"She's married," Kylie announced.

Makenna's green eyes snapped wide. "To Alec?"

"None other."

"Ye sound disapproving," Tara observed with a raised eyebrow.

Kylie snorted and held out the missive to her sister so she could read it for herself. Tara might think her judgmental, but she didn't know what Liza had suffered over the years.

Meanwhile, Makenna grabbed the unfurled parchment and began to scan it.

"I can't believe she'd be so reckless," Kylie muttered, unable to contain herself a moment longer. She felt like a pot of hot milk about to froth. Suddenly, all her frustrations of late boiled up inside her.

"To wed a former pirate, ye mean?" Tara asked.

"Aye!"

That got Makenna's attention. She glanced up from reading, her brow furrowing. "We knew they were lovers, Kylie," she reminded her. "Surely, ye realized it was just a matter of time?"

"She had the chance to forge her own path in life," Kylie shot back, pulse racing now. "Not to answer to any man except the clan-chief and the Bruce himself. But now she's Alec Rankin's wife, she risks sinking into his shadow. Before we know it, he'll be ruling Moy, not her."

Silence followed this outburst. Both Makenna and Tara were staring at her as if she'd just sprouted devil's horns. Indeed, she didn't usually have so much to say for herself. But she wouldn't choke down her anger any longer. Her altercation with Rae Maclean had loosened something inside her, and this missive had just pushed her over the edge.

Eventually, Makenna cleared her throat. "I don't think that will happen."

"Won't it?" Kylie pulled a face. "There is no chance Alec will stand back and let his wife make all the decisions. No man would."

"They aren't *all* controlling, ye know?" Tara replied. Her voice was still low, yet there was a glint in her smoke-colored eyes. "I hope ye aren't confusing protectiveness with oppression … there's quite a difference."

Kylie's pulse started to race. Of course, Tara would see it that way. She was wed to a man who respected her and treated her like a queen. But most marriages were like her own had been—or worse, for Liza had suffered terribly at Leod Maclean's hands. "I *know* the difference," she growled back.

Meanwhile, Makenna's brow had furrowed. "I know Errol treated ye poorly," she replied, eyeing her sister warily now. "But that's in the past now."

"Aye," Tara murmured. "Don't let one bad man stain yer view of all others."

Turning from her companions, Kylie stalked back to her window seat and snatched up her embroidery. Suddenly, she felt as if the two of them were ganging up on her. A blissfully wed woman, and a willful virgin. They hadn't lived in her shoes. They didn't understand.

9: DEAD AND GONE

"IT'S TOO BONNIE a day to stay cooped up indoors," Kylie announced, pushing herself to her feet. "Let's take our lessons outside today."

Both her charges looked up from where they'd been scratching out greetings onto their boards. Surprise flickered across their young faces. In the three weeks since their father's reprimand, they'd behaved themselves, but *they* weren't the problem this morning. *She* was. The walls were closing in on her. She needed to get out.

"I shall collect a basket for our boards and charcoal." Kylie went on briskly. "And we will stop by the kitchen and see if Cadha has any treats we can take with us."

"Where are we going then?" Ailean asked, eyeing her warily.

"We can take the path south along the coast … I shall teach ye while we walk."

Anticipation quickened inside her at these words. A brisk stroll, while they recited French drills, would help break the morning's monotony, and the exercise would settle her restlessness. Ever since her exchange with Makenna and Tara, after receiving Liza's letter, she'd felt on edge. The day following Liza's letter, she'd written a reply, congratulating the couple. Her sister wouldn't hear of her censure—and that was best.

In truth, she was embarrassed about her outburst. She'd taken care not to bring the subject up with Makenna or Tara again. Nonetheless, releasing the pent-up bitterness and resentment inside her—which hadn't really been about Liza's choices at all, but her own—had felt oddly liberating.

Rising to her feet, Kylie flashed her charges a smile. She then moved away from the table and collected a basket for their things. "Come on, lads … the day waits for no one."

Downstairs, Kylie and the lads stopped by the kitchen, where Cadha gave them some shortbread wrapped up in a soft linen cloth, to take with them. That delighted Ailean and Lyle, and by the time they passed under the portcullis and down the causeway leading out of the castle, both boys were capering.

It was a bright late August day, the kind that made one believe that summer might last forever. All the same, there was a fresh edge to the breeze that warned it wouldn't. They should make the most of the sunshine and warmth while they had it. A full turn of the moon had passed since Kylie's arrival at Dounarwyse, and summer was indeed waning.

They turned south then, taking the path that led above the crescent-shaped beach—where a group of men were taking turns at wrestling on the sand. A shaggy dog bounced excitedly around the wrestlers, its bark echoing across the water.

Kylie's lips quirked. Storm was up to his usual mischief. A few feet away from the collie stood a tall, broad-shouldered man with auburn hair. Rae Maclean looked on as two warriors grappled, moving side-to-side like crabs.

"I want to play with Storm!" Lyle said, his voice rising in excitement.

"Can we go down to the beach?" Ailean asked.

"Later," she promised. "When we return from our walk."

The trio set off, and Kylie began to pick out objects from around them, describing what she saw in French. "La mer est azur," she began, pointing out at the smooth blue swathe of the Sound of Mull. "Repeat after me."

"La mer est azur," both lads chimed in, their voices far more animated than they'd been thus far.

"Look, there's a boat!" Lyle called, pointing to what looked like a birlinn in the distance.

"Aye," she agreed, flashing him a smile. "Say it in French, Lyle."

The lad scrunched his face up before replying. "Un bateau."

"*Il y a* un bateau," his elder brother corrected him smugly.

"Well done, both of ye," Kylie answered. "Now, Ailean … tell me what else ye see." She was enjoying this. Why hadn't she made a game of their lessons before now?

Because ye take everything so seriously, lass. She always had. Perhaps it was time she relaxed a little, and let things unfold as they should, instead of worrying about the future. She desperately wanted her new life at Dounarwyse to work out, but fretting over it only hindered her progress here.

Ailean glanced around before pointing back the way they'd come. "Il y a un château."

There's a castle.

"Good! Now, shall we describe it further?"

They stopped a moment, and she taught them words to describe Dounarwyse broch. Strong. Big. Made of stone. Before they knew it, both lads were managing short sentences.

Finishing their chat about the broch, they turned south once more and walked a distance. Long grass rippled around them. Green hills, carpeted with heather and dotted with wooly, black-faced sheep, stretched west. It was a lovely morning indeed, and, as she walked, Kylie felt the last of her tension melt away.

With the warm sun on her face and the smell of sweet grass filling her nostrils, life seemed easier.

Eventually, they stopped for a spell and ate their shortbread. It was delicious: buttery and fragrant with the scent of heather honey. The lads then collected pebbles, and Kylie used them for a lesson on numbers. For the first time since she'd begun instructing them, Ailean and Lyle looked as if they were enjoying themselves. They giggled their way through the lesson, turning it into a game—and by the end, Kylie was laughing with them.

High-spirited, the party made its way back to the broch.

The fortress, perched high above the Sound, was visible from many furlongs distant, and Kylie found herself admiring it as she strolled along behind her charges. Dounarwyse's walls were lofty indeed. Meanwhile, the lads were busy collecting flowers and herbs on her instruction. They'd press them the following morning and have a lesson about the flora that surrounded their home.

It was hard not to feel lighthearted as she followed them and listened to their excited voices. They couldn't always go outdoors for a lesson—as the weather was changeable here on Mull—but she'd made the right decision taking them out today.

For the first time, teaching them didn't feel like a chore, and seeing them enjoy learning caused a kernel of warmth to germinate deep inside her chest. It melted the remnants of the bitterness still lodged there.

Maybe Makenna's right, she reflected, as a warm breeze feathered across her cheeks. *Errol's dead and gone*. For a while now, she'd been carrying resentment around like a yoke, but in doing so had just made life harder than it needed to be.

The world seemed brighter without it.

Following the path back to the broch, they soon reached the track leading to the shore. And as she'd promised the lads that they could see Storm, she let them scamper down to the beach. Halfway down the hill, Kylie's step faltered. The men had finished their wrestling and had all gone into the sparkling water for a dip. Maybe coming down here hadn't been a wise idea. It was too late though, for her charges had already reached the foot of the path.

"Storm!" Lyle shouted excitedly. "Come!"

The Highland collie was now lying near the tideline, gnawing on a piece of driftwood. However, upon spying the lads, the dog leaped to his feet, picked up his stick, and bounded toward Lyle and Ailean.

Kylie had just stepped onto the beach, her booted feet sinking into soft sand, when her gaze alighted on a man who'd just emerged from the water and was striding back into shore. His hair was slicked back, seawater running in rivulets down his strong body.

Kylie's mouth went dry, even as her heart kicked against her ribs.

Rae Maclean was walking toward her, gloriously naked.

10: I'D GIVE MY LIFE

MOTHER MARY, WHERE to look?

For a moment, Kylie froze, transfixed by the sight of the laird of Dounarwyse disrobed.

Maclean wasn't the only one naked on the beach. The others had also stripped off their clothing so that they could take a plunge after their training. But Kylie paid no attention to any of them.

Instead, she stared at *him*.

Maclean wasn't the first man she'd seen wearing nothing but his skin, of course, for she was a widow. Yet the leashed power of his body, the way the sun gleamed on his wet skin, accentuating every muscle, every scar, transfixed her.

"Lady Grant," Maclean's greeting jerked her out of her reverie. "A fine day, is it not?" His voice was low, and slightly breathless from his dip in cold sea water, yet his expression was veiled.

"Aye," she gasped, cutting her gaze away. Curse her, she could feel her cheeks warming. "I took the lads outdoors for their lessons this morning … I hope ye don't mind?"

"No." Kylie sneaked another glance his way to see the laird scooping up his discarded clothing. "As long as they're learning something … and not just doing as they please." She noted a reserve in his tone now, for he'd just reminded them both of the argument that had ended in a forbidden kiss.

"La mer est azur!" Lyle sang out then, as he danced about the sand with Storm, who now bounced excitedly after the stick the lad had just thrown.

"Le château est grand et fort," Ailean added with an impish grin.

The laird inclined his head, the edges of his lips tugging upward. Something relaxed inside Kylie as she marked his reaction. It was a relief to see him smile, rather than snarl, at his sons.

"Well said, lads," Jack called out. The captain had just donned his clothing a few yards away and was shaking water out of his shaggy auburn hair. "Ye'll be singing us courtly *chansons* in no time!"

"They'll certainly show up *yer* poor grasp of the French tongue," Maclean countered, his tone dry. However, when his gaze met Kylie's once more, it was warm. "Ye should make the most of the sunny weather if my sons enjoy taking their lessons outside."

Fortunately, the man had now pulled on his braies, although he seemed unperturbed by the fact she'd seen him in the nude. He now donned a loose lèine, the thin linen sticking to the hard muscles of his shoulders, chest, and upper arms.

She nodded, keeping her gaze firmly upon his face. "I shall."

Pulling on his boots, Maclean then glanced up at the sky. "Noon is close … we should get back to the broch."

The other men didn't need further encouraging, and they set off up the track that led from the shore toward the fortress.

Kylie brought up the rear with Lyle and Ailean—and their father.

To her consternation, the laird had dropped back so that he walked alongside her, his collie padding companionably at his heel. Presently, the lads drew ahead, finishing their collection of wildflowers and herbs, leaving the laird and Kylie in relative privacy.

Her heart fluttered at the realization.

It was the first time they'd been alone in a while.

"So, Ailean and Lyle are behaving themselves?" Maclean asked after an awkward silence.

"Aye," she replied stiffly.

Another silence fell before he cleared his throat. "I was wrong to intrude as I did that day … and to lose my temper also … but ye will tell me if my sons give ye trouble, won't ye?"

Kylie shot him a sidelong glance, to find him studying her intently. "Aye." Lord, she wished she didn't feel so uncomfortable around him now. "If that is what ye wish."

Something flickered in his eyes at her awkward response, and his lips parted as if he might say something. However, after a moment, he firmly shut his mouth, a muscle flexing in his jaw. "Did ye enjoy yer walk along the southern path?"

She nodded, relieved that he'd changed the subject. "The views are bonnie indeed." She gestured across the water then. "I like how ye can see the mainland from here."

He gave a soft snort. "Aye, it's a reminder Mull isn't a lonely isle in the midst of a wild sea … but part of something greater. Scotland." The pride in his voice was evident.

"The broch certainly has a great vantage point," she said, glancing up at the high walls that thrust up against the blue sky. "If anyone attacks, ye shall see them coming."

He gave another snort. "Not always … when the fog rolls in during spring and autumn … the likes of the Ghost Raiders use it to their advantage."

Kylie frowned as she recalled their attack on Lochbuie village at Bealtunn. A couple of them had even managed to get inside Moy Castle.

She suppressed a shiver at the reminder of how close Liza had come to dying. Her sister had been captive and ended up with a knife to the throat. The leader of the Raiders, a man named Ross Macbeth, had managed to climb the wall with a rope—with help from the inside—and had been intent on robbing the castle's strongroom. It was only thanks to Alec's intervention, and Liza's quick-thinking, that disaster had been averted.

"Ye've been busy of late with the wall around Dounarwyse village," she said then. "Yer tenants will certainly feel safer now."

"Aye … and we'll soon have daily patrols, morning and evening, along the coast." His voice hardened as he continued, "I'll not have those skull-faced shit-eaters sneak up on me again."

An awkward silence followed these vicious words. A fierce scowl now creased Maclean's face.

"What about the Mackinnons?" she asked, deciding it was best to move on from the Ghost Raiders, for the mention of them had blackened the laird's mood. "Do ye worry about them?"

He shrugged, his face relaxing a little. "Bran Mackinnon hasn't given me any trouble since the Battle of Dounarwyse … and if the whelp knows what's good for him, he won't."

Kylie drew in a deep breath before releasing it slowly. "I should tell ye that Makenna is betrothed to him."

His eyes snapped wide. "To Bran Mackinnon?"

"Aye."

"Ye have been keeping that news close."

She pulled a face. "Aye, well … it's a complicated tale … although it's tied up with the Battle of Dounarwyse," she replied before heaving a sigh. "To get the MacGregors onside, Kendric Mackinnon promised my father much … including a marriage alliance between his son and my father's firstborn daughter."

Maclean's brow furrowed. "Isn't Makenna the *youngest* of the MacGregor brood?"

"Aye … Da omitted to tell the former Mackinnon clan-chief that he'd already married his eldest daughter off. The only maid amongst us now is Makenna."

To her surprise, the laird gave a low laugh. "And it will be quite a match."

Kylie studied him, intrigued by his reaction. "Ye have met Bran Mackinnon then?"

"Aye … although the last time I saw him, the lad was on his knees outside the walls of Dounarwyse, splattered with blood and facing Loch's judgment. He's been sulking ever since."

"Well, once he and Makenna wed, he'll be too busy trying to tame her to focus on much else," Kylie replied, glancing up at the walls. She caught sight of a woman's silhouette there, her long hair blowing in the breeze. Although Makenna wasn't part of the Dounarwyse Guard, she spent much time prowling its walls as if she served here. "She won't take kindly to being robbed of her blades."

Maclean didn't reply, and when Kylie glanced his way once more, she marked the groove between his brows. Once again, he looked as if he wished to say something but was checking himself. "I haven't forgotten my promise to take ye and my sons up to Dùn da Ghaoithe before the summer's over," he said then. "We shall go at the end of this week … before this fine weather turns."

Kylie smiled, even as uneasiness fluttered up. She was relieved she and Maclean had cleared the air somewhat. All the same, she wasn't sure it was wise for her to spend a lot of time with him. "The lads will be excited," she answered, keeping the focus firmly on his sons. "And it'll be instructive for them too."

Kylie fought a wince then. How dry and prim she sounded.

The laird's lips quirked. "Ye certainly take yer role seriously," he teased.

"Of course," she replied, covering up her embarrassment with a firm tone. "It pleases me greatly to have found a purpose." If she kept this up, she really would turn into a stern 'duenna'.

"Aye," he murmured. "All of us need one."

Seizing the opportunity to steer the conversation away from herself, Kylie cleared her throat. "And what is yers, Maclean?"

His green eyes glinted. "What do *ye* think drives me, Lady Grant?"

Her pulse fluttered at the edge to his voice. Her first impulse was to glance away, but his gaze held her fast now, and something within her rose to the challenge. "I believe ye are committed to ensuring yer kin, yer people, and yer broch all thrive," she answered carefully. Her skin prickled then, as she continued. "Ye'd give yer life to protect Dounarwyse, and all it shelters."

His gaze widened. Perhaps he hadn't expected such a heartfelt response, yet she'd meant every word. How different he was from her late husband. Errol had cared so little about the well-being of his broch and lands that he'd gambled his wealth away.

"I would," he replied softly. "Although, just between ye and me … sometimes the responsibility weighs heavily."

Kylie inclined her head at this admission. Maybe Maclean had sacrificed too much to ensure Dounarwyse prospered. He was stoic, but his angry outbursts and irritation at his sons indicated that other emotions flowed just beneath the surface.

And after observing him over the past weeks, she was beginning to understand him a little better. He carried a burden upon his shoulders, and worried about keeping his tenants safe, but there was more to his volatility than that.

The man was frustrated. Embittered. Lonely.

Not for the first time, she wondered about his marriage. She and Makenna had speculated a little about it, but her gut told her now that it most definitely hadn't been happy.

We aren't so different then. The realization made her step falter.

Maclean's hand shot out, his fingers wrapping around her upper arm to steady her. The contact—the heat of his touch through her sleeve—made Kylie's breathing grow shallow.

"Thank ye, Maclean." How she wished her voice didn't sound so strangled. "Sorry, the ground is rough here … I wasn't paying attention."

The laird nodded, releasing her arm. They fell silent then, concentrating instead on climbing the steep, rocky path to the drawbridge. The clang of metal from the blacksmith's forge greeted them, as did the acrid tang of hot iron, when they passed under the portcullis. Beyond, the barmkin was busy. Lads were wheeling out carts of muck from the stables, and fowl clawed at fallen straw, searching for oat and barley husks.

As she stepped out into the cobbled yard, Kylie caught sight of a man and woman embracing before the entrance to the guard tower.

Jack had bent his lovely wife back over his arm and was giving her such a passionate kiss that his men had started hooting and jeering. Captain Maclean ignored them though, as did Tara, who merely wound her arms sinuously around his neck and hauled him closer.

A moment later, Jack scooped her up into his arms, kicked open the door to the guard tower, and carried her inside.

More catcalls followed, but the couple were clearly oblivious to them.

Kylie whispered an oath, her gaze remaining upon the doorway Jack and Tara had just disappeared through. "What a sight."

"The devil's cods," Maclean muttered. "Do they have to make such a spectacle of themselves?"

Surprised by his outburst, she cut him a glance, to see he was scowling. Deeply.

"Apologies, Lady Grant," he continued before she could reply. "My brother regularly forgets himself with his wife." His mouth pursed then. "See what I have to put up with."

She stilled. Aye, her instincts about him had been right. He *was* frustrated. Resentful, even. It seemed that the laird of Dounarwyse was jealous of the happiness his brother and sister-by-marriage shared.

Kylie's chest tightened then. So was she.

"Oh, come on … is that the best ye've got?"

"Aye." Panting, Makenna wiped her forearm across her sweaty brow. She then shot Tormod a rueful look. "I'm done."

"Can't handle me, eh?" he goaded with a smirk.

She snorted, still breathless from their sparring. "Hades, ye are full of yerself."

"Aye, but it's merited."

"I still managed to shove ye onto yer arse," she pointed out with a goading smile.

He grinned back, flashing those perfect white teeth once more. "I thought I'd let ye have one wee victory."

"Is that so?"

"Aye … ye are improving … but ye still aren't as good as me."

"Arrogant ass." Makenna pulled a face.

She then moved away from where they'd been fighting upon the terrace that sat high in the broch, between the eastern walls and the tower house itself, and began to unwrap the binding on her blade. "I hope ye enjoyed besting me." She then sheathed 'Arsebiter' at her side. "For that was the last time."

"Oh, aye?"

"I appreciate yer instruction … but I won't be sparring with ye any longer."

In truth, as much as she'd wanted to improve her skills, putting up with such a smarmy instructor had sorely tested her patience. She hungered to become a warrior to be reckoned with, but even she had her limits.

Misgiving arrowed through her then. *What are ye doing, lass?* By rights, she should have set off for Meggernie Castle days ago, yet she'd lingered here instead.

Tormod folded his arms across his chest. "Can't weather being beaten every time?"

Makenna eyed him warily, her mood sobering further. He was an attractive man, with his silky white-blond hair and tall, lean frame—and he fought like a fiend—but over the past days, she'd grown increasingly uncomfortable in his presence. Kylie was right: it was time to end her training with him.

"I'll be leaving soon," she replied with a shrug.

He snorted a laugh. "The Meggernie Guard can't do without ye?"

"No."

He sheathed his own sword. "I'm surprised the men at yer father's castle get any work done … with such a bonnie lass serving amongst them."

Makenna resisted the urge to sneer. Tormod's comments, which she'd brushed off during their initial sessions, had now started to vex her. The warrior didn't know when to hold his tongue. "I shall take my leave now, MacDougall," she said coolly. "I imagine ye have somewhere else ye'd rather be anyway."

He inclined his head. "On the contrary … I've enjoyed fighting with ye. Will ye take a drink with me in the guard hall?"

Makenna shook her head. "My sister is waiting for me." That wasn't a lie. Usually, at this hour, she and Kylie would share a wine together in the lady's solar.

"Lady Grant can wait."

"I think not." Makenna took a step backward then. "Thank ye for taking the time to train with me … but yer evenings are now yer own."

With that, she favored him with a nod, turned, and headed for the door that led down the guard stairwell to the barmkin. And as she walked away, the skin between her shoulder blades itched. The warrior was staring at her.

Eager to be out of his sight, she quickened her pace, pulled open the door, and entered the narrow stairwell. However, she'd only gone down a few steps when a hand closed around her upper arm, yanking her backward. The move was so fast that she didn't have time to retaliate or pull away.

The grip on her arm turned iron, and a hard male body collided with her back before a hot breath feathered across her cheek. "Not so fast, lass," Tormod rasped. "It's time ye thanked me … *properly*."

An instant later, a rough hand grasped hold of her left breast and squeezed hard.

11: NOT A MAN LIGHTLY CROSSED

MAKENNA CURSED.

AN instant later, she moved. Not away from her assailant but toward him. She drove her elbow into his gut and arched backward, attempting to smack him in the face with the back of her head. Unfortunately, though, the knave was standing on the step above her, which gave him an advantage.

All the same, the whoosh of the air escaping his lungs, as she winded him, was satisfying. Her surge of victory didn't last long though before he grabbed hold of her hair and yanked her head back.

Fire lanced across Makenna's scalp, even as fury slammed into her.

She'd felt safe back at Meggernie. Although some of the men were mouthy or flirtatious, none would have dared lay a hand on the clan-chief's daughter.

But they weren't in her family's castle now, and this warrior wasn't like any of those she'd learned to fight with.

Tormod MacDougall was dangerous; she'd known that from the moment she'd seen him try to throttle another man in the barmkin on the day she arrived here. But, foolishly, she'd thought she could both learn from him and keep the man at bay. Kylie had warned her to watch herself around him, but she shrugged off her sister's concerns.

I should have listened to her.

She hadn't met a man yet whom she feared—but underneath the anger that surged through her veins, anxiety now flared.

She'd driven her elbow into Tormod's stomach hard enough to bring most men to their knees, but the bastard still gripped her breast, his fingers digging in painfully.

It was clear exactly what he wanted—and he'd take it by force.

Panic bubbled up then. She'd always thought she'd be the last woman to be cornered by a randy man, or raped. This couldn't be happening.

But it was, and she had to get away.

She stepped up, the heel of her boot crushing his foot, and arched back once more. This time, the back of her head smacked into his nose.

Tormod cursed, stopped groping her breast, and ripped open her laced vest instead.

The devil was lithe in build, but he was deceptively, and formidably, strong. He pressed the length of his body against her then, his arousal grinding into her backside. "Feel that, lass," he growled. "Ye're going to enjoy having it plow ye."

Fury washed over Makenna in a hot tide. If the bastard tried putting his rod anywhere near her, she'd cut it off. Snarling a curse of her own, she deliberately let her body sag. The move caught him off-guard, and she lurched forward. Using the distraction she'd created to her advantage, she reached down and whipped out the thin blade she always carried in her boot.

Tormod didn't know it was there—but he was about to find out.

Not hesitating—even as his brutal fingers tore open the lèine beneath her vest and kneaded her breast cruelly—she drove the blade into his arm.

The warrior roared. And this time, he did release her.

Heedless of the steep stairs or the fact her lèine and vest were ripped open, her breasts exposed, Makenna fled down the steps.

"Bitch!" Tormod snarled, his voice echoing against stone. "Ye shall pay for that."

Panting, Makenna whipped around, pulling her lèine closed with her left hand, while she raised her knife with her right.

The warrior was right behind her, yet he halted at the sight of the blade glinting in the light of the cresset burning on the wall beside them. Blood coated his arm, for she'd cut through his leather wrist bracer, and feral rage glinted in his ice-blue eyes.

But Makenna was ready for him now. He wouldn't catch her unawares again.

"Another step, and it won't be yer arm I stab," she said coldly. "But yer cods."

"Do ye have anything to say in yer defense?"

Rae glared at the bloodied, defiant warrior who stood—flanked by Jack and one of the Guard—in his solar. In his opinion, there was nothing Tormod could say to defend what he'd done, but since he'd already heard Makenna's version of the facts, he'd give this cur his ear as well.

Tormod's lip curled. "I don't know what that harpy told ye, but it's all lies. She was willing."

"Ye attacked her in a stairwell and tried to rip off her clothing," Rae replied, biting out each word now. "It doesn't sound like a willing woman to me."

"Ye know what lasses can be like ... all keen one moment and skittish the next," Tormod replied, ignoring the gimlet stare Jack was giving him. "We were enjoying ourselves when she turned into a hellcat. She just—"

"I've heard enough," Rae cut him off, out of patience now.

He'd seen Makenna a short while earlier, her face streaked with tears, clutching the shreds of her clothing to her breasts as she ran up the stairs inside the broch. He'd just exited his solar and had been the first person to find her. Just as well, for she'd been in a state.

Tormod's expression shuttered, even if anger shadowed his gaze. He didn't appreciate being interrupted.

Aye, the man was a problem. But now he'd be dealt with.

"Ye shall spend the night in the oubliette ... and then I shall take the whip to yer back in the barmkin at first light tomorrow," Rae informed the warrior coldly. "After that, ye will leave Dounarwyse on foot ... without a horse, yer weapons, or any belongings." He paused then, letting his words sink in. "And ye shall *never* return here."

A nerve ticked in Tormod's cheek. "Ye should think twice before dishing out such punishment, Maclean," he said softly. "I'm not a man lightly crossed."

White-hot fire washed over Rae. The urge to draw the dirk at his hip and slice Tormod across the throat pulsed in his chest. With difficulty, he leashed the murderous impulse and growled, "Neither am I."

The whip lashed across the warrior's naked back, and Kylie flinched. An instant later, a bloody line appeared upon Tormod MacDougall's pale skin.

Drawing back his arm, jaw set, the laird let the whip loose once more.

MacDougall grunted this time.

At Kylie's side, Lyle made a sound in the back of his throat, and without thinking, Kylie reached out and put her hand on his shoulder. It was a bold move, and not one she felt overly comfortable making. Yet the lad surprised her by moving close and wrapping his arms around her legs.

Kylie's throat constricted.

Curse ye, Maclean … why do yer sons have to watch this?

Ailean stood to her right, his body rigid as he viewed the punishment. Kylie restrained herself from reaching out and putting a reassuring hand on his shoulder though. Ailean was two years Lyle's elder, and likely wouldn't take kindly to being fussed over.

The chieftain of Dounarwyse had made it clear that every resident of this broch would observe Tormod MacDougall's punishment, and banishment. It was a warning, that rape—attempted or otherwise—wouldn't be tolerated.

Nonetheless, with every lash of the whip, muffled gasps escaped the watching crowd.

Kylie's gaze shifted to where her sister stood silently to Ailean's left. Makenna had folded her arms across her chest as she looked on. Her face appeared hewn from stone this morning, every line of her body tense.

The whip lashed once more. A crisscross pattern of bloody welts now covered MacDougall's back. The man clung to a pole in the center of the barmkin, a guttural sound ripping from his throat with each cut of the bullwhip.

Bile surged up, stinging the back of Kylie's throat. She could understand why her sister might want to witness MacDougall's punishment, but she had no wish to view such violence.

She'd witnessed floggings before—for both her father and late husband had dealt out justice in their keeps—but the sight of it had always turned her stomach. She started to sweat then, nausea rolling over her once more.

If this continued, she'd be sick.

Mercifully, Maclean ceased the whipping then. Breathing hard, he lowered his arm and stepped back.

An uneasy silence followed the flogging. Many of those gathered around the perimeter of the barmkin shifted uneasily, their gazes downcast now.

Heedless to their reactions, the laird nodded brusquely to the guards who'd been looking on. They untied MacDougall and started dragging him across the barmkin toward the gates.

However, halfway there, the disgraced warrior surprised everyone by digging his toes into the cobbles. He then half turned, his gaze seizing upon where Makenna stood next to Kylie. His pale eyes sliced into her. "It isn't over between us, lass," he rasped, his voice carrying over the silent barmkin. "Ye shall see me again."

Makenna didn't move, didn't flinch.

"Enough," Maclean snarled. "Get him out of here."

And with that, the guards hauled the warrior away, across the barmkin and under the archway that led out of the fortress. There, they unceremoniously dumped him on the other side of the lowered drawbridge. He was still in clear view of all, and as Kylie looked on, MacDougall slowly, and painfully, pushed himself up onto all fours before staggering to his feet. The man was barefoot and clad only in a pair of braies. A freshly scabbed cut was visible on his right forearm. She'd heard he spent a rough night without food or drink in the oubliette—Dounarwyse's dank 'bottle dungeon', which could only be accessed by a trap door—and he now was leaving the broch with nothing, not even a pair of boots.

"Tormod MacDougall is hereby banished from Dounarwyse." The laird's gruff voice echoed through the morning air, drawing everyone's attention once more. "And if he ever returns, his life will be forfeit."

Another brittle silence followed this proclamation. The faces of those gathered around the edges of the barmkin, all of whom had witnessed the warrior's punishment, were set in grim lines. Kylie wagered that few of them were sad to see MacDougall go. However, the flogging had put them all on edge. It was a reminder that although their laird was a fair-minded man, he was capable of brutality too.

Across the yard from where the sisters stood, Tara held both her daughters close—her youngest slung across her front, the eldest perched on her hip. Her face was strained. Like Kylie, she hadn't wished to subject the bairns to such a sight. Arabella started to weep softly before Tara whispered soothing words. Then, casting the laird a look of censure, she retreated inside the guardhouse with her daughters.

It was time for Kylie to go back indoors as well. She was just about to murmur something to her charges—although neither of them would be in the mood to study plants this morning—when Maclean crossed to them, his long legs eating up the ground.

A moment later, he was standing before Kylie and his sons.

"We could all do with getting out of the broch for a while," he announced gruffly, his gaze sweeping over Lyle and Ailean before it rested upon Kylie's face. "I was going to leave it to later in the week … but let's take that ride up to Dùn da Ghaoithe."

12: THE UNRAVELING

A STIFF BREEZE pushed at Kylie as she climbed the last scree-covered slope to the top of Dùn da Ghaoithe. She could see why it had been named so—it certainly was exposed up here.

It had been quite a climb to reach the top, although the exertion was a welcome distraction after witnessing the violent flogging. The atmosphere within the broch had been tense when they'd ridden out, and it was a relief to depart for a short while.

Breathing hard, she stopped then, pushing away a strand of hair that had come free of her braid, and surveyed the panorama that stretched around her. She could see for miles in every direction from up here. To the east, the bulk of the mainland shadowed the sky, while to the southeast, she made out the proud outline of Duart Castle. Swiveling around, she surveyed the wood-clad landscape farther north before casting her attention southwest to where the isle's largest mountain, the mighty Ben Mòr, reared up. Her skin prickled then.

What a beautiful isle this was. To think this was her home now.

"What do ye think?"

Tearing her gaze from the view, Kylie focused on Maclean. The laird had stepped next to her, while his sons clambered over rock below them. Dùn da Ghaoithe was a high, rocky ridge with deep corries on either side. Both Lyle and Ailean were excited to finally visit it. Intrigued by the lads' squeals, Maclean's collie joined them. Storm's tail wagged as he sniffed at clumps of heather before he lifted his leg upon a boulder.

"Well, it was definitely worth the effort," she replied, lowering her gaze.

Silence swelled between them before he cleared his throat. "Is something amiss, Lady Grant?"

"No," she said quickly, glancing up once more. Maclean was watching her closely, his green eyes shadowed now. "I'm sorry ye had to see that earlier," he said, lowering his voice. Four of his men had joined them on their trip up to the top of the nearby mountain, but they were both standing far enough away to give the two of them some privacy.

Kylie swallowed. "Then why did ye insist I did?" She paused then, her brow furrowing. "Surely, yer sons could have been spared?"

The laird sighed before raking a hand through his short hair, leaving it in spiky disarray. "Ailean will rule Dounarwyse one day … and Lyle is likely to step into Jack's role eventually. Shielding them from what it means to be chieftain or a captain of Dounarwyse will only make the reality of it all the harsher." He grimaced then. "In truth, I must take some blame for what happened. If I'd gotten rid of MacDougall a month ago … yer sister would never have been attacked."

The roughness to his voice made Kylie's chest constrict. She didn't want him to take responsibility for MacDougall's actions. Indeed, he was the sort of man to shoulder such blame. "Ye weren't to know where things would lead," she answered with a shake of her head.

Their gazes met and held.

"Has yer opinion of me lowered then … after witnessing me flog MacDougall?" he asked quietly.

Kylie's breathing caught. She was surprised her opinion mattered. "Of course not."

"Ye aren't afraid of me now, are ye?"

Her chest constricted. What a contradiction this man was. He was as strong as an oak, yet there was also vulnerability to him. "No," she replied softly.

And she wasn't.

Their stare drew out until the laird severed it. He swung his attention east, his jaw tightening as if he was waging an internal battle. However, when he spoke once more, his tone was subdued. "How is Lady Makenna faring?"

Kylie swallowed a sigh. Her sister had begged off joining them on this trip, saying she wished to rest instead. "It's hard to tell," she admitted. "At present, whenever I ask how she is, she brushes me off."

"She's proud."

Kylie's pulse quickened. *Aren't we all?* "Aye, and tough too … but this has shaken her. I know my sister well enough to see it."

An excited squeal intruded then, and her gaze traveled to where Lyle had found a shiny piece of quartz and was showing his brother. Their eagerness made her smile.

"I'm relieved my sons seem to have rallied after seeing MacDougall flogged," Maclean admitted.

Kylie gave a soft snort. "Aye, well, fortunately, bairns live very much in the moment." She paused then before calling down to the lads. "Choose a few stones, and we shall study them at home."

The boys flashed her a grin at this before they started to fill their pockets.

"Ye are good with them," the laird noted.

"Am I?" Warmth filtered through her at his compliment. "I have no bairns of my own … so must confess I was nervous about how they'd react to me."

He gave a soft snort. "I didn't make building a rapport with them any easier, did I?"

"No … but Ailean and Lyle are starting to trust me now. I'd say the worst is over. They're both good lads."

"They are." Something in his voice made her glance his way. He was watching his sons with a shadowed gaze. "Do they remind ye of yer wife?" she asked gently.

He tensed at this question, and she immediately regretted being so bold. Her nosiness was getting the better of her. She was about to apologize when he replied, "Lyle more than Ailean. He has her looks." He gave a rueful shake of his head then. "Their characters are Maclean through and through though."

She arched an eyebrow. "How so?"

"Both fiery, pigheaded, and stubborn … no different to Jack and me at the same age."

Kylie smiled. "So, ye too were full of mischief once?"

A laugh rumbled up from his chest, and it warmed Kylie to hear it. The laird of Dounarwyse showed far too little mirth. "I was. If there was a prank to be made … or a trick to be played … I was likely at the center of it."

She observed him with interest. It was hard to reconcile the serious man he'd become with the light-hearted lad he'd once been. Suddenly, she was curious to know more about the events that had shaped Rae Maclean. However, now wasn't the time or place for such conversations. She was relieved though that they'd spoken frankly about other matters. She didn't want there to be awkwardness between them.

"Would ye have supper with me in my solar, this eve?" he asked then, taking her by surprise.

Kylie stiffened. The last time they'd been alone in his solar, he'd kissed her. All the same, a while had passed since then, and they'd patched things up. He'd put the incident behind him and was clearly trying to mend things between them. She should let him. And so, after a moment, she nodded. "Very well."

Rae's mood gradually lightened on the way home. He'd needed to get away from Dounarwyse for a few hours, to put this morning behind him. When he'd ridden out of the broch earlier, he'd been tense, his blood still boiling after dealing with Tormod MacDougall. The knave's parting words to Makenna had made him long to string the whoreson up by his neck from the walls. But since the flogging had already upset many of the broch's residents, he didn't wish to traumatize them further.

Even so, it was only when they'd reached the top of the mountain ridge that the anger finally drained from Rae. Guilt had needled him then. Maybe his decision to force everyone in the broch to watch MacDougall's punishment had been a little harsh. His sons were still wee, after all.

Ye need to be softer with them. Aye, and he would be. Ailean and Lyle would leave childhood behind soon enough. From now on, he'd let his sons enjoy their innocence and freedom while they had it.

Ailean rode double with him now, his arms wrapped around his father's waist, while Lyle traveled perched in front of one of the laird's men. Kylie followed close behind on her sure-footed garron as they picked their way down the mountain slopes. As soon as they reached the foothills, they quickened their pace to a brisk canter. Storm bounded next to Rae's courser, a streak of white, grey, and black against the swathes of heather surrounding them.

It had been a good day out, an overdue adventure for his sons. The lads had been pestering him to take them to the top of Dùn da Ghaoithe for a while, but he'd kept putting the trip off.

Dounarwyse lay just a few furlongs distant now—and for the first time in a long while, Rae felt almost at peace with himself and the world.

Indeed, he'd felt so at ease with Kylie earlier, as they stood shoulder-to-shoulder, looking out over the spectacular views, that he'd invited her to supper.

Was that wise?

Probably not. His invitation had been impulsive, and he'd marked her hesitation.

He'd then braced himself for her refusal and inwardly chided himself for feeling relieved when she'd accepted. The truth was, he liked talking to Kylie and didn't want to spend yet another evening with only his thoughts for company.

It's just a meal between a laird and the woman who tutors his bairns, he told himself firmly. *Where's the harm in that?*

By the time they clattered into Dounarwyse's barmkin, the broch's stone gilded by the early evening light, supper was approaching. Both lads were exhausted after the day's adventures, and Rae carried Lyle upstairs to his bedchamber, with Ailean at his heel.

Esme was waiting with a hot bath for the lads.

Usually, Rae would have left the maid to her task then, but something made him linger this evening. Was it guilt? He'd been such a grumpy bastard with Ailean and Lyle of late. He intended to remedy that.

To everyone's surprise, he sent Esme away to fetch the bairns' suppers and set about bathing his sons himself. Kylie would be joining him shortly for supper in his solar, but in the meantime, it pleased him to see the lads splashing around in the large iron tub together. He wanted them to relax in his company, as they once had.

Ailean grumbled good-naturedly while Rae washed his hair, although Lyle wailed when his father accidentally got soap in his eyes. Ailean then called his wee brother a 'mewling babe', and Rae had to pull them apart as they started scrapping.

These two were just like him and Jack at the same age. As the elder, Rae had often teased his wee brother—behavior that usually ended in a fight.

A few stern words reminded both lads of their manners, although Storm, excited by the noise the bairns were making, nosed his way in then, licking Ailean and Lyle's faces until they squealed. Muttering, Rae pushed the collie aside. However, thinking this was a new game, Storm barked, reared up on his hindlegs, and raced at him.

The collision nearly sent Rae headfirst into the tub.

"Storm wants to play!" Lyle laughed.

"Does he?" Entering the chaotic spirit of the evening, Rae shoved the dog playfully away. "Off with ye then!" His sons giggled as, once again, Storm backed up, gave a feisty bark, and then barreled into him.

By the time Esme returned with their suppers—two bowls of leek and haddock stew with fresh oaten bread—father and sons were all laughing while Storm bounced around them, his barks echoing through the bedchamber.

The lass murmured an oath under her breath as she surveyed the scene. "That was a ruckus indeed, Maclean," Esme observed. "I could hear ye from the kitchen."

Grinning, Rae rose to his feet and ordered Storm to go and sit by the bed. "Aye, sorry about that." He then nodded to his sons. "Come on, lads … let's get ye dried and dressed."

It was a mild evening, and so the hearth was unlit. Even so, Ailean and Lyle perched on stools before it, while Rae sat cross-legged on the sheepskin nearby, watching them eat. After the day's adventures, both boys were ravenous.

And as Rae observed them, his throat tightened. He'd missed out on much of late. He'd let loneliness and bitterness, and his worries about the security of Dounarwyse, blinker him. But the truth was his sons mattered as much to him as his responsibilities as laird. He couldn't let them think otherwise.

"Can I have a riding lesson tomorrow, Da?" Ailean asked as he wiped up the last of his stew with a scrap of bread.

"I'm out on patrol tomorrow, lad," Rae replied. Ailean's green eyes guttered, and he added. "But next week, I will give ye a lesson … ye have my word."

"Can I have one too?" Lyle asked eagerly.

"Ye are too young," Ailean shot back.

"Am not."

"Ye can watch me teach Ailean," Rae cut in before another squabble erupted. He knew how it was, the rivalry between brothers. "And once it's done, I'll let ye sit on the garron's back and lead ye around the barmkin."

Lyle nodded eagerly at this, while Rae pushed himself up and rose to his feet. He then glanced at where Esme was folding clothes in the corner of the bedchamber. "Ye can finish up there, lass. I'll put the lads to bed, tonight." It was strange, but he was loath to be parted from his sons this evening—almost as if he wished to reassure himself that all was well.

This announcement earned wide smiles from both boys.

A short while later, Lyle and Ailean were tucked up next to each other in bed, with Rae lying on the edge.

"Tell us a tale, Da," Ailean said, his gaze gleaming in the light of the lantern that burned on the table next to the bed.

"Aye!" Lyle exclaimed. "The Headless Horseman!"

Rae sighed, even as he swallowed a smile. "Don't ye ever get tired of that one?"

"No!" They both chorused.

Once, when Donalda was still alive, he'd recounted that story to them often. But it had been a while since he'd tucked his sons into bed, let alone told them any tales.

Before his wife's death, Rae had been the one to put them to bed in the evenings. He hadn't been close to Donalda, yet he enjoyed the uncomplicated affection his sons had lavished upon him. He'd always had a flair for storytelling, and the delight on his sons' faces, as he told them of fairies, wulvers, and giants, had been a sight indeed. But when their mother died, he hadn't known what to do with their grief, or how to ease it, and so had taken a step back from them.

He regretted that now.

Do they remind ye of yer wife? Aye, they both did, although not in the ways he'd explained to Kylie earlier in the day. Their eager faces and earnest gazes brought back memories of his distant marriage and everything he'd longed for and never found.

Trying to ignore the ache that rose under his breastbone, Rae cleared his throat. He then began the story his own father had told him. Suddenly, he was transported back in time, with Baird Maclean's powerful voice rumbling through his bedchamber.

"Once, many years ago, there lived a young man called Euan. He was the son of a powerful chieftain and dwelled upon a crannog on the southern coast of Mull. He was proud and ambitious, and wanted to rule ... but his father was hale and strong and that wasn't to be."

"Did he want his father's lands?" Ailean asked.

"Aye," Rae replied. "He coveted them ... and wouldn't stop nagging his old man to give him some more."

"But he refused," Lyle added. "And then they went to battle against each other!"

"Aye." Rae raised an eyebrow. "But who's telling his story, me or ye?"

"Ye!" Lyle clutched his father's hand, and something that had been locked tight inside Rae's chest for a while now unraveled.

13: THE ART OF COUPLING

KYLIE WAS ALREADY waiting for Rae in his solar, seated on one of the high-backed chairs, when he finally entered, Storm at his heel. The Highland collie went straight to her and pressed unabashedly against her legs. Laughing, she stroked his ears.

"That dog isn't bothering ye, is he?" he asked, his brow furrowing. "He can be a terrible pest, at times."

She flashed him a smile. "Not at all." Meanwhile, the collie nudged her with his nose, encouraging her to continue.

He whistled then. "Come, Storm … leave the poor woman be."

Flashing him a disappointed look, the dog moved off and settled onto a sheepskin before the unlit hearth.

"Wine?" he asked then, as he moved to the sideboard.

"Aye, thank ye."

He poured them two cups of plum wine, and had just handed Kylie hers, when a knock came at the door. "Supper," a female voice sang out.

"Aye," Rae called. "Bring it in."

Two lasses from the kitchen brought in trays of freshly baked bread, stew, cured sausage, cheese, and apples. It was a simple meal, but there was plenty of food, and it was exactly what Rae was in the mood for this evening.

He moved to the table and took his seat. "Sorry I was so late joining ye for supper … I put the lads to bed, and they insisted on a tale."

Kylie's mouth curved once more as she took her place opposite him. "What story did ye tell them?"

"Lyle's favorite … the Headless Horseman." He pulled a face then. "Both lads love the bit where a claidheamh-mòr lops off Euan's head, while his horse gallops away with his corpse held in place by the stirrups."

She winced. "A grisly tale, that one."

"Aye … just the kind wee lads love … especially since it happened on Mull."

"So, have ye seen this grisly specter yerself?" she teased.

He shook his head, his mood sobering then. "No … but my brother has."

That got her attention. "Aye?"

He took a sip of wine and set down his cup before picking up the basket of bread and offering it to her. Kylie took a slice, although her gaze remained upon him. He wasn't going to get away without telling her the tale.

"Do ye know how Jack and Tara met?" he asked after a pause.

She shook her head.

"Tara is a Mackinnon of Dùn Ara … daughter to the former clan-chief. Around four years ago, my brother stole her away in an act of revenge."

Kylie's eyes snapped wide. Clearly, despite that Tara had spent time with Kylie and her sister, she hadn't divulged her history. "Why would he do such a thing?"

"Kendric Mackinnon killed our father … they'd met to discuss land rights, and their discussion erupted into an argument … one that ended in my father's murder." Rae's mood shadowed then, as it always did when he remembered the tragedy. "I was thrust into the role of chieftain at the age of seventeen … too busy learning how to rule to nurse hatred and revenge. But Jack did."

Kylie's brow furrowed at this. Meanwhile, Rae busied himself with slicing some cheese and sausage and placed them onto the trenchers before them.

"So, Jack abducted Tara with the intention of doing her harm?" she asked after a moment.

Rae nodded. "He intended to sell her to a pirate." She murmured an oath at this, yet he continued. "Jack's act was rash and foolish … he ended up on the run with her. It wasn't long though before he realized his mistake … before he lost his heart to his enemy's daughter." He paused then, giving his head a rueful shake. "One morning, on the western slopes of Ben Mòr, they spied the Headless Horseman."

Her lips parted. "Isn't it supposed to bode ill for the blood-kin of any Maclean who sets eye on it?"

He nodded. "Ye know yer Mull folklore, it seems."

She gave a soft snort. "Liza told me the tale when I was at Moy Castle."

"Aye … that's how the story goes … and when we nearly lost Loch's sister, Astrid, at the Battle of Dounarwyse, we believed the superstition might be true."

He favored her with a wry smile then. "But Astrid rallied, and here the rest of us are four years on … very much alive."

Kylie swallowed a mouthful of bread and cheese, all the while stealing glances at the man seated opposite her.

What a tale that had been.

She had no idea of Jack and Tara's unconventional match. The woman had given up everything, including her kin, to be with the man she loved. *Tara never told me she's a Mackinnon of Dùn Ara.*

"Why has this story never reached my ears?" she asked finally, breaking the silence between them. "I'd expect all of Mull to know of it."

Maclean huffed a sigh. "While Tara's father still lived, it was dangerous to let on the whereabouts of his daughter … so we kept things quiet," he replied. "Bran Mackinnon knows his sister lives at Dounarwyse, of course … but there's little he can do about it." He eyed her then. "Few people outside this broch even know that Tara is a Mackinnon. She's gotten used to not talking of her origins."

Taking the warning, Kylie nodded. "Well, ye can rest assured that I won't be spreading gossip," she answered. All the same, she'd have to tell Makenna—especially since she was betrothed to Tara's brother. "Seventeen is young to have taken on the mantle of laird," she said after a pause. "Ye must have found it difficult."

His fingers tightened around his cup of wine. "Harder than I ever admitted to anyone." He grimaced then. "Jack named me a 'fazart' for not avenging our father's death, and I hit back … our quarrel led to a ten-year estrangement."

Kylie stilled at this revelation. "And did ye *marry* young too?" she asked softly.

The laird's features tensed. "No … I was one and twenty when I took Donalda as my wife." He then pushed away his trencher, and the remains of his meal, and leaned back in his chair, eyeing her over the rim of his cup. "As ye might have guessed … we weren't overly happy together."

Kylie wasn't sure how to respond. Indeed, she'd speculated on the laird's marriage, yet hadn't been bold enough to ask him directly about it. All the same, he'd heard her unvoiced question.

Silence swelled between them before he lifted his cup to his lips then and took a deep draft. "Donalda was a good woman, and it was a fine match, for she was the daughter of a MacDonell chieftain. She was an excellent mother and chatelaine too, but things between us were …" He trailed off there, cutting his gaze away. "Distant."

Kylie picked up her cup and took a large gulp. Curse her, she now heartily wished that she hadn't led them onto this subject. It was clearly one that put him in ill humor. Earlier, she'd been enjoying the laird's company. They'd had an exhilarating day out, and their conversation when they'd stopped atop Dùn da Ghaoithe had made her relax in his company.

"It didn't help that Donalda's womb took a long time to quicken. Seven years, in fact … and only after she went to see a herbwife for help," he spoke up once more, taking Kylie by surprise. "She didn't welcome my touch … but forced herself to do so to give me sons." A deep groove furrowed between his eyebrows at the memory. "It made me feel like a beast … as if each time I lay with my wife, she barely suffered it."

"Didn't ye try to make coupling … pleasurable … for her?" The moment the question slipped from her tongue, Kylie slammed her mouth shut. Hades, what was wrong with her this evening? Mortified, she took another gulp of wine.

Maclean's attention cut back to her, his mouth quirking, even as his gaze remained shadowed. "I did my best … but Donalda was my first … my *only* … lover."

Kylie's pulse quickened. She had only herself to blame for the turn this conversation had taken. She wasn't sure how she'd expected Maclean to respond, but she hadn't seen this admission coming.

"Apologies," he said, flashing her an embarrassed smile. "This isn't a conversation fit for a lady."

She snorted before reaching for the wine jug, refilling both their cups. "Really? I was the one who instigated it."

"Coupling doesn't disgust ye then?"

She flashed him a veiled look. "No … I was wed once, remember?"

His jaw tightened, and she swore she saw something akin to jealousy flash in his eyes. "Yer husband pleased *ye* then?"

She let out a long, slow exhale before shaking her head. It was her turn to divulge details now, and only right too since he'd been candid with her. "At first … until Errol grew frustrated that I never got with bairn." She broke off then, her chest constricting at painful memories. "He was desperate for sons, ye see … and fathered three of them on local women." A familiar ache rose in her chest at this admission. "Things were never the same between us after he strayed from my bed … I stopped enjoying our coupling after that, for I could never trust him enough to relax in his arms again."

Maclean didn't answer immediately. She didn't blame him either. She'd said more than enough. Too much, in fact. What was it about this man that made her blurt out her unfiltered thoughts? This gruff, enigmatic chieftain had a strange power over her.

"Ye didn't deserve such treatment, lass," he said finally, his voice roughening. "No woman does."

"Aye, well … no man wants a barren wife," she answered ducking her head so he wouldn't see the bitterness in her eyes.

He made a noise in the back of his throat. "For a while, Donalda and I both worried that we wouldn't have bairns … but never did I consider straying from her bed because of it."

The ache under her breastbone deepened. "That's because ye are a decent man, Rae. If only there were more men like ye." She swallowed then, cursing herself for addressing him by his first name. He should remain 'Maclean' to her. It was proper.

She was still railing at herself, when he answered, "I'm not that decent." His voice was low, but something in it made her chin kick up. "If I were, I wouldn't ache for ye, *Kylie*." The expression on his face made her pulse flutter in the hollow of her neck. Her breathing now came in short, shallow gasps. The man was looking at her as if he wished to devour her.

Tension crackled in the air between them. She didn't speak, for she didn't want to break this delicious, forbidden enchantment that had spun between them. However, what she wished to admit was that this infatuation wasn't one-sided. She ached to tell him she hadn't forgotten their kiss or that the sight of him naked on the shore that day had made her imagine a host of inappropriate things.

The silence swelled, and then Maclean pushed himself up from the table.

Her belly clenched in disappointment. He thought he'd taken things too far and was about to end their conversation. "I should be honest with ye as well," she said huskily. "It seems only fair."

A muscle flexed in his jaw. "Aye?"

"Aye." She broke off there, swallowing as her throat tightened. "The truth is … I … I want ye too."

His lips parted, and for a moment, he merely stared at her. And then, to her surprise, he turned and moved to the bookshelf behind him. Taking down a slim wine-red leather-bound volume, he handed it to her. He then lowered himself back down onto his seat.

Pulse still skittering, Kylie viewed the leather cover. "The Art of Coupling," she murmured before glancing up at him, confused. "What's this?"

"Ye are right … I was unsure of myself when I first wed … but then I found this on my father's bookshelf" —Hades, the man was blushing now— "that spoke of how to bed a woman." He gave a soft snort then. "I read it from cover to cover, but when I attempted to do some of the things I'd read with Donalda, she screeched like a banshee."

Kylie swallowed. "Ye read a book about … *coupling?*"

"Aye." He paused then. "Open it … if ye dare."

Her breathing caught. There had been no mistaking the challenge in his voice.

He'd just thrown down the gauntlet, and she'd answer.

Jaw setting, Kylie flashed him a feisty look before settling her attention upon the book once more. Aye, her face was likely glowing like a coal, but she wouldn't be cowed. He thought she didn't have the spine to look inside this book. But he was wrong.

Even so, when she opened the volume at a random page and scanned the words that had been written there, her breathing choked off.

When yer lover's quim is suitably wet … rub her juices over yer swollen member and—

"By the Saints." She shut the book with a snap. "Where did yer father get this?"

"I have no idea," Maclean replied. "He never spoke to me of it, obviously … but he and my mother were happily wed. He must have gone to some lengths to please her." Their gazes fused then, the moment drawing out. "Ye can borrow it, if ye wish?"

Kylie flushed hot. Her first instinct was to throw this volume back at him and leap to her feet before making a hasty excuse and fleeing the solar.

But she didn't. Instead, an odd, kindling excitement flickered to life in the cradle of her hips. She was so aware of the man seated opposite. Even though the table separated them, she marked every detail about him, including the shallow rise and fall of his broad chest as he watched her.

Maclean was waiting for her to refuse, for her to hand the book back with a shake of her head and a look of reproach.

But she wouldn't. Once again, a strange boldness had gotten its claws into her. "Very well," she replied finally. "I shall. Thank ye."

Silence fell between them, and when the laird shattered it, his voice was strained. "As I said, I'm not a 'good' man, Kylie. If I were, I wouldn't imagine going through that book … page by page … and doing everything it describes to ye."

She stopped breathing altogether at these words. Squeezing her thighs together, for her quim was aching now, she stared back at him.

Rae's lips lifted at the corners, although his gaze had now turned bleak. "Aye, lass … I am *that* depraved." He raised a hand, scrubbing it through his short hair. "And if ye don't wish to remain at Dounarwyse in the wake of such a revelation, I shall understand."

Kylie searched his face, marking the self-recrimination plastered over it now. What a tortured man he was—passionate yet ashamed of it. Sadness constricted her throat then. How lonely he must have been over the years. "I don't want to leave, Rae," she said softly.

His brow furrowed, tension rippling through his broad shoulders. "Ye don't?"

"I admitted I wanted ye too, didn't I?"

"Ye did … but I thought—"

She shook her head. "I have no wish to get emotionally 'entangled' with anyone again … or to ever take another husband … but yer words don't shock me." She paused then, her pulse lurching before she blurted out, "On the contrary … I find them intriguing."

He gave a shaky laugh, reached for his cup, and drained it. And when he set it back on the table, she noted a slight tremor in his hand. "I don't want to remarry either," he admitted, his tone roughening once more. "But nor do I want to spend the rest of my days living as a monk."

Kylie stilled at these words. Was he celibate? Surely, a man as attractive as him could easily find a servant to warm his bed? Meanwhile, the laird's gaze met and held hers. "Do ye intend to remain chaste?"

She considered his words a moment before letting out a soft laugh. "I'd rather not ... but it isn't the same for women as men." She couldn't help but inject a chiding edge into her voice. "Ye can visit brothels and take lovers with impunity ... but a widow cannot. Not if she doesn't want folk to whisper behind her back." She broke off then, dropping her gaze to where her finger now traced the patterns of the oaken table. She couldn't believe they were discussing such things.

"Ye could take a lover in secret."

Her heart started to thump against her breastbone. She knew where this conversation was heading, and she was suddenly skittish. "I could."

"And if yer lover didn't make emotional demands on ye ... if he didn't try to trap ye in marriage ... would ye consider such a liaison?"

"I don't know," she replied hoarsely. "Relationships often sour once the initial excitement fades ... the situation could get ... complicated."

"What if there was a time limit?" he asked, his voice lowering once more.

"What do ye mean?" Her voice was little more than a croak now, sweat bathing her skin. She'd never had a conversation like this. It was both erotic and alarming, and it made her feel as if she were spinning out of control.

"What if I took ye to my bed from the first of September ... and we spent the autumn and winter months working our way through The Art of Coupling," he replied, his gaze gleaming now. "But once the first spring bulbs flower, we ended our involvement to prevent unwanted emotional entanglement. After that, this ... *hunger* ... would be sated."

14: THE LAIRD'S WICKED GAME

KYLIE'S CHEEKS WERE flushed, her full lips slightly parted, and her lush bosom now rose and fell sharply. But it was her eyes that caught and held Rae's attention. Her pupils had enlarged, making her gaze dark and limpid.

He was playing a dangerous, wicked game.

Nonetheless, his proposal had been made, and there was no withdrawing it.

What in Hades are ye doing? The voice of sanity and reason whispered to him. *The woman will think ye an immoral wretch.*

Aye, but he was. He'd thought about little else of late except plowing the lovely Kylie. And after the conversation they'd just had—an exchange he'd remember until the end of his days—he knew she wanted him too.

And he hadn't lied before. He wasn't in the market for another wife. Nor was he wanting to lose his heart. No, what he needed was to make up for years of frustration and longing, with this woman.

Only her.

He wasn't sure why he'd shown Kylie that book—desire must have turned him momentarily witless—all the same, her reaction to it surprised him. She had the appearance of a stern widow at times, with her plain kirtles and spinsterish hairstyles that would ward most men off; but from the moment he'd met her at Moy Castle, he'd sensed the raw sensuality just beneath.

And after that torrid kiss they'd shared, he knew that bedding her would be a delight.

Even so, he'd now started to sweat like a priest in a brothel. What if he'd completely miscalculated? Was he about to make an utter fool of himself?

"Ye want us to become lovers … for six months?" she asked finally, as if to reassure herself she hadn't misheard him, and the huskiness to her voice sent a jolt straight down to his rod.

"Aye … we shall make a game of it," he replied, thinking on his feet now. "Once a week, when the rest of the broch slumbers, ye shall come to me." His voice grew strained then as his groin started to ache. "And we shall choose chapters from the book to follow … ye may pick out which ones, if ye wish?" He halted at that point, worried that he'd gone too far. There was a fine line between lewdness and lechery, and perhaps he'd just crossed it.

"Have ye thought this through?" she asked, raising an elegant eyebrow.

"No," he admitted with an embarrassed snort. And he hadn't. He'd had lusty thoughts about the woman he'd hired, but he'd never conceived of making such a proposal to her. "If I'm honest, all of this is new to me, lass. I'm making up every word as I go."

She inclined her head. "And what about the fact I share a chamber with my sister?" she pointed out. "Surely, Makenna will notice if I sneak out of bed?"

"I shall arrange for ye to have separate bedchambers, if ye wish?"

Silence followed his confident response. Hades, it did sound as if he'd planned all this.

Her smooth throat bobbed. "Can I have a day or two to think on things?"

His pulse started to thump in his ears. Well, she hadn't rejected him outright. That was a start. "Of course."

"Very well." She pushed herself up from the table then, favoring him with a smile, even if her cheeks were still flushed. He couldn't read her gaze now though; she'd deliberately veiled it. "I shall bid ye good eve then."

He rose to his feet, nodding to her. "Good eve, Kylie." How he liked saying her name. He also enjoyed hearing her address him familiarly as well, although she didn't do so now.

Instead, Kylie nodded back and stepped away from the table. An instant later, she checked herself. Moving forward once more, she retrieved the book he'd lent her and tucked it under one arm.

And then, without another word, she walked from the solar, leaving him staring after her.

A salt-laced breeze drifted in through the open window, cooling Kylie's flushed cheeks.

Sitting on the window seat in the lady's solar, winding wool onto a spindle as she conversed with Makenna and Tara, she'd made the mistake of thinking of the game Rae had proposed. A mistake, for the moment she did—her mind instantly conjuring up torrid images—she'd started to sweat.

Luckily, her companions were too focused on each other to pay her much attention, for Makenna had just told Tara about the bargain their fathers had struck. It was Sunday, and there was no class today. Instead, after returning from the Sunday service in the village kirk, Ailean and Lyle were outdoors having their first riding lesson with their father.

As soon as the sisters had awoken at dawn, Kylie told Makenna of her discovery about Tara. Likewise, Makenna had news for her as well.

There was a ferry for Oban leaving mid-morning the day after next, and she would be on it. The time for her return to Meggernie Castle was well overdue.

Nonetheless, her sister's announcement had made a lump rise in Kylie's throat. She'd swallowed it though. Of course, Makenna wished to resume her role in their father's Guard while she was still able. Not only that, but MacDougall's attack had soured her stay at Dounarwyse. She'd want to put it all behind her. All the same, the thought of her sister leaving filled her with irritational fear. She didn't confide much in others, but her younger sister was still her rock. In truth, she sometimes felt an irritational stab of jealousy toward Makenna—for the lass had always gotten more attention than her—but knowing she was nearby made her feel secure.

Kylie cleared her throat then, focusing on Tara. "Ye aren't upset that I told Makenna about ye and yer brother?" she asked, suddenly aware that she might think her a gossip. "The laird did tell me to keep quiet about it … but I thought my sister should know."

Tara shook her head, although her expression remained strained. "Don't fash yerself," she replied softly. "I'd have told ye both myself" —her gaze flicked to Makenna then— "if I'd known ye were betrothed to Bran."

Makenna managed a tight smile in return. "Sorry … I should have mentioned it." She grimaced then. "In truth, I try not to think about the alliance our fathers made."

Tara didn't reply to this candid comment, and Makenna shifted uneasily in her chair. "So, ye haven't spoken to him since the Battle of Dounarwyse?"

Tara shook her head, her silvery eyes clouding. "He made it clear the day of the Mackinnon's defeat that I was dead to him."

Makenna's brow furrowed at this news, grooves etching on either side of her mouth.

Kylie also tensed. Was her sister's betrothed intractable … the sort of man to nurse grudges?

As if sensing their worry, Tara sighed. "Our father was hard on us both … my brother especially. He wished for a brutish, blood-thirsty son, but Bran was a sensitive lad. He'll be bitter now … but he isn't like his sire."

"He isn't?" Makenna didn't look convinced.

Tara huffed a weary sigh, casting aside the clothing she was mending. "The bad blood between the Macleans of Duart and the Mackinnons of Dùn Ara runs deep. My brother was on the losing side of the battle between our clans … he saw men he'd grown up with die."

Her throat bobbed then, her voice growing husky as she continued. "He sees me as a traitor."

"Ye didn't betray him," Kylie pointed out gently.

Tara's full lips quirked in a smile that didn't quite reach her eyes. "I fell in love with the enemy … that's betrayal in my brother's eyes."

"Aye, well, it seems as if he's cursed with a rigid temperament," Makenna sniffed.

Tara smiled once more, and this time, her gaze warmed. "Something *ye* shall no doubt cure him of."

Makenna muttered a curse at this before stabbing her needle into the pillowcase she was embroidering: a field of yellow and white daisies. She wasn't just adept with a dirk, but was also a talented seamstress. Back at Meggernie, Kylie remembered her younger sister embroidering by the light of a lantern, long into the evenings. "It remains to be seen if yer brother will even present himself at Meggernie Castle at Bealtunn," she pointed out. "He might decide he'd rather not honor his father's debt."

"Oh, he'll be there," Tara replied softly, sadness edging her voice now. "Honor is important to Bran … he'll not break a promise."

Makenna screwed up her face and set aside her embroidery. "Enough about me," she muttered. "I'd rather not dwell on what's to come." She then rose from her seat and went to the table a few yards away, where a leather bag sat. Kylie had noted it earlier, but their conversation—and thoughts of Rae's proposal—had distracted her. Now, Makenna reached into the bag and withdrew a slender leather sheath attached to a wide strap. Turning to Kylie, she held it out to her. "Here … this is for ye."

Putting down her spindle, Kylie took the weapon. "Good Lord, what am I supposed to do with this?"

Makenna snorted. "I had it made especially for ye before I left Meggernie. It's a lady's dagger, designed to be worn strapped to yer thigh. Whenever ye go for a walk beyond the walls of Dounarwyse, or to market, ye should wear it."

Kylie frowned. "Do ye really think the world such a dangerous place?"

Her sister's gaze never wavered. "I would sleep easier back home if I knew ye wore it."

They stared at each other, and Kylie thought of refusing. However, it would be churlish to push away such a thoughtful gift, and so she nodded slowly.

Makenna's lips curved. "Take a look at it then."

Carefully, Kylie took hold of the grip and drew the dagger from its leather sheath.

Across the room, Tara gave a low whistle. "Look at that wicked blade."

"Aye," Makenna said proudly, her gaze still fixed on Kylie. "Remember our lessons … if someone attacks ye, go for the sensitive spots."

"Aye, the groin, throat, or belly," Kylie answered with a wince.

Makenna nodded, her smile widening into a grin. "Ye were always better with a blade than Liza," she admitted with a wink. "Faster … with a truer aim."

Kylie raised an eyebrow, even as she warmed under the unexpected compliment. "I was?"

"Aye … now, strap it on then … let's see how it fits."

With a sigh, Kylie carefully resheathed the weapon and rose to her feet. She then pulled up her skirts and strapped the blade to her right thigh.

Makenna gave a nod of approval. "Perfect."

Kylie muttered something under her breath before adding. "Ye speak as if I'd just donned a fine amber necklace."

Her sister gave a low laugh. "This is far more beautiful … and useful." Their gazes met once more. "Promise me ye'll wear it."

"Don't weep … or ye'll have me howling like a bairn."

Kylie hiccoughed, swallowing hard to loosen her tight throat. It felt as if someone were throttling her this morning. "I'm trying." It was no good though, the tide inside her wouldn't be stemmed, and hot tears started to flow down her cheeks.

"Och!" Makenna stamped her foot, her moss-green eyes overflowing now as well. "I warned ye!" Her sister pulled Kylie into a hard hug, and they clung together for a few moments.

Meanwhile, in the barmkin, a wind whipped in through the open gates, scattering straw and tugging at the women's hair. The sun had just risen, and it wasn't giving out much warmth this morning. Makenna would be glad of the fur-lined cloak she wore when she took the ferry across the water to Oban. Her sister had a long day of travel ahead of her; indeed, it would take her well over a week to reach their family home in Perthshire.

"Thank ye for staying here with me," Kylie whispered, her voice catching. "Although I wish I'd insisted ye leave sooner … maybe if I had, MacDougall wouldn't—"

"There's no point in worrying about such things," Makenna cut her off, giving her ribs one last squeeze before releasing her. Stepping back, she knuckled away the last of her tears and squared her shoulders. As always, her sister looked ready for action, with a quiver of arrows and a longbow slung across her back, a dirk at one hip, and her longsword, 'Arsebiter', at the other. She was dressed in her sturdiest kirtle and surcote, and underneath, she wore leather chausses. Makenna had left her long red-brown hair unbound, although she braided it at the sides to keep it out of her eyes in the wind. Her sister looked both formidable and striking.

"Ye focus on yerself now … and making a success of yer new life," Makenna said firmly. "Ye have made a good start. I want ye to be happy here."

"I will be," Kylie replied, wishing she sounded more convincing. Guilt speared her then, for she hadn't said anything about her attraction to Rae, nor had she told her about the kiss they'd shared or the conversation they'd had over supper a couple of days earlier.

And because she was so adept at hiding things, her sister suspected nothing.

A hollow sensation settled in her chest then, a familiar feeling of loneliness. Why had she always found it so hard to let others—even her sisters—in? She could have told Makenna about Rae, for she wouldn't have judged her, but whenever the urge had risen, she'd quashed it.

"I shall miss ye," she said huskily.

Makenna cleared her throat. "And I ye, dear sister." Her lips curved then. "I expect regular missives from ye, mind … not like Liza, who only writes when prompted."

Kylie nodded. "I promise."

Makenna moved back then, heading toward the garron that was saddled and ready for her. Captain Maclean and two of his Guard would escort her south to Craignure and ensure she safely boarded the ferry. Although Tormod MacDougall had been banished from Maclean lands, they didn't want to take any chances.

Turning, Makenna glanced over at where Rae stood on the steps to the broch, flanked by his sons. She then raised a hand in farewell.

The laird of Dounarwyse nodded. "A safe journey home, Lady Makenna."

Makenna sprang up onto the pony's back then, sliding her booted feet into the stirrups, and adjusting her weapons. She cast Kylie a final glance, and their gazes held for a few moments. Then, Makenna gathered the reins and turned her mount around, following Jack and his men out under the portcullis.

Kylie watched her leave, her chest aching.

"I'm hungry." Lyle's voice drew her attention. "Is it time to break our fast yet?"

"Aye, lad." Rae scooped the boy up, setting him upon his shoulders. He then took Ailean's hand. It pleased Kylie to see him more demonstrative with his sons. The adoration on their faces whenever they looked at him was plain to see. "Let's go up and get stuck into some fresh bannocks."

"Can I have another riding lesson today?" Ailean asked, flashing his father a cheeky smile.

Rae snorted. "Ye always have to push it, don't ye? Today, Lady Grant will be teaching ye … but if ye study hard this week, I shall take ye out again on Sunday." He glanced over at Kylie then, their gazes meeting across the barmkin.

The impact of it—the first time she'd made such direct eye contact with him since their supper together—made her stomach swoop like a diving swallow. He'd given her a couple of days to think over his proposal, and hadn't pushed her for an answer, yet he'd want one eventually. And, in truth, she wasn't sure how to respond.

Just six months of carnal intimacy—an adventure of sorts— and then she could return to being a chaste widow. It tempted her, and it cowed her too. Kylie had never been the sort to flout the rules—but there were times when her self-imposed cage frustrated her. What would it be like, to set herself free from it, if only for a short while?

The moment drew out, and then Rae's lips tugged into a smile that made her belly flutter. "Will ye join us in the solar, Lady Grant?"

Kylie's pulse skittered. She had to find a way to calm herself around him. "Aye," she replied.

He nodded, his smile still lingering, before he tore his gaze from hers and turned, retreating up the steps to the broch with his sons.

Heart thumping against her ribs, Kylie followed.

15: SNOWDROPS AND BLUEBELLS

KYLIE SHUT THE book firmly, even as her pulse raced like a bolting hind.

Ever since Rae had loaned it to her, she hadn't dared read it. Instead, she'd slipped the volume under her mattress and tried to forget it. But the book's presence burned like a coal in her mind—and so, this morning, with a blanket wrapped around her shoulders, she'd retrieved the slim volume and started it, at the beginning.

Staring down at the innocent-enough cover now, she leaned her head back against the wall.

Satan strike her down, she didn't know what to make of what she'd just read. She wasn't an innocent, and yet many of the things she'd read had surprised her, shocked her even.

The book was lewd, detailed, and frank in its opinions and descriptions. She wondered who had written it. And for what purpose? As a manual?

Her mind churned as she splayed a hand over its smooth leather cover.

It was the first day of September—nearly a week had passed since she and the laird had taken supper together.

He needed his answer.

She lifted her other hand then, placing it to where her pulse fluttered at the base of her throat. Rae wanted them to work their way through this book, for her to choose chapters. Excitement quickened in her belly, clutching as she imagined doing some of the things she'd just read.

Errol hadn't done any of it. His approach to coupling had been fast and furious. In the early days, she'd found him exciting, even if he didn't seem to care if she reached her peak or not. But this book focused on the woman's pleasure, as much if not more so than the man's.

It had been a revelation.

Sucking in a deep breath, Kylie closed her eyes. *No one will know.*

None of her kin were here. She was on her own at Dounarwyse now. If she and Rae were careful, which he'd assured her they would be, they could embark on this six-month journey of discovery before concluding things in the spring, without anyone within the broch being the wiser. She could enjoy the pleasures of the flesh without having to deal with the negative consequences and complications of actually being in a relationship.

And ye would have delicious memories to hold dear.

Kylie's heart kicked, and her eyes snapped open.

The Saints forgive her, she really was considering this. "Daft woman," she muttered aloud. It felt odd to have this bedchamber to herself, although it was just as well at present, for she couldn't have read this lewd book without piquing Makenna's interest. It had been another reason to wait before opening it. "Ye don't even know if he will please ye."

However, even as the words slipped off her tongue, her belly clenched once more. Rae's kiss had promised her that, even if he was inexperienced in the art of pleasing a lover, he'd take to this game with enthusiasm. And for her part, she was so hungry for him that just the sight of the man made her feel dizzy with lust.

No, whatever the coming months would bring, if she agreed to this, the laird of Dounarwyse wouldn't disappoint her in bed.

And yet, still, she hesitated.

Kylie was a woman who liked to think through every decision meticulously. All her sisters had once teased her about her cautious ways, and she'd answered that someone had to make up for *their* recklessness. Someone had to think about the consequences of irresponsible behavior.

If she agreed to this, she'd experience the thrill of pleasure and freedom for a few moons—but she'd also be taking a huge risk, with her reputation and her position here.

Cursing, Kylie set aside the book and threw back the blankets, swinging her legs over the side. She'd drive herself mad if she kept going around in circles, chewing over the rights and wrongs of this. One of the maids would be up soon, to help her ready herself to break her fast with the laird and his sons.

It was time to face the day—and Rae Maclean.

"Very well, Maclean. I accept yer proposal." Kylie's words made Rae's pulse leap. "Just six months mind … the moment we spy the first snowdrops bloom, we shall stop."

He inclined his head, hope quickening within him. "Snowdrops flower early … ye could have waited for bluebells." Indeed, the first snowdrops usually peeked their bonnets up in mid to late February, even braving snow and ice to do so, while bluebells didn't flower until March.

Kylie's jaw firmed at these words, and she folded her arms across her chest. "Snowdrops."

Rae had been teasing her, of course, but he sensed she was too on edge to be played with, and so he nodded.

The pair of them stood in his solar. They'd broken their fast, as usual, with his sons. But instead of leaving with Ailean and Lyle, and taking them straight to the lady's solar, where they'd begin their morning's lessons, Kylie had bid them to go ahead while she spoke to the laird. Alone.

Rae had known why, although he'd steeled himself for her to decline him.

Over the past days, she'd been on edge in his company, often refusing to meet his eye when he sought her gaze out. In truth, he'd started to berate himself for making her so uncomfortable. This morning he'd awoken out of sorts. It was September the first, the beginning of autumn. If she didn't seek him out to give him her answer, then he wouldn't speak of his 'game' again.

Of course, he'd had a few days to regret his rash behavior. He'd hired Kylie to teach his sons, not warm his bed. She was a lady, not one of those lusty lasses at *The Barnacle*.

He didn't wish for the complication of a relationship, but he wanted Kylie, and the force of his longing for her made his gut ache, made his breathing grow shallow whenever she walked into a room. His appetite for food had lessened over the past few days as he'd waited for her answer, and when she'd asked to speak to him this morning, he'd started to sweat.

But she'd accepted.

All the same, he had to be certain that she didn't feel coerced into this. "Are ye sure this is what ye truly want?" He asked, stepping close to her.

"Aye." Her voice was husky now. "I have thought of little else these past days."

Heat ignited in his belly at this admission, but even so, he persisted. "If ye feel uncomfortable and would rather I withdraw my proposal, I can. Yer position here isn't in jeopardy … and it never will be."

She inclined her head. "It sounds as if *ye* are the one who's had second thoughts?"

He huffed a laugh before moving closer still. They were near enough now that he could have reached out and drawn her into his arms. All the same, he restrained himself. Servants were due to appear at any moment to clear away the trenchers from the table behind them. He'd made the rules of this game clear, and he'd follow them. "No," he said softly. "I just want to reassure myself that ye are a willing party."

She lifted her chin, her luminous oak-colored eyes holding his. "I am."

He smiled, even as his pulse started to hammer in his ears. "Tonight then?"

A tremor went through Kylie, her soft lips parting slightly. "Aye," she whispered back. "When do ye wish me to come to ye?"

"Late," he replied. "Wait until yer candle burns down … and knock on my door thrice."

Kylie made her way down the stairs, padding softly in her slippers. It was indeed late. The candle in the lantern at her bedside had burned down to a melted stub. As soon as it had, she'd risen from her bed and thrown a woolen cloak about her shoulders, pulling up the hood. Then, tucking The Art of Coupling under her mantle, she slipped from her bedchamber.

There wasn't likely to be anyone about at this hour. All the same, she glanced around her before heading down the shadowed hallway to the landing. The laird's solar and bedchamber sat on the first floor of the broch. A door led between them, while two external doors faced the landing.

Stopping before the left one, Kylie inhaled deeply and straightened her spine—even as her heart thumped against her ribs.

Heavens, she was close to losing her nerve.

She'd hardly eaten anything at supper, for her stomach had closed, and had barely paid any attention to the conversation at the table around her. All she'd been able to think about was that in a few hours' time, she'd be naked in the laird's bed.

Excitement tightened her chest then, her breathing growing shallow. And when she lifted her hand to knock, she noted that it shook slightly.

Clenching her fingers into a fist, she took a deep breath and knocked three times as Rae had instructed.

And then she waited.

A heartbeat passed, and then another, before the door swung open.

Rae Maclean stood there, clad in braies and a loosely tucked lèine. She'd expected to find him looking a bit rumpled and sleepy, yet he appeared as wide awake as she was.

Wordlessly, he stepped aside and gestured for her to enter, and Kylie did, before he closed the door behind her. She then pushed down the hood of her cloak, as he turned to her once more.

For a few moments, they merely stared at each other.

Kylie drank him in, noting the way his tunic was unlaced at the throat, revealing crisp whorls of auburn hair upon his chest. The soft glow of the hearth to his left kissed his skin, brought out the red in his hair, and darkened his green eyes.

Her pulse started to race once more. How she wanted to throw herself at him.

There was no doubt about it, the laird of Dounarwyse was a fine-looking man. He wasn't classically handsome, not in the way his brother was, but there was an intensity to him, an undercurrent of sensuality, that made Kylie's senses reel.

"Ye brought the book?" he asked finally, breaking the silence.

She cleared her throat before casting him a shy look under her eyelashes. "Aye." She handed it to him. "Here ye are."

He took it, and his lips curved into a slow smile that lifted years from his face. "Have ye read it?"

She nodded. Aye, she had. Thoroughly. In truth, some of the acts described in here were far too adventurous for her. Some of them had made her blush up to her hairline, while others made her curious.

Rae moved back from her then and set the volume upon the edge of the large canopied bed that dominated the chamber. Upon entering, Kylie's attention had been so fixed upon the laird that she hadn't taken the time to observe her surroundings. However, she did so now. The chamber was comfortably furnished with sheepskins upon the floor. A large tapestry, depicting a bucolic scene of fields against the backdrop of mountains, dominated one wall, while a large hearth burned opposite the bed.

Storm sat by the fire, scratching under his chin with his back paw.

Rae's gaze traveled to his dog before he gave a low whistle and headed to the door that led through to his solar. "Come on, lad … ye can sleep next door tonight."

The collie gave him an affronted look.

"Off ye go." Rae opened the door and gestured.

Slowly, Storm rose to his feet. He then padded through into the solar, head low, tail down.

"I think he's taken offense," Kylie noted, smiling despite the nerves that now fluttered like moths in her belly.

Rae gave a soft snort. "That's because I indulge him too much." He closed the door firmly behind the collie. "However, having my dog watching me bed ye will put me off."

Kylie giggled at this. She couldn't help it. The relationship between the laird and his Highland collie could be a comical one, and it eased the tension in the bedchamber just a little. Still smiling, she removed her cloak and hung it up by the door.

And when she turned to face Rae once more, she found him watching her intently. And the naked desire in his eyes made her knees weaken.

Of course, she looked far different from usual. Her hair, while not unbound, was braided loosely down her back. It wasn't coiled tightly around the crown of her head or above each ear like during the day. And instead of a high-collared surcote over a kirtle, she wore nothing but a linen night-rail.

Rae's throat bobbed as he raked his gaze down the length of her.

The heat in his eyes made her feel as if she'd burst into flames at any moment.

His lips parted then, and she glanced down to see that her breasts—unrestricted by clothing and swollen with arousal—thrust against the thin material. The man would have been blind not to see her peaked nipples.

"Ye are so bonnie," he said huskily.

She swallowed, dizziness sweeping over her. If he kept looking at her like that, she'd soon be on her knees, begging him to take her. "What happens now?" she whispered.

"Now, ye choose a chapter, and we shall follow its instructions."

Kylie's pulse fluttered in her throat.

His lips tugged up at the corners once more, even as his gaze remained limpid. "Aye, lass … I want ye to decide what we do, remember?"

A moment passed, and then she moved to the large bed and picked up the book.

After reading it numerous times over the previous day, she knew exactly which chapter she wished to begin with. Nonetheless, she didn't want him to think she'd given this a lot of thought, and so she took her time leafing through the pages before handing the open book to him. "This one."

Rae scanned his gaze down the page, and she watched his pupils flare wide, even as his body stilled. "Aye," he said, his voice tight with anticipation. "This is perfect."

16: FOLLOWING INSTRUCTIONS

RAE GLANCED UP, focusing on her once more, his lips quirking. "Shall I undress ye first?"

"No," she murmured, her voice catching as nerves got the better of her. And with that, before she lost her courage altogether, she stepped close to him, tugging his lèine from his braies.

Rae's smile widened, and he set the book down on the bed once more. He then caught the hem of his lèine and pulled the tunic over his head in one fluid movement.

Breathing shallowly now, Kylie raised a hand and trailed her fingertips down, from his collar bone—over the hard planes of his chest, and over the crisp curls of hair that covered it—to his belly. She halted at the waistband of his braies then before beginning to unlace them.

Curse her trembling hands, she wasn't doing this gracefully. Of course, the last time she'd been intimate with a man was with Errol. Even though it had been a long while, this felt strange—illicit.

Rae didn't seem to mind her fumbling though. He patiently waited as she undid his braies and then pushed them down over his hips. His rod sprang free—long, thick, and hard.

Kylie's breathing caught. Then, without thinking, she ran her fingertips along the proud, quivering length of it, tracing the vein that bulged against the velvety skin. He groaned at her gentle touch, and she slid her fingers around his girth, squeezing gently.

Rae made a strangled noise before catching her by the wrist. "No, lass," he said throatily. "We're following the instructions, remember?" With that, he kicked off his braies. Reaching out, he fisted the linen of her night-rail and pulled the flimsy garment over her head.

An instant later, she stood there naked save for her slippers. Aware of Rae's hot gaze upon her body, she kicked off her slippers and raised her gaze, watching him observe her. And the hunger on his face made desperate need clutch at her belly.

Like the rest of her sisters, Kylie's body was strong and lush. The MacGregor women were small in stature yet sturdily built. "Made for bearing bairns and working hard," their mother had often quipped. She'd sometimes wished for a slenderer form, although the way Rae was staring at her right now made her feel like the most desirable woman ever born.

Her skin prickled, her breathing hitching when he stepped in close. He reached out, drawing her heavy braid over one shoulder and removing its tie. He then unwound the braid, letting her hair fall in waves over her shoulders.

"Ye have no idea how much I've longed to let yer hair down," he said huskily. "To tangle my fingers through it."

She stared up at him, her heart pounding as he did just that.

Then, cupping her face with his hands, he leaned in for a slow, sensual kiss.

The heat of his mouth, the slide of his tongue, made her melt into him. She kissed him back, and within moments, their embrace went from slow and exploratory to hungry. Groaning a curse, Rae ripped his mouth from hers then, his lips trailing down her jaw to her throat. "So lovely," he rasped, lowering himself to his knees before her, his hungry mouth fastening upon her swollen, aching breasts.

She bit down on her lower lip as he sucked on each engorged nipple, grazing it with his teeth and teasing it until she writhed against him. Her hands lifted to his head, sliding through his short hair and pulling him closer still as his mouth grew hungrier. With each suck, her quim throbbed.

This wasn't described in the chapter she'd opened, although she was pleased he'd started with lavishing attention upon her paps. Indeed, she was enjoying it so much that a soft cry of disappointment escaped her when he drew back and rose to his feet.

His magnificent rod bobbed before him, and her greedy hands reached out to stroke it once more. However, with a soft laugh, he stepped back before nodding at the bed. "No," he murmured. "The book … remember?"

Huffing an oath, she watched as he moved to the bed and stretched out onto his back, as the book instructed.

Nervousness fluttered through Kylie then. What would happen next wasn't a mystery. She'd read this chapter carefully. She knew how things would go. Nonetheless, something inside her quailed. What they were about to do was so intimate. What if she didn't enjoy it? What if *he* didn't? What if—

"Come here, lass." Rae's husky voice intruded upon her spiraling thoughts.

She padded toward the bed, nervously wetting her lips with the tip of her tongue. "So, ye have never attempted the *soixante-neuf* before?"

He shook his head, even as his eyes hooded.

"I haven't either," she whispered. Breathing quickly and shallowly, she climbed onto the bed. However, instead of turning away from him and straddling his face, as the book instructed, she hesitated. "What if I smother ye?"

Rae's low laugh rumbled across the bedchamber. "That's not likely."

Her pulse started to thud in her ears. "But—"

"Ye won't," he interrupted her, gently yet firmly. His eyes glinted wickedly then. "Although, if ye do, there are worse ways to go."

"Rogue!" She swatted her hand at him, but he caught her wrist and drew her around before lifting her into position.

Her breathing stilled, and she closed her eyes as he gently spread her thighs wide, exposing her to him. Heat flushed over her, sweat beading upon her skin. She started to tremble then, her need quickening as he stroked her bared inner thighs. His fingers then spread her wider still before he pulled her down, his mouth covering her sex.

And when his tongue started to circle and flick, as the book instructed, the pleasure that arched through her loins made her choke down a cry. He was only getting started though, for his relentless tongue continued. Her soft panting filled the chamber as he worked her.

But she couldn't forget that *soixante-neuf* required them both do to their part.

Trembling under his sensual onslaught, she leaned toward his groin.

His rod was rock-hard now, its smooth, rounded head slick with moisture as it thrust up to meet her. And when she cupped his heavy, tight bollocks, his shaft jerked. "Magnificent," she whispered, squeezing slightly.

He rewarded her with a low groan, and then his tongue speared into her.

She gasped, her body starting to quiver.

Trying to concentrate on her task, she leaned close and took the head of his shaft into her mouth, sucking gently at first, while her fingers wrapped firmly around the base of him.

She sighed. He tasted salty, musky—delicious. With a groan of her own, she drew him deep into her mouth, letting the tip of her tongue glide down his length as she went.

His body jerked before he growled a curse, his breath feathering against her sex. "Slowly," he panted, "Or I'll spill too soon."

She took his advice, leisurely sliding her mouth up and down his rod. She removed her hand from its base, and with each slide attempted to bring him deeper. He was big, and soon the head of his shaft hit the back of her throat. However, a wild excitement had now quickened in her lower belly, her wet mouth sliding easily down his swollen length.

He made a strangled sound in the back of his throat, his hips lifting off the bed.

And all the while, his mouth continued to devour her, his tongue teasing the swollen bud nestled within the petals of her sex.

This felt even better than she'd expected. Her entire body tingled, every nerve set alight by his touch. At the same time, she felt as if she were molten wax, and he were a bright flame.

Fumbling for his hand that gripped her hip, she grabbed it, and placed it on the back of her head, encouraging him to guide her.

Grunting, he tangled his fingers into her hair and pushed her onto his swollen member, canting his hips each time she brought him deep into her mouth and throat. Pleasure coiled in her lower belly, the tender flesh between her thighs throbbing as she worked him in a frenzy now, grabbing hold of his thighs to anchor herself. Her legs jerked with each glide and flick of his tongue, heat building and coiling—until she lost control.

Throbbing waves of pleasure rippled out through her groin and lower belly, and she literally saw stars as she shuddered and writhed against his hungry mouth. Her raw cry would have echoed through the chamber—likely waking the broch—if his rod hadn't gagged her.

Rae thrust his hips hard up then, driving his shaft into the back of her throat, his body quivering as he spilled.

She drank him down greedily, and as he slowly withdrew from her mouth, she licked him clean.

In the aftermath, she lay there boneless and panting. Her wits felt scattered to the four winds, and sweat bathed her limbs.

Wordlessly, Rae lifted her off him, and she rolled sideways, turning so that she leaned her cheek against his belly.

Still trembling from the force of her peak, Kylie tilted her head to meet his gaze and found him staring down at her. His cheeks were flushed, his fern-green eyes the color of polished jade. "Ye studied that chapter well," he rasped.

She gave a breathless laugh. "So, I know how to follow instructions?"

"Aye … the teacher makes a fine student."

He held out a hand to her, and she took it, allowing him to draw her up against him. Lying in the cradle of his arms, listening to the steady thud of his heart against her cheek, she felt truly at peace for the first time in a very long while. The realization unnerved her slightly. *Careful.* Aye, the things they'd just done to each other had been exciting, freeing, but this was just a game. An exploration of all the things they'd both missed out on over the years. That was all it meant.

She couldn't get too comfortable with this man.

"I can hear ye thinking," he said eventually, rousing her.

She snorted. "Aye?"

"Ye don't regret what we just did, do ye?"

"No," she replied honestly and without hesitation.

"What is it then?"

She didn't answer immediately. In truth, she didn't want to share her thoughts with Rae. It was best he believed she was in control of her emotions. If he suspected she was already struggling, then he might decide to end things after tonight.

Panic fluttered up then. *We've only just begun.*

"I'm thinking about what position to choose for when we next couple," she said eventually.

Laughter rumbled through his chest. "Aye?"

She shifted up onto one elbow and gazed down at him, her fingertip trailing down his sweat-damp chest, tracing the whorls of hair there. "Aye," she murmured.

He raised an auburn eyebrow, and when her hand traveled lower to his belly, something hard and hot nudged it. Kylie's core clenched in response. Despite that she'd just peaked, she was desperate to have him inside her.

"Ready for more?" he asked.

She nodded.

Rae lifted a hand to stroke her face. "I will ensure to withdraw before spilling," he assured her.

She favored him with a soft smile, even as her chest tightened. It was kind of him to worry about such things, yet he didn't need to. "My womb will not quicken if ye release inside me," she assured him. "I'm barren, remember?"

His eyes shadowed. "Are ye sure? I do not wish to—"

She raised her hand, placing her fingers upon his lips to silence him. She didn't wish to discuss this. She and Errol had lain together often enough for it to be clear something was amiss with her, and the fact he'd sired three bairns with local women was proof enough. She couldn't bear children. "I am sure."

"What's next then? Do ye wish me to fetch the book?" he asked after a pause.

"Aye … I will need to re-read this one," she replied with a teasing smile. "For it's complicated."

He raised an eyebrow at that, inviting her to explain herself. Yet she didn't elaborate. Instead, she retrieved The Art of Coupling and leafed through it, until she found the right place. "Here it is," she murmured. "*The Spider.*"

"The Spider?"

"Aye." Dropping her gaze back to the open book, she scanned the page. "It says it requires some flexibility … so hopefully, we can manage it." He made a sound in the back of his throat at this, but she continued. "So … I lie on my back and hook my legs over yers. My hips should be raised a little above yers … while yer legs go underneath and bend to the side of my body."

He screwed his face up, as he tried to visualize her instructions. "And then?"

"We rock back and forth until we find a rhythm that suits us." Putting the book to one side, she shifted onto her back. "Sounds straightforward enough."

Rae huffed a laugh. "If ye say so." He moved around then, positioning himself between her spread thighs. His rod stood up like a banner, and the sight of it, waiting for her, made need quicken like wildfire in her loins. After some twisting, they managed to get into position. And when Rae slowly slid into her, filling her, stretching her, she bit back a deep groan. Heavens, he felt good. She was still wet and tender from her climax earlier, and he entered her easily.

Trembling now, she braced herself on her elbows while Rae leaned back on his hands. However, as they started to rock, Kylie hissed in pain.

Rae immediately halted, concern furrowing his brow. "Have I hurt ye?"

"No." She muttered an oath then. "I've got cramp in my hip."

He remained still, waiting until she nodded to him. They began to rock once more.

"Cods!" The cramp had seized her hip again, worse than before, and had spread to the back of her thigh. "I think we might have to choose another position."

"Good idea … my back is killing me," Rae grunted as he withdrew from her. A moment later, he rolled onto his back and pulled her astride him.

She huffed a surprised laugh. "That was a deft move, Maclean."

His mouth curved into an embarrassed smile. "Aye, well … I'm a quick learner too." A blush stained his cheekbones then. "I've always wanted a woman to ride me."

She flushed at these words. She too had never coupled in this position. Errol had preferred Kylie under him as he plowed her.

She took hold of Rae's shaft and positioned it between her thighs. They both groaned as she rolled her hips and eased his long thick length into her once more. Staring down at his face, she took in his parted lips, the way his eyes now hooded with lust.

"Do ye remember this position in the book?" he asked huskily.

"Aye."

"Any advice then?"

Heat flared low in her belly. She wasn't used to taking the lead, and yet excitement quickened within her at the thought of being in control for once.

"Grip my hips," she instructed, thrilling at this new role. She'd never have dared to make such demands of her late husband. But Rae's breathing quickened at her words, and he obeyed, his strong hands moving to her hips, his fingers pressing into the soft flesh. "Lift me slowly and move my hips in a gentle circle as ye do so."

He complied.

"Aye," she breathed, as pleasure rippled through her core. "Lower me onto yer rod again … the same way."

He did before repeating the act, again and again. And with each sensual roll and slide, she felt herself growing wetter and needier. A throb started deep within her quim, one that craved more. And the instructions in The Art of Coupling told her how to get what she wanted.

She widened her legs even further and leaned forward, bracing herself on the bed with her hands on either side of Rae's head. And then, as he slid her down to the hilt of his member, she ground herself hard against him.

Pleasure clenched and rippled low in her belly, causing her to gasp. "Oh, aye," she whimpered.

Rae groaned, sweat beading on his brow as his eyelids flickered. "Christ's blood," he ground out. "How am I supposed to last when ye make sounds like that?"

She tried to laugh, but the coiling hunger in her core screamed to be sated. And so, she started to ride him, her breasts swinging in his face as she ground herself against him whenever he drove deep. He had lifted his hips now, rolling his own hips with each thrust, until they both unraveled.

His eyes closed then, his head falling back against the pillow.

Relieved that he'd severed eye-contact, Kylie also looked away. It was too intense, too intimate, to hold his gaze while they coupled. Who knew what he might see in her eyes when she was at her most vulnerable?

Instead, she rode him with abandon, biting down hard on her bottom lip—for she knew she'd start screaming if she didn't—until she peaked violently and gave herself up entirely to pleasure.

17: THE AFTERMATH

RAE AWOKE TO a wet tongue lapping his cheek and hot dog breath.

Eyes snapping open, he found Storm in his face. His collie had somehow managed to open the door between the solar and his bedchamber.

He cursed, just as the collie licked him again—and this time got a mouthful of dog tongue. Spluttering, he lurched up out of bed. "Out, Storm!"

The shaggy dog withdrew, tail wagging.

Wiping his mouth with the back of his hand, Rae rose from the bed and crossed naked to the nightstand, splashing his cheeks with water. He then cast Storm a dark look. The collie sat a few feet away, watching him expectantly. "Ye are a right troublemaker, lad," he muttered. "But ye got yer wish … I'm up now."

It was hard to stay grumpy at his collie though—not after the night he'd just had.

Bedding Kylie had surpassed all his expectations. Lying with her was the closest he'd ever felt to true freedom. She'd been lustier and more adventurous than he'd anticipated, rousing a passion within him that had left him reeling. She'd slipped from his bed in the early hours and returned to her own, leaving him to sleep. And he had. Like the dead—until his rude awakening.

He went through his morning ablutions swiftly, concluding his bathing and brushing his teeth with a hazel stick dipped in salt. He then threw on a fresh lèine and braies and buckled his dirk around his hips before making his way through into the solar.

He'd risen later than usual, and his sons and their tutor were already seated at the table, awaiting him. A large tray of fresh bannock, cut into wedges, sat between them, and the wee lads were eyeing it hungrily. However, they were loath to dig in before their father arrived.

"Morning, Da!" They sang out, and Rae favored them with a smile. How differently he behaved toward them these days. Until recently, he'd greeted them both with a scowl each day.

"Morning, lads." He then shifted his gaze to Kylie, who was watching him with a veiled gaze. "Sorry … I overslept."

"I know," she said softly. "That's why Lyle let Storm into yer bedchamber."

Rae snorted, casting his youngest son a mock-frown. "Is that why I awoke to foul dog breath in my face?"

Both boys started laughing at this, while Rae took his usual place at the head of the table.

They began their meal then, amidst his sons' companionable chatter. Rae helped himself to a large wedge of bannock, smeared it with butter and honey, and ate with relish.

After the night's activities, he was hungry this morning. As was Kylie, he noted. Usually, she only ate a single wedge of bannock—aye, he noted such things about her—but this morning, she managed *three*, washed down with a large cup of weak ale.

They didn't speak for a while, preferring to let Ailean and Lyle fill any silences. Ailean was enthusing about the pony he was learning to ride on, while Lyle was pestering him to let him help groom it.

"Did ye sleep well?" Rae asked Kylie eventually, meeting her eye.

To his pleasure, her cheeks went a charming shade of pink. "Aye," she murmured. "Like a stone."

"All is well this morning then?" He didn't know why he was asking her this, only that he wished to reassure himself that she hadn't awoken to regrets. *He* certainly hadn't.

Their gazes held before she licked honey off her lower lip. The sight of her darting pink tongue sent a signal straight to his groin, and his rod sprang to attention. Curse it, he wouldn't be able to rise from the table until the wood in his braies subsided. "Aye," she replied, her voice slightly husky now.

Rae's pulse quickened. How was he supposed to control himself around this woman? He'd been the one to stipulate that they'd meet in his bedchamber only once a week, but he regretted that now. He wanted her in his bed *every* night from now until spring.

Easy there, lad, the voice of reason checked him then. *Once a week is sufficient. Ye don't want to do anything foolish, do ye?*

His mood sobered at the reminder. No, he didn't.

This arrangement was so that they both could enjoy the pleasures of the flesh they'd missed out on over the years—without getting entangled in a relationship.

After Donalda's death, he'd made himself a promise. Marriage was a burden, and since he already carried much upon his shoulders, he wouldn't take another wife.

Rae's chest tightened then as he thought of Donalda, guilt spearing through him. The poor woman hadn't meant to be a burden. She'd done her best. But being wedded to her had felt like a life sentence on The Bass Rock. Loneliness had dogged his steps of late, but he'd felt even more alone when he'd been married. He wouldn't make such a mistake again—which meant he needed to keep the lovely Kylie at arm's length.

Even so, her luminous gaze and the blush that had deepened upon her cheeks made it difficult not to stare at her now.

Yanking his gaze away, Rae reached for his cup of ale and took a deep draft.

He had to be careful.

The mist swirled in—its cool kiss feathering across Rae's cheeks.

"The sea fret is as thick as porridge this morning," one of his men grumbled behind him. "We'll ride straight into the water at this rate."

Rae cast a glance over his shoulder. "That's why we need to be out here," he pointed out. "The Ghost Raiders sail in on days like this."

The warrior's brow furrowed. *"The Night Plunderer* could be out there, Maclean." He gestured to where a bank of thick, drifting mist obscured the Sound of Mull. "Right in front of us … but we'd never know."

"Aye, but we're waiting for them."

Rae turned back to face the direction of travel and raked his gaze over the fog-shrouded landscape. He'd sent Jack and a party of warriors to scout the coastline north of Dounarwyse, while he took his party south.

His jaw tightened then. *We're ready for ye this time, ye bastards.*

No, he wouldn't be taken unawares this year. The wall around Dounarwyse village had been completed at the end of summer, and he now posted guards around it after nightfall. The defenses would prevent the Ghost Raiders from sacking the hamlet.

Those reivers had plagued his thoughts for a while now— even so, this morning, he found it difficult to brood on them as he often did.

A day had passed since the best night of his life, and he kept catching himself grinning like a fool at the most inconvenient moments. Indeed, his mood was so buoyant that he'd caught his brother watching him quizzically earlier that morning, when they'd talked in the barmkin before setting off on their patrols.

"I thought ye'd be scowling at the sight of such thick fog," Jack had noted, his gaze narrowing. "But ye look almost cheerful about it."

Rae had hurriedly schooled his features into a more solemn expression at this observation, for Jack was as sharp as a boning knife and would wonder why his surly elder brother was walking around with a daft smile upon his face.

Even so, as he'd ridden out with his men, a sense of well-being had settled over him. He felt a decade younger this morning.

It hit him then—as the rumble of waves on the shore below drifted through the damp air, and somewhere in the mist, a goat bleated—how *smothered* he'd felt over the years. He'd been weighed down by responsibilities he'd taken on too young. But Kylie Grant had blown into his life like a spring storm and freed him from his troubles. Thanks to her, he could breathe once more.

And now, as he rode amongst the swirling mist, another smile tugged at his lips.

He was ready for the Ghost Raiders and now bedded a beautiful, lusty lady once a week. Life was looking brighter than it had in a long while.

"Lady Grant."

Kylie's head jerked up, mortification prickling her skin as she focused on the lad seated across from her. How many times had Ailean said her name? He was looking at her quizzically now.

Embarrassed to have been caught a thousand leagues away, she cleared her throat. "Aye, Ailean?" Curse her, she needed to concentrate. Instead, she'd been reliving her delicious encounter with the laird of Dounarwyse, and wishing the days would pass faster so that she could go to him again.

"I've finished."

She smiled. "Good … let me see what ye have written."

The boy handed her his pine-wood board, and she read the sentences he'd painstakingly etched upon it.

I am called Ailean Rae Maclean. Rae Baird Maclean, chieftain of Dounarwyse, is my father.

"Well done," she murmured, glancing up to find Ailean watching her intently. She couldn't let thoughts of Rae distract her. She'd been hired to teach his sons, and that had to be her focus. She'd moved to Mull to gain a modicum of freedom and independence—as much as a woman was allowed—and she had to carry out her role well to ensure her place here remained secure. "Yer hand is improving." She flashed him an encouraging smile. "Soon ye shall be ready to write with a quill and ink, like yer father."

"Will I too?" Lyle asked, glancing up from where he was still writing. The lad sat next to Kylie this morning upon a long bench.

"No," Ailean replied with a snort. "Ye are too wee. I shall write with a quill *long* before ye do."

In response, Lyle muttered an oath and was about to jam his elbow into Ailean's ribs when Kylie caught his arm.

"Of course, ye will," she said firmly. "Yer brother is only riling ye."

"Baby," Ailean muttered, and Lyle's blue eyes started to gleam with unshed tears.

Kylie cut Ailean a quelling look before she focused on his little brother once more. "Ailean will always be yer elder," she said gently. "And ye must get used to it."

"But I want to learn to ride … to write with a quill," he replied, his voice a trifle querulous.

"And ye shall." She paused then before giving a rueful shake of her head. "I have two elder sisters and two younger … I know what it's like to compare yerself to a sibling." Confusion shadowed his gaze at these words, so she continued. "My two elder sisters, Sonia and Alma, are beauties … while my two younger siblings, Liza and Makenna, have fiery natures that make them impossible to ignore. Growing up, they received all the attention … while I sometimes felt invisible."

"Ye are bonnie too, Lady Grant," Ailean piped up then, his voice contrite. He didn't like being ignored in favor of his brother. "*And* fiery."

She flashed Ailean a smile before focusing on Lyle once more. "The point remains that in families there will always be rivalry." Her mouth quirked again. "And there are some *benefits* to being the younger sibling, ye know?"

"There are?" Lyle looked doubtful.

"Aye, yer father will be harder on his firstborn and more lenient with ye. And ye can learn from Ailean's experiences and mistakes too … and avoid some of them."

"I can?"

"Aye."

"I won't make any mistakes," Ailean said boldly.

Kylie huffed a laugh and reached across, ruffling his mop of auburn hair. "Aye, ye will, lad … we *all* do."

"That is a lovely tune … I haven't heard 'Wild Mountain Thyme' in a long while."

Seated on the window seat in the lady's solar, continuing the embroidery that Makenna had left behind, Kylie glanced over at where Tara had just entered the chamber.

"Thank ye," Kylie replied, embarrassed. In truth, she preferred to sing when she was alone. Her voice wasn't as good as some of her sisters', or her mother's. "It's always been my favorite." Her gaze shifted to the tray Tara carried, bearing a jug and two wooden cups. "What have ýe brought?"

Tara flashed her a smile. "The first of the apple wine … I thought as the mist is finally clearing, we could share a cup."

Kylie grinned back. Indeed, it was a relief to see the world again. The last tendrils of fog were now rolling out to sea, revealing one of those autumn afternoons when the light was golden, and every detail outdoors stood out in sharp relief. From her vantage point by the window, she had an arresting view over the pastures and tilled fields that rolled west of the broch. The sight had been so bonnie that she'd been compelled to sing.

Casting aside her embroidery, she made space on the window seat while Tara placed the tray on a nearby table and poured them cups of wine.

"How are ye faring since yer sister left?" Tara asked, bringing over the wine and perching next to her. The sunlight burnished the woman's red mane, making it look as if it were aflame. Kylie had never seen anyone with such bright hair.

"Well enough," she answered with a half-smile. It wouldn't do to appear too exuberant, or Tara would wonder at the reason. "Although, I do miss Makenna." She paused then. "I worry about her too."

Tara's mouth curved, even as her silvery gaze shadowed. "That is only natural … all of us fret about our siblings."

"Aye … but Makenna is a proud one and wedded to serving in our father's Guard." Her brow furrowed, and she took a sip of the sweet apple wine. "I fear yer brother may be disappointed in his bride."

Tara snorted. "On the contrary, Makenna is likely exactly what Bran needs." Her mouth kicked up into another smile then. "A strong-willed man requires a woman to match him."

Kylie smiled, even as she thought about her own marriage. Errol had been dominant, yet she'd smothered her feisty nature to please him. It hadn't worked. Perhaps if she'd shown more spirit, things might have been different between them. Shaking herself free of a past she couldn't change, she eyed Tara. "Well, it's fortunate for Jack that ye have a nature to match yer hair."

Tara threw back her head and laughed, and when her gaze met Kylie's once more, it sparkled. "I'm glad ye came to live with us," she said, still smiling. "As much as I love it here, I've missed having someone to talk to." She paused then, sobering. "Donalda and I were never close … but I can be myself with ye."

Kylie took this admission in with interest. "What was she like?"

"Quiet … self-restrained," Tara replied with a rueful shake of her head. "I don't think I ever saw her and Rae bicker … not like Jack and I do." She paused then. "Donalda was an excellent chatelaine though … I always admired the way she managed the broch."

Kylie nodded at this yet refrained from asking anything else. It wouldn't do to appear too interested in the laird's wife.

Meanwhile, Tara continued to drink her wine, observing Kylie over the rim of her cup.

Her gaze had turned speculative now, and Kylie tensed. "What is it?"

Tara shook her head. "I'm not sure … I can't put my finger on it … but somehow, ye are different today."

"I am?" she replied, taking care to appear amused rather than flustered by this observation.

"Aye, there's more color to yer cheeks, yer eyes are brighter, and ye smile more readily." Tara paused then, her lips curving. "And I caught ye singing like a bird just now."

Kylie's pulse quickened, even as she shrugged. "Maybe living at Dounarwyse suits me."

Tara's smile widened. "I'd say it does."

18: MY SHIP AND MY SWORD

Castle Coeffin, Isle of Lismore

One month later …

RAMSAY MACDONALD DIDN'T like to be interrupted when he was drinking. He had a jug of mead at his elbow, and his companions had just started another round of knucklebones, when the stranger entered the hall—and he could tell by the beeline the man was making for him that he wished to talk.

Tall, fair-haired, and with a swagger that made Ramsay scowl, the man reminded him of the laird of this castle. Duncan MacDougall's hair was more white than blond these days, yet the resemblance was striking. The same high cheekbones. The same ice-blue eyes.

Taking another pull of mead, Ramsay tracked the newcomer right up to his table. The man then halted before him and folded his arms across his chest. "Ross Macbeth?"

Ramsay grunted. These days he didn't go by his real name—he hadn't done so in nearly four years. Ramsay MacDonald was a wanted man and so was Ross Macbeth. "Aye, what's it to ye?"

The stranger gave him a wolfish smile. The bastard had perfect white teeth. "My name's Tormod MacDougall."

"Good for ye."

"My uncle says ye captain that cog moored on the docks."

"Aye." Ramsay drained the last of his mead and poured himself some more. He wasn't drunk enough to bandy words with this bore. "What of it?"

"He tells me ye and yer men are the 'Ghost Raiders'."

Ramsay pulled a face. The laird of Castle Coeffin had a big mouth. Over the past months, the MacDougalls had given Ramsay and his men a safe port. They had no love for the Macleans of Mull, having had a long-running dispute over fishing rights. Even so, Ramsay knew he was likely outstaying his welcome by now.

He'd promised Duncan he'd get back to raiding the Isle of Mull's coastline in the autumn, and he would.

Still grinning, and unbothered by Ramsay's cool welcome, Tormod dragged a stool over from a nearby trestle table and took a seat. It was growing late, and the castle's hall was empty save for this table where Ramsay and his crew lingered. The laird had long since retired with his wife to his chambers upstairs. "Fear not," the arrogant newcomer drawled. "I have a bone to pick with the Macleans of Mull too."

Ramsay sneered. He didn't care and wished this fool would stop his yapping and leave him in peace.

Undaunted though, Tormod continued. "My uncle says there are two Macleans ye hate the most … Loch Maclean, and his cousin, Jack."

Ramsay stilled. Had he said that? He must have been in his cups when he let that slip. He'd gone by his real name back when he and Jack had crossed paths. These days, he was usually careful not to reveal much about the events that had led to his exile. "Is there a point to yer blether?" he asked sourly.

"Aye." Tormod drew his stool closer, his pale blue eyes gleaming intently now. The hair on the back of Ramsay's neck prickled. There was something about this warrior that made him uneasy. He smiled too much, yet his eyes were as cold as lumps of granite. "I used to work in the Dounarwyse Guard. Did ye know that Jack Maclean leads it these days?"

Ramsay set his cup down on the table before him with a thump.

Around him, his men ceased their game of knucklebones, keen gazes swiveling his way. But their captain ignored them. Instead, his gaze remained riveted upon Tormod. The man didn't know it, yet he'd just handed Ramsay a prize.

The location of the individual he'd long fantasized about killing.

He hated Jack even more than he did Loch Maclean. Loch's cousin had crossed him on two occasions. The first was when he, Loch, and Finn MacDonald had bested him and his friends in a fight at the Craignure Inn nearly five years earlier—an incident that had resulted in Ramsay's banishment.

The second time had been a year afterward. Ramsay and his fellow outcasts had been living rough in the glens and hills south of Ben Mòr when they stumbled across Jack and a woman. The Mackinnon clan-chief's daughter had tried to get them to help her, with some tale about how Jack had abducted her.

Ramsay hadn't cared. He'd tried to abduct Tara so that he and his friends could all take their turns plowing her, but Jack had stopped them.

Riding away, injured, with his friends lying dead behind him, had been a bitter gall to swallow. Ramsay had nursed his hatred ever since.

"Ye didn't know, did ye?" Tormod leaned close, his handsome features tightening.

Ramsay didn't reply.

"Jack has done well for himself. He's grown indispensable to his brother … and wedded a clan-chief's daughter … Tara Mackinnon."

Heat started to pulse in Ramsay's gut.

Jack and Tara. He wanted revenge upon them both.

Curse it, he was sober now. It was as if all the mead he'd downed tonight had been water. Gaze narrowing, he fixed Tormod with a long, hard look. "What do ye want?"

"Dounarwyse broch and all its lands."

Ramsay stared at him a moment before laughter broke free. Likewise, his men guffawed around him. But the laird's nephew's smile faded.

His stillness was unnerving, and Ramsay's mirth quickly died away. "And why?"

"Let's say that, like ye, I have a score to settle. I intend to put the laird of Dounarwyse and his smug brother to the sword and rule in their stead."

Tormod halted then, his mouth twisting. "It would be fitting, for a MacDougall to take Dounarwyse … for it was my forefathers who built that broch, not the Macleans."

Ramsay shook his head. He didn't care who'd built Dounarwyse. As much as he wanted Jack Maclean dead—and as much as he'd love to make Tara his whore as an additional punishment—he lived in the real world, unlike MacDougall. The fool's arrogance was something to behold. "Christ's blood," he growled. "What did Rae Maclean do … steal yer woman?"

Tormod's eyes glinted. "It doesn't matter. All ye need to know is that I will have vengeance … and Dounarwyse."

"Many have tried and failed to take that broch, lad." One of Ramsay's men pointed out. "What makes ye think ye can?"

Tormod swiveled slowly, his gaze raking over the warrior who'd spoken. "While I was living at Dounarwyse, I made it my business to learn its secrets." His attention flicked back to Ramsay. "And I discovered a hidden way into the fortress."

Silence settled at the table, everyone's attention riveted upon the newcomer now.

Ramsay's crew had been ill-tempered of late. *The Night Plunderer* had never been caught—but Leod Maclean's death and the loss of all the coin he was hoarding on their behalf had left a sour taste in everyone's mouth, as had their failed attempt to rob Moy Castle's strong room. News would have spread that the Ghost Raiders were men, not wraiths, and soon folk would see them as nothing more than guised pirates. Things had gone ill this past summer for Ramsay and his crew, and they'd all been wondering what the future held.

But Tormod MacDougall had gotten their attention.

"Aye?" Ramsay said finally, his tone veiled. "And what's that?"

"A storm drain inside the eastern curtain wall," Tormod replied, his mouth curving once more. "Most castles don't have them … but Dounarwyse gets lashed with rain every spring and risks flooding otherwise. The drain is only opened once a year though … during early spring when the rains come." He paused then, his gaze never leaving Ramsay's. "The tunnel empties out on the rocks beneath the broch. I climbed up it last spring when we lifted the iron hatch. It's narrow, and ye must contend with flowing water when it rains, but wide enough for men to navigate in single file. Ye can crawl the tunnel at first, and then ye must climb. The rock is rough though, and it's easy enough to find hand holds."

Another silence followed this explanation.

Ramsay considered Tormod's words, turning them over and over before replying, "Ye make it sound easy … but it can't be."

"Easier than ye'd think." The warrior flashed him another toothy smile. "We'll spend the next months recruiting more raiders … and then, once winter ends, we shall sail into a perfect storm. Heavy rains. Guards tired after winter. Shortening nights. I know the broch's routines, the movements of the servants and the guards … and the layout of the tower house." He leaned in once more. "If we time it right, Dounarwyse will be ours."

Ramsay quirked an eyebrow. "*Ours?*"

Tormod shrugged. "All right, *mine*. But if ye agree to help me take the broch, I shall give ye half of any wealth we find." His eyes gleamed. "And ye can take yer pick from the women too."

Moments passed after this declaration. Meanwhile, Ramsay's mind worked furiously.

He could have it all. Revenge against the Macleans. Jack Maclean's head. His enemy's spitfire wife chained to his bed— and enough coin to set him up for life.

For the first time in a long while, hope filtered to life in Ramsay's chest. Finally. Freedom from the grudge he'd carried like a heavy shell upon his back was close. All he had to do was ally himself with Tormod MacDougall.

Ramsay didn't like him much, although he didn't warm to most people. He didn't trust him either. Nonetheless, he reminded himself that it was he, not Tormod, who held all the power here. It was his ship and his crew. His rules. Tormod might have the arrogance of ten men, but he was still outnumbered. If Ramsay decided to take Dounarwyse for his own—and he well might—there was nothing this turd could do about it.

And so, he nodded. "Very well, MacDougall," he said slowly. "Ye have my ship and my sword." With that, he spat on his palm and held it out.

Tormod grinned back and, without hesitation, grabbed Ramsay's hand with his own, locking the two of them together in an iron grip.

Ramsay then glanced over at where his men looked on. "Looks like we'll be staying on here until spring, lads."

19: JUST THE TWO OF US

Dounarwyse broch, Isle of Mull

Two and a half months later …

"GIVE THAT TO me, ye toad!"

Kylie sprinted out of the broch in pursuit of the bounding Highland Collie, who had swiped the plaid shawl she'd been slinging around her shoulders as she stepped out of the lady's solar. Storm had then shot down the stairs like a fleeing squirrel. Cursing, Kylie picked up her skirts and followed him.

She'd hoped to catch the dog in the entrance hall below, but a servant had just opened the doors to fetch water from the well.

Storm slipped past the lad and out into the brilliant white of a snowy afternoon.

Kylie slowed as she navigated the slippery steps leading down to the snow-covered barmkin.

They were icy and treacherous, and she didn't fancy taking a tumble. Nonetheless, when she reached the bottom, she trudged toward where Storm bounced and tossed his head, her shawl fluttering behind him like a flag.

"Enough of this game!" she called out in exasperation as the dog darted away whenever she drew close. "That's my shawl, and ye are slobbering over it!"

But Storm hadn't finished yet. The snow had fallen thickly three days earlier, and the collie had been lively ever since. His white-tipped tail stood up like a plume as he pranced around the perimeter of the barmkin. Above, the sky was a hard blue, and the air was so cold that her cheeks prickled. Storm didn't mind the chill though. If anything, it made him friskier. He then darted inside the open granary door.

"I've got ye!" Kylie shouted, victorious, as she raced after him and pushed through the narrow gap.

Inside the musty-smelling building, where a glowing lantern hanging from the roof illuminated neatly piled sacks of oats and barley, she came to an abrupt halt.

In the center of the space stood a tall man with a fur mantle about his broad shoulders. A servant stood with the laird, etching marks onto a sanded pine board.

Rae plucked her scarf gently from his dog's jaws. Meanwhile, Storm sat down meekly at his master's feet, feigning innocence.

"This is yers, I take it?" The laird raised an eyebrow, his mouth quirking.

"Aye," she panted. "Yer dog is a menace!"

A grin flowered upon the chieftain's face, an expression that made her stomach dip as if she were on a high swing. "Aye, he's a rogue all right." He glanced at the servant then. "That's all for now, Muir. I'll finish up here."

The man nodded, cast Kylie an amused grin, and handed Rae the board. He then exited the granary, leaving them alone.

She approached her lover, belly fluttering. Even after four and a half months at Dounarwyse, just the sight of the laird made her feel like a giddy lass. They'd continued their wicked game ever since the beginning of autumn, meeting every Sunday night, for lusty encounters. She'd thought that after a month of trysts, she might begin to tire of the arrangement they'd made—but she'd been wrong.

If anything, each meeting just made her hungrier for him. Waiting for Sunday to arrive made each week feel interminable. It was Saturday now, two days before Yule, and need coiled in her belly. *Tomorrow.*

Reaching out, she took back her shawl. However, her breathing caught as their hands brushed. It was as if everything was still new between them. When would her craving for him subside?

Likewise, Rae stilled at the contact, his eyes darkening in the soft lantern light.

And then, catching hold of her wrist, he drew her against him, his mouth slanting over hers for a lusty kiss.

It was reckless and foolish, and she should have pushed him away and chastised him, but instead, she stepped into Rae, her lips parting for him.

A groan rumbled through his throat, and his arms went around her. The next thing she knew, he'd twisted her left and walked her back, away from the gap Muir had slipped through and out of sight of the barmkin.

Pressed up against a pile of sacks, Kylie melted against Rae, her hands sliding up his thick gambeson and linking around his neck as she met his kiss wildly.

Lucifer strike her down, she was daft letting herself respond to him like this. Of late, she'd given herself a strict talking to, reminding herself daily of her purpose at Dounarwyse. This was a new start. She had a good life amongst people she respected. Her friendship with Tara had deepened, and she'd developed a strong rapport with the servants here too. Her charges' behavior had significantly improved as well. With the cold weather, they couldn't venture out on their walks as often as in the summer, and Kylie had worried Ailean and Lyle would play up. But they hadn't.

The independence that she had found here sometimes made her feel giddy. No, she wasn't a lady laird like Liza, and, aye, she worked for the laird of Dounarwyse, but her role gave her a sense of purpose and achievement. Her *arrangement* with Rae allowed her to explore the urges she'd long quashed, and there was a freedom in that too.

The life she'd built here was too important to put at risk— yet here she was, grinding her breasts and groin against the laird, just yards away from where a servant drew water from the well. She could hear the splash of water and the thud of wood against icy stone.

Rae ripped his mouth from hers then. "God help me," he whispered, his breath feathering across her ear. "I want ye, lass."

"And I *need* ye," she breathed back. It was difficult to focus, especially when his tongue traced the shell of her ear. She trembled against him, need pulsing between her thighs. "But not here."

Breathing hard, he drew back, his gaze searing hers. "Meet me upstairs then," he said, a rasp to his voice. "Wait in the solar, and I shall join ye shortly."

Kylie's pulse started to race, excitement churning in her belly now.

She *should* remind him of their agreement—that they only ever met on Sunday nights under the cover of darkness and never in the middle of the day. But as their stare drew out, hunger shivering between them, all common sense fled. "Aye," she replied huskily.

Rae moved back, his hands clenching and unclenching at his sides as if he was fighting the urge to step close once more, to lift her skirts and plow her right here amongst the sacks of grain.

Breathing shallowly now, Kylie tore her gaze from his, slung her shawl about her shoulders, and turned. She then walked on unsteady legs to the door.

Bathed in sweat, his body quivering as pleasure quickened in his loins, Rae watched Kylie in the looking glass.

She perched upon his lap, her legs spread open across his thighs. He sat on the edge of the bed and had dragged the tall looking glass from the corner of the chamber so that they could watch themselves couple in it.

This had been one position in The Art of Coupling he'd been eager to try for a while. He'd told her early on she could choose the positions, but he couldn't help himself now. All the same, he'd been shy to suggest it. But when he'd summoned the nerve this afternoon, his lover had agreed without a beat of hesitation.

The light of the blazing hearth a few feet away gleamed on Kylie's sweat-slick skin and upon the neatly coiled braid that wrapped around the crown of her head. Usually, he unbound her hair before taking her, but this afternoon, there hadn't been time.

Instead, they'd flown at each other the moment he'd entered the solar and closed the door behind him. Rae had then scooped her up into his arms and carried her through into his bedchamber, where they'd ripped each other's clothes off.

He'd forced himself to slow down then and had taken the well-thumbed book off the shelf by his bed. Kylie's mouth had curved as she watched him, her oaken eyes darkening with anticipation.

She loved this game as much as he did.

His lover shuddered then, as his fingers stroked between her spread thighs, and her head dropped back against his shoulder. In response, Rae grazed his teeth along the column of her neck.

"Christ's blood, ye are glorious," he ground out, his gaze returning to the looking glass. "Just look at ye."

Her swollen breasts rose and fell sharply as she lowered her chin and shifted her attention to their reflection. There she was, opened wide for him, her lush body bared. A flush rose to her cheekbones then, and her lips parted as she slowly circled her hips against him, bringing him deeper.

Their gazes met in the looking glass, and held for the barest instant, before hers hurriedly slid away.

It always did at intimate moments.

Rae was no better, he supposed. The idea of looking deep into her eyes while he took her made something inside him quail—for there was an intimacy to the act that flustered him. But whenever he got up the courage to do so, Kylie either closed her eyes or turned her head to one side.

"Plow me, Rae," she gasped then. "From behind."

They slid to the floor, and he took her on all fours upon the sheepskin, between the bed and the looking glass. There, he gripped Kylie's hips and rode her hard.

Meanwhile, she shuddered and groaned, her head hanging between her braced shoulders. "Oh, Jesu," she gasped, the desperate edge to her voice making heat ignite at the base of his spine. He was close now. She arched her back with each thrust, her arse pushing up against him.

And as he drove into her again, she shattered, a choked cry ripping from her throat. They were making too much noise this afternoon, yet he didn't care. He could think of nothing except losing himself inside this woman.

At that moment, he caught a glimpse of her face in the looking glass. The flush on her cheeks had spread down her neck now. The ecstasy that suffused her features made something constrict deep in his chest.

Tightening his grip upon her hips, he drew back once more, raising her up. And this time, he looked down at where their bodies met, and where she clutched at him, pink and wet.

The sight was so erotic that his release slammed into him like a battering ram, and he thrust deep one last time. Blood thundered in his ears, and pleasure shot up his spine.

"Kylie!" he choked as his loins spasmed once more and he ground into her. In response, she gave a raw, guttural groan.

They collapsed on the sheepskin, spooned together with Rae still buried to the hilt inside her heat. And for a while, neither of them spoke. He couldn't have formed a coherent sentence if he tried. Over the past months, their coupling had been passionate, surprising even, but the force of his climaxes still took him by surprise.

Afterward, it felt as if he were drifting amongst the clouds, bathed by sunlight.

Eventually, he roused himself from the torpor that risked sending him to sleep. Reaching up, he stroked the back of his hand over Kylie's soft cheek. "I got carried away, lass," he murmured, suddenly concerned that she hadn't yet said anything. "I didn't hurt ye, did I?"

"No," she said, her voice deliciously husky. "That was …" Her voice trailed off, as she searched for the words to describe what they'd just done.

Rae's lips curved. "Wild?"

She gave a soft, shaky laugh. "Aye."

They fell silent once more, while he gently stroked the tender skin of her shoulder and flank. She had such a soft, delicious body—one that he'd developed an obsession with. It had become a challenge at mealtimes not to stare at her. Every gesture she made, no matter how innocent, caused his gut to ache with longing. And his rod often stood to attention at the most inconvenient of times.

The truth was that once a week wasn't enough.

He craved to take her to his bed *every* night.

Rae didn't tell Kylie so though, for he didn't want to alarm her. He was aware his feelings for his lover had grown more intense of late, but he was equally aware of the agreement they'd struck. As such, he kept his thoughts to himself now.

Even so, he wanted more than just her body. They often talked after coupling, and shared most meals together, with his family present, of course. But despite his vow to keep an emotional distance between them, he now wanted to spend time with her, alone—to unravel her secrets and learn her innermost thoughts.

"As it's Yule, I wish to invite ye to supper with me this eve," he said, breaking the silence between them once more. "Will ye accept?"

"Just the two of us?" she asked sleepily.

"Aye." She didn't answer immediately, and, curse him, his belly tightened in response. Despite that their encounters often blazed hotter than a smith's forge, Kylie kept her emotions on a tight leash. The woman could be inscrutable, and now was one such occasion.

A pause lengthened between them before she finally replied, "Is that wise, Rae?"

He loosed a sigh before leaning his head forward and skimming his lips over her shoulder. "It's just supper … nothing that should make anyone suspicious." He paused then. "And it's been a while since we shared a meal together alone."

She shivered, a sigh of her own escaping as his lips trailed up to her neck. Her braided hair made it easy for him to caress her there, and he gently nipped her skin with his teeth. The soft sound she made in the back of her throat then—and the way she sinuously ground herself back against him, causing his rod, still buried inside her, to harden—caused his thoughts to scatter.

"Very well," she replied, her voice breathy now. "Just one supper can't hurt."

20: STRAYING OVER THE LINE

SEATED OPPOSITE RAE, Kylie helped herself to a slice of walnut-studded bread and tore off a crust, dipping it into the bowl of thick mutton and neep stew. Then, taking a mouthful, she chewed slowly.

"This is delicious," she murmured, reaching for her goblet of wine. "Just when I think Cadha can't improve on her skills, she surprises me."

Rae's lips tilted into a boyish smile. "Aye, there's nothing like a hearty stew when there's a blizzard outside."

Indeed, a snowstorm had blown in with the gathering dusk, and outdoors, snow fell in thick, silent drifts. Nonetheless, it was cozy inside the laird's solar, with the fire crackling and Storm—not making mischief at this hour—curled up before it.

Kylie took another mouthful of stew and searched for something to say.

What was wrong with her this evening? She was usually so comfortable in Rae's company—never at a loss for words. But not now. In the aftermath of their torrid joining earlier in the day, a lump of dread had settled in her belly. That afternoon, she'd helped Tara make Christmas wreaths downstairs in the hall, with the help of Ailean and Lyle. They were decorating the hall for Yuletide with banks of candles and garlands of ivy and pine. It now smelled like a forest glade. However, Kylie had found it difficult to focus on her task. And as afternoon slid into evening, her uneasiness had grown.

She and Rae had strayed over a line.

They had to cross back.

Clearing her throat, she picked up her goblet then and took a fortifying gulp. "We should be more careful in the future," she said softly. "Someone might have seen us today ... or heard us."

His features tightened at these words. "Aye." His voice roughened slightly. "Ye are right."

Relieved by his agreement, she took another sip of wine. "We still have another two months of our ... *arrangement* to go ... but I think it's important we remind ourselves of the rules."

He nodded, even as his green eyes shadowed. "Ye believe I have forgotten them?"

"No ... but I think we've both gotten careless." Good. She was being firm. It eased the panic that thumped at her breastbone. "We meet to enjoy each other once a week, to explore the things our past lives denied us. But come the spring, we will have to step back and resume our old roles once more."

Rae held her gaze, an emotion she couldn't quite place flickering over his face. His lips parted then as if he might say something.

However, after a moment, he closed his mouth firmly. "And that's what ye wish for?" he said finally, his tone veiled now. "For us to go back to our old relationship after the winter?"

Alarm flared once more, and her pulse fluttered. Was he questioning their 'game' now? "I think it is wise, do ye not?" she replied carefully.

Silence fell in the solar again, broken only by the crackling of the hearth and the soft whuffling sound of Storm's breathing. The dog was now fast asleep.

They continued their meal, although Kylie had lost her appetite, as tension rose between them.

After a while, Rae pushed away his half-eaten bowl of stew and leaned back in his chair, swirling his goblet of plum wine before him. "Aye … it's wise," he admitted gruffly. "I suppose I've gotten greedy of late. Being with ye is like being shown a fabulous banquet that I can only sample but never feast upon."

Kylie flushed hot at these words. Rae feasted upon her every time they were alone in his bedchamber. Her body still hummed from how he'd taken her that afternoon, and heat pooled in her lower belly when she reminded herself that the following day was Sunday, and soon he'd take her again.

"Ye *are* greedy, Maclean," she said, her lips quirking. "Insatiable, even."

He huffed a laugh, even as his gaze remained serious. "Aye … ye are quite a woman."

Warmth rose to her cheeks. "I'm glad I please ye."

"Oh, ye do." He paused then. "But more than that, I am truly myself when we are together."

Kylie fought the urge to squirm in her seat. Suddenly, it felt overly hot in this solar, and the collar of her kirtle seemed to be choking her. She knew she should say something revealing in return, but her tongue wouldn't form the words. "So, ye no longer feel as if ye have missed out on the pleasures of the flesh?" she asked eventually.

"No," he replied, his gaze steady. "Ye have given me memories to cherish."

Her throat tightened then. Mother Mary, she needed to change the subject. It wasn't a good idea to continue down this road. The truth was that the connection between her and Rae wasn't just physical. It was deeper. He knew it, and so did she. Over the past weeks, trust had started to build between them, and a bond was forming.

Nonetheless, she was as committed as ever to stopping their liaison with the spring.

Just the thought of what might happen if they didn't made her feel as if she were falling headfirst into an abyss.

And it terrified her.

"With ye, I have discovered another world, Kylie," Rae admitted after a pause. "But after all of this is done, I want things to remain amicable between us. I wish us to be friends."

Kylie's heart kicked hard against her ribs. *Friends.* How could she see this strong, kind, sensual man as a friend again?

Cease this! She gave herself a sharp mental slap.

Rae wasn't the problem at present; she was her own worst enemy.

Dropping her gaze to her bowl of unfinished stew, she drew in a steadying breath before replying, "Of course."

Kylie departed swiftly after supper, saying that she'd promised to help Tara finish decorating the hall. Rae had hoped they'd take a wine together by the fire and relax in each other's company for a while. However, he could see she was anxious to leave—indeed, impatience bristled off his lover—and so he let her go without comment.

In the aftermath, he poured himself a large cup of wine and crossed to the hearth.

He was seated in his chair, staring at the dancing flames, while Storm slumbered, unconcerned by his master's brooding, when a heavy knock sounded at the door.

Rae pulled a face. He recognized the manner of the knock, and since it didn't belong to Kylie, he didn't wish for company. "What is it, Jack?" he barked.

The door swung open, and his brother strode in, shaking snow off his heavy fur cloak before hanging it behind the door. "That's a warm welcome," he greeted him. Jack's cheeks were flushed with cold, yet his gaze was bright. He was a happy man. It emanated from him.

Rae had never admitted such to his brother, but ever since Jack and Tara had come to live at Dounarwyse, he'd been secretly envious of the bond they shared. Their obvious passion for each other and easy rapport had stood out against the reserve between Rae and Donalda. Even after over a decade of marriage, there had been no spontaneous affection between them, whereas his brother and Tara couldn't keep their hands off each other.

And then, after Donalda's sudden sickness and swift death, his brother's contentment gradually chafed him even sorer.

Rae had decided not to wed again, and he wasn't the sort to casually take a lover—or he hadn't been before Kylie came to live in his broch. All he could see before him was a lonely life where he sacrificed his wants for the good of his people.

But since taking Kylie to his bed, his bitterness had eased, as had the anger that had soured his belly for so long. For the first time, he was truly enjoying the pleasures of the flesh with a woman ripped from his dreams. He too had tasted joy, but this evening, it felt as if the warm cocoon he and Kylie had wrapped themselves in had fallen away.

She was deliberately taking a step back from him, and there was nothing he could do about it.

And to his chagrin, a kernel of resentment formed deep in his belly at the contentment upon his brother's face. He should be pleased for him—for he knew the trials that Jack and Tara had endured to be together—but this evening, it was difficult to summon charitable thoughts.

"What has got ye in a mood?" Jack asked, eyeing him as he strode to the sideboard and poured himself a generous cup of wine.

Rae didn't answer. Meanwhile, Storm rose from the fireside, gave a languid stretch, and padded over to the Captain of the Guard, plume-like tail wagging. Jack ruffled the dog's long curly coat as Storm pushed against him. "At least someone is pleased to see me."

"I'm sure Tara would be," Rae replied sourly.

"My lovely wife is busy finishing the decorations for the hall with Lady Grant." Jack crossed to the chair next to Rae and lowered himself into it. He then stretched his long legs out in front of him, crossing them at the ankles. "I know better than to intrude on such a task."

Rae grunted.

Jack took a swallow of wine, regarding him under a furrowed brow. "What's *wrong* with ye, this eve?"

"Nothing."

Jack snorted. "Liar … but if ye wish to keep yer own counsel, that's fine by me."

"Any news from the Watch?" Rae asked then, deliberately shifting their exchange from him to more practical matters.

"None … it's been blessedly quiet of late."

Rae nodded, frowning. "I expected to hear word of the Ghost Raiders by now … but it seems they didn't reive anywhere in The Western Isles this autumn." Indeed, September through to early November had been foggy. Rae had ensured he had patrols out every evening during the risky months, keeping an eye on the nearby villages, and the coastline for any sign of *The Night Plunderer* lurking in the mist. However, not only had they not bothered his lands, but it seemed they'd left everyone else alone too. It was odd, and their silence made him nervous.

"Maybe their thwarted attack at Moy at Bealtunn scared them off," Jack suggested.

Rae's lips thinned. He too wanted to believe that, but a tension deep in his chest told him the raiders were merely biding their time. Even the joy he'd found with Kylie couldn't distract him from it. "That's what they want us to think," he said after a pause. "They'll wait until we get complacent and then strike." He paused then, flashing his brother a hard smile. "But at least we're prepared now."

Jack's auburn brows knitted together. "Aye, although we haven't had fog for a while … now it's cold enough to freeze off Lucifer's balls."

Rae snorted. "No, but in spring, when the sea fret rolls in again, we must be ready."

Silence fell between the brothers then. They slowly sipped at their wine while Storm picked up an old ox bone and began gnawing it before the fire.

"How are my nephews progressing with their studies?" Jack asked finally when it became clear that Rae wasn't going to restart their conversation.

"Impressively." Rae glanced his brother's way to find Jack watching him, his gaze slightly narrowed. "They both had a brief exchange with me in French yesterday."

Jack smiled. "It seems their tutor has gotten that rambunctious pair in hand."

"Aye," Rae replied cautiously. "It would seem so."

"Ye did well to hire her. I knew she'd work out."

Rae nodded, although he now fought a growing uneasiness at the direction his brother was heading in. He didn't wish to discuss Kylie at present.

"Ye two appear to get on well," Jack observed then.

Rae stilled. Cods, his brother was like Storm on a scent. Taking a fortifying gulp of wine, he then shrugged. "Well enough."

"On the contrary, brother … before she came to live here, ye were growing increasingly dour. But of late, I've actually seen ye smiling … often." He paused before grimacing. "Although not this eve."

"Don't look for things that aren't there," Rae replied, even as he started to sweat.

"Have ye thought about wooing her?" Jack pressed on.

"No," Rae replied curtly.

"Why not?"

"Because I don't wish to wed again."

Jack frowned. "Ye told me that after Donalda died, but I thought it was grief talking. Surely, now that time has passed, ye could consider finding yerself a wife?" He paused then, his green eyes twinkling. "I know Lady Grant comes across as a little spinsterish at times … but ye know what they say about women who—"

"That's enough," Rae cut him off sharply. "We aren't speaking about the *lady* I've hired to instruct my sons in such a manner." His pulse was racing now. He had to find a way to still his brother's flapping tongue. The trouble was, Jack was far too observant; he always had been. They'd never spoken of Rae's marriage to Donalda, or how he'd felt about his wife, but sometimes, Rae had marked the knowing glint in his eyes.

Nonetheless, he wasn't going to discuss Kylie with him, and he definitely wouldn't be telling him about the game he'd tangled himself in—one he was losing control of.

Jack's eyebrows shot up. "I wasn't." He gave his head a shake. "Christ's teeth, ye *are* a tetchy bastard."

21: ALL GAMES MUST END

Two months later …

"CAN WE GO a little farther?"

Lyle's face was so hopeful that Kylie couldn't help but smile. "Very well … just a few furlongs more," she replied. "But then we must return to the broch."

"Aye," Ailean piped up. "I don't want to miss out on venison pie."

"That's right," Kylie agreed, still smiling. "Neither do I." She too had heard about the delicious noon meal Cadha and her assistants were preparing. The laird and his men had been hunting a week earlier and brought back two young hinds. And now that the meat had hung long enough, venison pie had been promised—a treat indeed.

Kylie continued walking along the path, while the lads ran ahead. They'd just finished a conversation in French. It had been stilted, but the longest exchange either of the lads had managed so far.

They always did better when they were outdoors, walking with her. However, this winter had been bitterly cold. It was now heading toward late February, and large patches of snow still covered the ground, while the rest of it had turned to mud.

All three of them were bundled up in leather and fur, yet the wind still chapped their faces. All the same, it was a joy to be out of the broch. The boys had run about like excited puppies since the moment they passed under the gates. It was hard not to smile, and as she walked, a feeling of contentment settled deep into her bones. She'd never fitted in anywhere as she did at Dounarwyse.

They crossed over a bridge then, spanning a burn that ran down the cleft between two hills before emptying out into the Sound. Rushing water foamed and bubbled over smooth rocks.

"Where is all the water coming from?" Ailean asked, halting on the bridge and peering over the wooden railing.

"From there." Kylie pointed to where smooth green hills rose to the west. "The snow is melting on higher ground and turning into water."

"When can we go exploring?" Lyle asked, his round cheeks flushed with cold and excitement. "I want to climb Dùn da Ghaoithe again."

"I'm sure yer father will take ye out," she replied. "For spring isn't far off." Her belly clenched as she said these words. Spring loomed on the horizon. Despite the chill in the air, there was a warmth to the sun that hinted that winter was drawing to a close.

And soon, the game she and Rae had embarked upon would also end.

The trio resumed their walk, Ailean and Lyle skipping ahead once more before they picked up sticks and pretended to duel.

As she watched them, Kylie's mood, which had been light when she'd left the broch, darkened.

It had been a mistake to think about Rae. After their conversation at Yule, they'd resumed their weekly liaisons, with her tiptoeing to his chamber every Sunday night. And in the interim, the laird hadn't asked her to join him for a meal alone or strayed beyond the limits they'd established.

She'd been grateful.

In truth, she'd braced herself for Rae to make another attempt to deepen their relationship. But he hadn't. Part of her had been disappointed, yet she crushed that response whenever it tugged at her. They spent much of their time together in bed, but they talked a lot too. Their exploration of The Art of Coupling had allowed her to learn a lot about the chieftain of Dounarwyse, and about herself.

He had a dry sense of humor, a sense of the ridiculous, and tenderness that took her breath away sometimes—while she was bolder and more adventurous than she'd even thought. But more than anything, she liked who she was when she was with him. Rae made her feel safe.

And that was part of the problem. She liked the man far too much.

That wasn't part of their agreement.

All the same, ever since their supper together at Yule, she'd marked a change in him. He was still as hungry for her each week, as passionate, but there was a slight reserve in his manner when they weren't abed. And when she observed him at mealtimes, or when she saw him on the walls with his men or talking to Jack in the barmkin, he seemed a little subdued.

Was she the cause?

Clenching her jaw, she picked up her skirts and stepped over a large puddle. *By the Saints, think about something else!* Her gaze slid left then, over the rough surface of the Sound. The wind had whipped it up this morning, although the shadow of the mainland was sharp against a robin's egg blue sky.

Perthshire, and Meggernie Castle, lay in that direction.

Longing tugged at her chest, not for her lover this time though. Indeed, she'd received a letter from Makenna the day before, with news from Meggernie, and reading her sister's missive, and her complaints about the Campbells pushing south again, had left her unsettled. Two days before getting word from Makenna, a letter had also arrived from Liza. All was well at Moy, and Liza planned to visit them at Bealtunn.

Of course, this news had pleased Kylie—despite that she still didn't approve of her sister's marriage—yet it couldn't shift the discomfort that sat on her chest like a boulder these days.

The nagging intuition that she was heading for disaster.

Anxiety fluttered up once more, although she tried to ignore it. *Life is good,* she told herself firmly, *and ye'd do well to stay focused on the progress ye have made with Ailean and Lyle.* Aye, she had. The lads were learning swiftly now. These days, they came to their lessons with an enthusiasm that warmed her.

"Look!" Lyle exclaimed then, throwing aside his stick and racing away down the path. "Snowdrops!"

Laughing, Ailean took off after him.

Quickening her pace, Kylie followed them to where a patch of slender green shoots—with delicate white bonnets that waved in the wind—grew farther up the path, poking up through a patch of melting snow.

Indeed, they were snowdrops—spring flowers that were symbols of hope and friendship in adversity.

"Spring is here!" Ailean said, flashing her a grin. "At last!"

Kylie forced a smile in return. "Almost," she replied, even as her belly dropped to her boots. "We haven't reached March yet … don't wish time away, lad."

She was a coward. She should have told Rae that day of her discovery.

After all, she'd made it clear. As soon as the first of the snowdrops appeared, their game would conclude.

But she hesitated, waiting until two days later, after they'd lain together again.

Kylie collapsed panting against Rae's sweat-slick chest, her body trembling in the aftermath of their passion, pleasure still pulsing through her womb. And as she lay there, and the world stopped spinning, her thoughts turned to the flowers she'd seen glistening in the late winter sunlight.

It's time.

Finally gathering her courage, she propped herself up onto an elbow and gazed down into Rae's ruggedly handsome face. His eyes were still closed.

"I've seen my first snowdrops," she murmured.

His eyelids flickered open, and his gaze shadowed, before his mouth curved into a wry smile. "So did I … a couple of days ago now … but I was loath to tell ye."

Kylie grimaced. So, they were both fazarts. She decided not to admit that she too had hesitated to tell him. She'd wanted one last time together.

They both had.

Rae huffed a sigh then. "Our arrangement is at its conclusion then?"

She nodded, even as an ache rose beneath her breastbone. "Aye, all games must end … sooner or later."

Their gazes fused before he finally replied, "Never have six months passed so quickly. It seems the blinking of an eye since we opened The Art of Coupling."

She gave a soft snort. "Aye, but we've worked our way through it now." Her breathing quickened then. "And … these days, we need no guide."

"No." He lifted a hand, brushing Kylie's hair back from her face. "I will miss this … closeness."

As will I. How she wanted to say those words, yet she stopped herself. Making such an admission would make severing this connection even harder.

Something shifted in his eyes then, and she tensed, bracing herself for him to ask for another month or two. She'd told herself before coming to him tonight that she'd remain strong. If he suggested such a thing, she was to deny him. The past six moons had flown, yet at the same time, it was too long. Each murmured conversation they had, in the aftermath of their coupling, each tender, unguarded moment, brought her closer to the brink of falling into a chasm.

Kylie had to pull herself back from it.

But Rae surprised her.

He didn't ask for more time or try to wheedle another promise out of her. Instead, he continued to look up at Kylie as his thumb caressed her cheek. And the softness of those fern-green eyes made her want to weep.

How easy it would be to love this man, to open herself up to him.

Nonetheless, being his lover for a spell was one thing, remaining in that role longer term was another. She could see trouble ahead and would do all she could to prevent it.

The moment drew out, and awkwardness stole over her. Clearing her throat, she favored him with a brittle smile. "There's no need to look glum just yet, Maclean," she teased, even as the ache under her breastbone intensified. "The night is still young … ye can have me again, if ye wish?"

He laughed before, to her surprise, shaking his head. "If tonight is the last we shall have together, then I'd rather spend the rest of it *talking* to ye, than swiving ye." His mouth curved once more, even if his gaze remained solemn. "Going forward, things will be different."

Kylie swallowed, even as she cursed this man for his decency. Couldn't he be selfish and callous, as Errol had been? Couldn't he say something that would make it easier to harden her heart against him?

Usually, Rae fell asleep after Kylie left him.

But not tonight.

Listening as the door whispered shut one last time, and his lover stealthily made her way back to her bedchamber, he stared up at the beams crisscrossing the ceiling above.

His self-restraint amazed him. So many times over the last few hours, he'd ached to tell Kylie that he was in love with her. And yet, he'd somehow managed to swallow the words, to let their last night together pass without a declaration that would likely end in his humiliation.

No, it was one that *definitely* would shame him.

She'd made her wishes clear. He might be pining for her like a lovesick youth, but she remained emotionally reserved. Sometimes, and tonight was one such occasion, it felt as if there were an iron door between them. She'd let him get close over the past months, but at a certain point her shields had come up, and there was no getting past them.

Of course, he'd known this moment was near. He'd been out riding when he'd seen the snowdrops.

Too soon.

He'd pushed his discovery to the back of his thoughts then and gotten on with his day. All the same, he'd dreaded this evening.

After their final tumble, he'd wanted to converse with his lover intimately for a while, for he enjoyed the closeness that had developed between them. He'd never felt so comfortable with a woman, so accepted for himself—and on a selfish level, he wished to have one last exchange he could revisit whenever loneliness sank its claws into him. But things had been awkward after Kylie had told him she'd seen her first snowdrops. Instead of talking, they'd merely held each other. And when she'd finally risen from the bed and pulled her night-rail back on, before slinging her cloak about her shoulders, he'd felt as if she were taking a piece of him with her.

Smitten fool.

Aye, he was.

Rolling over, Rae buried his face in the pillow and growled the saltiest curse he knew. This game had been his idea, but he'd overestimated his ability to be able to share his bed with Kylie Grant for six months and not fall for her.

She had managed though, and the realization left a bitter taste in his mouth.

22: A LOCK AND KEY

THE RAIN HAMMERED against the curtain wall, the skies above the color of lead.

Squinting out at the misty landscape beyond, while water ran off the brim of his sealskin hood, Rae grimaced. The spring rains had started early this year. Usually, they didn't get a deluge until April, but it was only the beginning of March, and the weather had turned. The last of the snow had melted with the end of February, the air had warmed—and heavy rain clouds had rolled in.

To the east, the Sound of Mull churned, white caps foaming. Unsurprisingly, no birlinns or cogs sailed between Mull and the mainland this morning.

Rae muttered a curse under his breath. He'd ordered a shipment of oats from Argyll—as a harsh winter had depleted their stores—but it would be delayed now. Turning from the view, he strode back along the walls, to the slippery steps that led back down to the barmkin. Large puddles had formed upon the cobbles, where two bairns splashed like waterfowl.

An instant later, their mother rushed out of the kitchen, her voice carrying through the pattering rain. "Look what ye have done ... yer new trews are filthy!" she shouted, waving a wooden spoon. "Get indoors, the pair of ye!"

The two lads hurriedly obeyed, ducking out of the way of her spoon as she took a swipe at them.

"Remember when we used to do that?"

Rae turned from watching the bairns disappear to see Jack approach, his long legs eating up the space between them. Like his brother, the Captain of the Guard wore a hooded sealskin cloak.

"Aye," he replied, with a half-smile. "Ma used to come after us with a wooden spoon too when we went back indoors, dripping and muddy."

Jack smiled back, although the expression was wistful. Shona Maclean had possessed a fiery temper, but they'd adored her. She'd also been big-hearted and affectionate—and her laughter had filled the broch. Her death had been sudden, a tumble down the tower house stairs had broken her neck. Their father had loved his wife deeply, and he was never the same afterward, although Baird's death had come little over a year later.

"We were trouble, weren't we?" Jack said, halting before him.

Rae snorted. "*Ye* were." He glanced around him then, his focus shifting from the past to the present. "The barmkin is close to flooding, Jack ... we will need to open the storm drain earlier than usual this year." His attention rested for a moment on the iron door inset into the eastern wall. A drain ran around the edge of the yard, and a small gap at the bottom of the iron allowed some water to escape. Usually, once the spring rains began, they would open the storm drain for a few weeks, allowing the barmkin to drain properly. "Ye'd better get the lads to unlock it this morning."

"I shall see it done."

Rae glanced back at Jack, to find his brother scrutinizing him.

Ignoring his penetrating look, he cleared his throat. "Once the rain eases, I shall lead another patrol south. I don't trust how quiet things have been of late." He halted then before growling, "The Raiders will attack again … soon."

"Maybe they won't," Jack suggested, cocking an eyebrow. "Have ye considered that?"

"They will … I feel it in my bones."

Jack huffed a sigh. "Aye, well … a man should always trust his instincts." His brow creased then. "Ye don't have to lead the patrol though … that's why ye have me, remember?"

"Don't worry, ye won't be sitting around on yer arse," Rae shot back. In truth, he was desperate to get away from Dounarwyse for a while. Of late, he'd started to feel as if the walls were closing in. "I'll send ye and the lads north again."

Jack nodded slowly. He was still frowning, and remorse tugged at Rae. He'd just snapped his head off for no good reason—something he'd done with increasing frequency of late—but he needed Jack not to question him.

His brother's gaze shadowed then, his lips parting, as if he was about to ask him something that Rae wouldn't—and couldn't—answer.

"I'll see ye at the noon meal," he said, stepping away from him abruptly. Then, before Jack could say anything else, he turned on his heel and stalked back inside the broch.

Storm was waiting for him, heavy tail thumping on the floor, inside the entrance hall. Usually, the sight of his dog roused a smile from him, yet not this morning. Fortunately, Storm didn't care what mood he was in. The canny collie had remained inside this morning, having taken one look at the hammering rain and deciding it was more pleasant indoors. As always, he fell in behind him as Rae took the stairs up to his solar.

Stepping into a chamber that was often his refuge, his escape from the demands of running the fortress, Rae stripped off his cloak and hung it up by the fire. However, no sooner had he done so when his chest tightened and his breathing grew shallow—and suddenly, dizziness assailed him.

Satan's cods, what's wrong with me?

Even being alone in here, with the roaring fire warming the damp air, didn't make him feel better. The sacking on the two windows had been rolled down, to keep the rain out. Unfortunately, it also kept the smoky air in. He felt as if he were being suffocated.

Crossing to the nearest window, he rolled up the sacking. He then placed his hands on the stone still and leaned forward, sucking the fresh air into his lungs. Eventually, the tightness in his chest eased, as did the lightheadedness.

Meanwhile, Storm pressed up against his leg and gave a low whine. The collie *had* noted that something was amiss, after all. Rousing himself, he reached down and stroked the dog's head. "I'm better now, lad," he murmured. "Don't fash yerself."

But, even as he spoke, something deep inside his chest twisted.

He wasn't any better. Not really.

Three long weeks had passed since his final night with Kylie, and with each day, he'd started to feel worse. How he missed her.

It was torture living under the same roof, seeing her at mealtimes, or watching from the window as she went out on her regular stroll with his sons, and not being able to talk to her frankly. Numerous times since that night, he'd been about to invite her to supper or to take a cup of wine with him in his solar in the evening.

But on each occasion, he'd choked the words back.

His hand still resting upon the window ledge curled into a fist.

He'd thought he'd handle things better than this. He'd lived long enough to know what disappointment was, what loss and loneliness felt like, but he'd been unprepared for this. Kylie had warmed his soul, and her absence made him feel as if winter had returned.

Storm gave another whine and pushed his nose insistently against his master's thigh, and in response, Rae huffed a bitter laugh. "Ye know I'm lying, don't ye?" He pulled a face then. "I'm not hiding this well."

No, Jack wasn't the only one in his household who'd noticed something was amiss. Both his sons had been unusually quiet at mealtimes, watching their ill-tempered father with worried gazes. No doubt, they thought they'd done something to make him that way. His grumpiness had also made the servants jittery, and he'd caught Kylie giving him a probing look once or twice.

He was miserable—and yet she appeared unmoved. She was different these days though, a little withdrawn.

Rae swallowed and pushed himself off the window ledge. He then moved to the sideboard and poured himself a large cup of plum wine. He never drank this early in the day, but today, he'd make an exception.

Things couldn't stay as they were.

Something had to be done.

"I must speak to ye, Lady Grant." The rumble of the laird's voice made Kylie glance up as she rose from the table. The noon meal had just ended, and around her, the hall was emptying out. Tara had just gotten to her feet and was struggling with wee Grace, who squalled unhappily in her arms. The bairn was getting her first teeth and wasn't herself.

Meeting Rae's gaze squarely for what felt like the first time in weeks, she forced a smile, even as her pulse took off. "Aye, Maclean?"

He nodded, his mouth compressing into a stern line. "Join me in my solar shortly."

And with that, before she could say a word, he moved away from the chieftain's table and left the hall.

Kylie watched him go, marking the tense set of his shoulders, even as her belly sank.

She'd been waiting for this—the moment that the laird would realize he didn't want her residing in his broch any longer—but even so, nausea washed over her.

"I won't join ye in the solar this afternoon, I'm afraid." Tara cast Kylie an apologetic look as she carried her squalling daughter away. "Grace needs me."

"It's no bother," Kylie called after her. "I might take a rest in my chamber instead."

The women had fallen into a pleasant routine over the winter, where Tara would leave her daughters with a maid for an hour or two while she and Kylie embroidered, wove, or sewed in the lady's solar. It was something they both looked forward to—although Tara's distraction today was a blessing. Kylie wagered that after her meeting with the taciturn laird, she wouldn't be in the mood.

Instead, she'd be packing her bags.

Heart in her throat, she made her way from the hall, past where the men were donning their sealskin cloaks to venture out into the driving rain once more. The air inside the hall was musty with the odor of wet wool and leather, and despite the rise and fall of voices, Kylie could hear the hiss of rain against the walls.

But it was difficult to pay attention to her surroundings, not when Rae awaited her upstairs.

She climbed the stairs slowly, prolonging the inevitable, and found the solar door ajar when she arrived on the landing. It was clear she was to enter.

Clearing her throat, she pushed open the door. "Maclean?"

Rae turned from where he'd been standing by the hearth, while Storm rushed to her, tail wagging.

"Close the door," the laird said softly.

Patting Storm's head with one hand, Kylie pushed the door closed behind her with the other. "Ye wished to talk to me?"

He nodded, his face the most severe she'd ever seen it.

Mother Mary, he *was* going to dismiss her.

Her heart started to kick against her ribs then, panic bubbling up. Curse her, she'd really made a mess of her new start. Dounarwyse felt like home these days, but it wouldn't for much longer—and she only had herself to blame. She'd let lust addle her wits and cloud her judgment. Rae had enjoyed their game, but now her presence here clearly chafed him. He didn't like that she hadn't wished to continue. Like most men, he liked to be the one in charge.

"I can't go on like this."

She started to sweat, even as her mouth went dry. "Excuse me?"

He moved toward her, halting when they stood around three feet apart. Meanwhile, Storm sat down between them. The dog had gone still; he'd even stopped wagging his tail, as if he sensed the gathering tension in the solar.

"I'm miserable," he said roughly. "Every morning, when I wake up, I have a blessed moment of relief before it feels as if a mule has just kicked me in the guts. I then force myself to go about my day … but all I can think about … is *ye*. We're worse than strangers now, lass, and I hate it. This longing is killing me. I—"

Kylie exhaled sharply. "Rae, I don't think—"

"Let me finish."

She clenched her jaw, swallowing down panic and the words that now burned on her tongue. She didn't want to allow him to continue. They'd made an agreement, and he was ruining everything. Even so, she remained silent as he'd asked.

"It started as a game … a way to make up for everything we'd both missed out on … but it became much more to me," he said huskily, his gaze never leaving hers. "I'm sick with love for ye, lass … and it's become unbearable."

Fear washed over her at these words, cold and prickly. "Then I should go," she gasped, even as her blood started to roar in her ears. God's troth, she felt like fleeing right this moment—picking up her skirts and running from Dounarwyse, never to return.

"No." Rae stepped closer, nudging Storm out of the way with his knee. He then placed his hands upon her shoulders.

Kylie's breathing hitched. It was the first time they'd touched since their last night together. The heat of his palms through her clothing, and the gentleness and strength of his fingers, made it difficult to concentrate. But she had to.

"I don't want ye to go," he said, his voice urgent now. "I want ye to stay … to be my wife. We are right together. We *fit*. Like a lock and key. Let me love ye, Kylie. Please."

She stared back at him, even as fear hammered against her ribs. "But ye told me ye never wanted to wed again?" She couldn't help but let an accusing edge creep into her voice, for in truth, she felt betrayed.

He swallowed. "I did. But that was before I spent time with *ye*." His gaze searched her face. "Donalda and I were never right for each other … but ye and I are."

"Ye don't know that," she burst out. "We spent a few months enjoying each other's bodies … that doesn't mean we'd be happy together."

"That's just an excuse, and ye know it," he shot back, his grip on her shoulders tensing a little. "We did far more than lie with each other. We talked. We learned of each other's pasts. We got to know each other. We grew to *trust* each other."

Shaking her head, she gently extracted herself from his grasp and stepped back, creating much-needed space between them.

A nerve ticked in Rae's cheek. "Ye are afraid," he said roughly. "And ye believe clenching yer heart like a fist will keep ye safe from harm … but it won't. All it will do is drain the joy from yer life. A clenched fist can hold nothing."

Her chest started to ache. "I've made my choice, Rae … please accept it."

"So, ye don't love me?" he asked, his voice barely above a whisper.

"No." Dizziness assailed her then, but she held fast.

He flinched at that. She'd wounded him, and the knowledge made her feel sick. But the fear was greater.

He moved back farther from her, and cold air rushed in between them. Storm tried to push his master back toward her, but Rae ignored the collie. "Ye want to leave then?" His voice was flat and his expression had veiled now, as he too shored up his defenses.

Kylie swallowed hard to loosen her painfully tight throat. Curse it, she'd entered the solar fearing that he'd send her away. But now he'd made it her decision. She didn't want to leave Dounarwyse and the life she'd made for herself, yet after this conversation, she couldn't remain here. "Aye," she replied roughly. "As soon as possible."

23: THE MOMENT TO STRIKE

Castle Coeffin, Isle of Lismore

Two days later …

"THE RAIN is slackening," Tormod announced as he strode up the gangplank. "We need to make for Mull."

Straightening up from where he'd been coiling a heavy oiled rope, the captain of *The Night Plunderer* scowled. "It's a bit early, isn't it?"

"Aye, but since it's been pissing down for over three days now, Rae Maclean will have opened the storm drain in the east wall. It's time."

Captain Macbeth's scowl became a glower, yet Tormod pretended not to notice. He was a belligerent bastard. His crew minded him, and until now, Tormod had pretended to do so as well.

However, he wasn't missing out on this opportunity.

Leaden clouds hung over the Isle of Lismore this morning, so low that they obscured the top of Castle Coeffin's tower house. But as Tormod had noted, the rain wasn't as heavy as it had been for the past days. It had lessened from a steady drumming downpour to a thick mist.

They had to go.

"We don't need to hurry," Macbeth muttered, placing meaty hands on his hips. "The spring's barely begun."

"On the contrary, if we delay, we'll make things harder for ourselves." Tormod stepped up onto the deck and halted before the big man. "As the days lengthen and the nights grow shorter, morale will rise within the fortress. They'll be at a low ebb right now. The winter was a bitter one, and the rain has been relentless. The guards on the wall will be tired and ill-tempered. This is the moment to strike."

Tormod marked then that their conversation had drawn the attention of the other members of Macbeth's crew. They halted in their tasks, turning to watch their captain and the man who'd recently joined their ranks eyeball each other.

"MacDougall has a point, Captain." One of them, a grizzled warrior named Harris, spoke up. "Best to hit them when they least expect it."

"Aye, once spring is in full flush, and the mists roll in, they'll be wary," another crewmember added. "They'll be on the lookout for us."

"Indeed." Tormod flashed both men a smile. "The lads have raised worthy points."

It pleased him that two of the crew had voiced their agreement. He'd worked hard over the winter to develop a rapport with the crew of *The Night Plunderer*. Ross Macbeth was the only one who didn't like him—but then the captain didn't like anyone really. When he wasn't prowling the deck of his cog, bellowing orders at his men, Macbeth locked himself away in his cabin. Tormod had noted the distance between the captain and his crew and had worked to exploit it.

When they stormed Dounarwyse, he wanted them *all* on his side.

Macbeth didn't suspect it yet, but his days in charge were numbered.

Tormod was a leader, not a follower, and once they took Dounarwyse, he didn't want to share his plunder, or power, with Macbeth. Once Rae Maclean and his brother swung from the castle walls, he'd take a knife to Macbeth's throat. Right now, though, he needed the man.

Excitement tightened his chest then.

He couldn't wait to return to Dounarwyse and have his reckoning with its laird.

Maclean would rue the day he ever lifted a whip to him. The humiliation of it still burned like a coal in his gut. Makenna MacGregor had witnessed his punishment too, although he'd clawed back some dignity by having the last word as he left. He'd meant those words—she *would* see him again. He'd seen fear flare in her moss-green gaze, and it had thrilled him. Makenna was more courageous than most *men*, yet he'd pierced her armor. He'd shown her that she was weaker than she believed.

It was a pity the lass would no longer be in residence at Dounarwyse. She'd have returned to her father's castle in Perthshire by now. One day, he intended to have Makenna for his own—but first, he would win himself a broch.

Meanwhile, a few feet away, Macbeth eyed him. Even though his strong jaw was covered by a thick beard, Tormod saw it flex. He wasn't happy, and yet knew he was outnumbered.

"All right then," he growled, his mouth pursing. "We'll set sail tomorrow morning." He moved forward then, one thick finger stabbing into Tormod's chest. "But mark me, MacDougall ... we aren't raising anchor until ye sit down with me and explain every detail of this plan of yers."

Tormod didn't react, even if he longed to do nothing more than grab that finger and snap it like a twig. Instead, he favored Macbeth with a slow smile. "As ye wish." He nodded left then, toward the captain's cabin. "Shall we?"

Dounarwyse broch, Isle of Mull

Later the same day ...

Standing at the window in the lady's solar, looking east as a murky grey day slid into an equally grim twilight, Kylie fought the urge to weep.

She'd been dueling with herself all day, telling herself that she needed to be strong. All the same, the urge to bawl like a bairn clawed at her.

The past days had been the hardest of her life, especially after she'd broken the news to her charges and Tara that she was leaving.

Ailean and Lyle had both burst into noisy tears. Then, the lads shocked Kylie by rushing to her, throwing their arms around her legs, and begging her to stay. She'd felt like a beast denying them, even as she'd mouthed a flimsy excuse about her family at Meggernie needing her.

Rae's sons hadn't understood, and the hurt in their eyes had cut her like a blade to the belly.

But she'd remained dogged to her purpose. After their final conversation, Rae had told her that a ferry for Oban was due in three days' time. He'd ensure she was on it.

Tara too had gotten tearful. She'd also been harder to lie to than Ailean and Lyle. Her silver eyes had been troubled afterward. "But I thought ye loved living here?"

"I do," Kylie had replied with a wavering smile. "Yet I've missed my family terribly of late. Meggernie is where I need to be."

Tara had given her a penetrating look then, and her breathing had caught. Her friend didn't believe her, yet, as if sensing Kylie's brittleness, she didn't push.

Telling everyone had been awful, but it was done now. Three days had passed—and tomorrow morning, Rae's men would accompany her to Craignure and put her on the ferry.

Dragging in a ragged breath, she continued to stare out the window. After days of heavy rains, the weather was finally starting to improve. Thank the Saints, or the ferry might not leave in the morning. Nonetheless, a wet mist hung over Dounarwyse this evening. Everything around her looked grey.

Of late, the world had lost its sparkle, and a knot of misery had lodged tight in her throat.

A clenched fist can hold nothing.

Rae wasn't a fool. He knew she was afraid. But the harder he'd pushed, the higher her fear had swarmed. In the end, nothing he'd said would have made any difference.

A tear escaped then, scalding her cheek as it trickled down to her chin. A second one swiftly followed. Her throat burned now as she fought the storm inside her.

The whisper of the door opening behind her made her startle.

"There ye are." Tara's voice filled the lady's solar. "I thought, since it's yer last evening here, we might—" Her voice cut off as Kylie hurriedly knuckled away her tears and turned from the window to face her. Tara's features tightened. "Sorry ... I shouldn't have burst in like that."

Kylie managed a brittle smile, even though there was little point. Tara could see she'd been crying. "This is yer solar too," she replied huskily. "Of course, ye can enter whenever ye wish."

Tara nodded before cautiously approaching her. And then, before Kylie could protest, or step away, she enfolded her into a tight hug.

She went rigid initially, panic fluttering in her chest, yet Tara's hold merely tightened. A moment later, she gave herself up to it. Liza and Makenna weren't here to comfort her, but she trusted Tara too, and it was exhausting remaining so stoic.

Tears started to trickle down her cheeks once more, and she hiccoughed, swallowing a sob.

Eventually, Tara drew back, her gaze searching her face. "I don't understand," she said softly.

She hiccoughed again and hurriedly wiped at her wet cheeks. "Apologies ... I'm not myself this evening."

"If it pains ye to leave Dounarwyse, then why are ye doing so?"

She shook her head as her throat constricted. Curse Tara, she meant well, but this conversation wouldn't help her. "It's complicated," she said, her voice hoarse. Stepping back, she sniffed. "But it's best I go."

Tara's eyes narrowed. "Jack thinks something has happened … between ye and Rae … and I didn't believe him initially." She paused then, her expression shadowing. "Yet now I do."

Kylie's heart lurched. She didn't reply, for her tongue felt as if it had welded itself to the roof of her mouth.

All the same, her silence was damning, and Tara's mouth curved into a gentle smile. "Aye … my husband is more perceptive than me, it seems." She paused then, searching her face once more. "Is it really so bad to be in love with him?"

Dizziness swept over Kylie. "I'm not—" she croaked.

However, Tara cut her off. "He's a good man … one of the best."

Her chest started to ache. "I know," she whispered.

"Did he do something to offend ye?"

Kylie dragged in another shaky breath and turned from her friend, moving to the window again. Cool, wet air feathered across her heated cheeks, soothing her a little. "No," she whispered.

"Then why are ye so upset?"

Silence fell between them, and Kylie let it lie. Her pulse started to race. She couldn't spill her guts to Tara—and not just to preserve her own dignity, but for Rae's sake too. It was too private, too raw. "I'm sorry … but I" —she broke off there and dragged in a deep, shaky breath, swallowing the sob that clawed its way up— "I c … can't talk about it."

"Don't fash yerself, hen," Tara answered softly. The scuff of her slippered feet followed as she drew near once more. A moment later, her hand rested on Kylie's shoulder. "I'll not pry it out of ye."

24: READY TO LEAVE

The Sound of Mull

STANDING ON THE deck of *The Night Plunderer*, his legs bent slightly at the knee with each roll of the cog, Ramsay MacDonald stared west.

He couldn't see it, yet the Isle of Mull lay there, shrouded by night and a curtain of mist.

Ramsay clenched his jaw and scowled into the darkness. As much as he hated to admit it, that weasel Tormod was right. This morning was the perfect moment to strike Dounarwyse. The rain had eased off, making the Sound easier to navigate. It would also mean they wouldn't be washed out of the storm drain when they tried to climb it.

MacDougall was a canny one. Two clever for Ramsay's liking. He didn't trust men as intelligent as the newest addition to his crew. Over the past months, he'd marked the way Tormod had befriended the other raiders. In the evenings, Ramsay didn't drink or dice with his men, but Tormod did. He often heard him jesting with them or ribbing one of his crewmates.

Ramsay had stayed alive over the past years by listening to his gut—and it told him that Tormod wasn't to be trusted.

He needed the warrior to get into Dounarwyse and take it successfully, for Tormod's knowledge of the broch and its routines made him indispensable. For the moment. However, once the broch was taken and Rae and Jack Maclean were dead, Ramsay intended to kill Tormod and take Dounarwyse for his own.

Why shouldn't he? He'd suffered more at the Macleans' hands than Tormod ever had. He deserved recompense. He'd rule the broch *and* Tara. A smile tugged at his lips as he imagined all the things he'd to do the haughty bitch. Maybe, he'd keep Jack alive for a while so he could watch.

"Not long now." A familiar voice cut through his lascivious, vengeful thoughts, and he glanced over his shoulder at where a tall, lean form approached, picking his way through the slumbering figures of the warband they'd amassed over the long winter: fifty men ready to take Dounarwyse. The moon was trying to break through the cloud above, and a few shafts of moonlight had managed. It glinted off Tormod's pale hair and frosted his haughty face.

The hair on the back of Ramsay's arms prickled.

"No," he replied gruffly. "We're almost close enough to drop anchor." Ramsay frowned then. "Maybe we should go in now, the dead of night has always worked well for us Ghost Raiders."

"Not yet," Tormod replied, stepping up to his shoulder, his own gaze fixed upon the dark western horizon. "Just before dawn is better. The Guard will be close to changing, and those on the wall will be weary." He glanced Ramsay's way then. "I've thought long and hard about this day over the past months, Captain. My plan is a good one.”

Ramsay gave a soft snort at this before asking, “So, we’ll need to wade through water to get to the tunnel entrance?”

Tormod nodded.

“And there won’t be any guards around?”

“No … the drain empties amongst the rocks directly beneath the broch. If we use mist and darkness as a cloak, no one watching from the walls will see us either.”

“And how easy will it be to climb up the drain?”

“Not very … but we’ll have our weapons tied to our backs.”

“Great,” Ramsay grumbled. “I hate cramped spaces.”

Tormod shrugged. “It might be a bit of a squeeze for a man of yer girth … but it's manageable.” Ramsay scowled at this. He didn’t appreciate the snide edge to the younger man’s voice.

“As soon as we’re clear of the tunnel and in the barmkin, we will split into our teams,” Tormod went on. “Ye shall go with those securing the walls, and I will lead my team into the broch to deal with the laird.”

Ramsay pulled a face. “No … Harris and four others are handling the gate,” he answered, his tone hardening. Indeed, he’d confirmed this with the lads the day before while Tormod had been out recruiting the last of the men who’d join them. He wasn’t going to let this interloper dictate all the details of this attack. “*I’ll* storm the guard tower with Will, Nathair, and Coll … that’s where Jack Maclean and his family sleep.”

Tormod’s lean frame tensed. “That’s not the plan we agreed to.”

Ramsay snorted. “I don’t give a pig’s arse about yer plan … I told ye from the start that I wanted Jack’s head and his wife as my prize. The others can secure the walls, trap the guards in the barracks, and get to the bell tower to prevent anyone from raising the alarm. But I'll have my revenge first." Of course, his plans were a little different from those he admitted, for he intended to maim Jack, take him captive, and then draw his suffering out. However, Tormod didn't need to know that.

Something ugly rippled over his companion's face at these words. It was fleeting, yet in the moonlight it was unmistakable, and Ramsay stilled. His right hand, which hung at his side, flexed as he readied himself to draw his dirk. MacDougall acted like everyone's friend, yet it was a thin veneer. The man didn't like to be crossed, and he hated that Ramsay was in charge here.

Moments passed, and Ramsay's fingers brushed the grip of his dirk. Aye, he was ready.

However, the warrior didn't move. "Very well," he said eventually, "As ye wish."

Tormod lowered himself into the water, clenching his teeth as the chill hit him. Satan's turds, it was freezing. Around him, he heard the gentle splash of the other warriors doing the same, before someone muttered an oath.

"Quiet," Macbeth hissed.

Tormod cast a narrowed gaze around him, barely able to make out the shapes of the thirty men who'd accompanied him. They were ready, as was he. The remaining twenty men—warriors he'd spent the last few months recruiting and then training—waited onboard *The Night Plunderer* for their signal.

As soon as the guards at the gate were dealt with, one of the Raiders would wave a black flag from the ramparts, signaling that it was safe for them to sail in and drop anchor. The rest of their men would then enter the fortress and help secure it. The pirate cog was heavy with supplies—sacks of grain, wheels of cheese, barrels of pickled herrings, among other items—which would ensure they'd outlast a siege. One of the first things Tormod would do, once the broch was his, was take fowl and goats from Dounarwyse village, as well as all the food and grain he could find.

With a force of fifty men, no one within this broch would be able to resist them. And it would mean that Tormod would have his own sizable guard to take on Loch Maclean when he tried to take the fortress back.

The Ghost Raiders had sailed again, but this time, they'd cast aside their long black cloaks, mailed gloves, and eerie horned sheep skulls. Tonight, they were men again—fell and dangerous.

Of course, their captain was among them, although Tormod wished he wasn't.

Earlier that night, he'd been tempted to draw his dirk and slam the blade through Macbeth's throat. He'd longed to watch desperation and pain flare in the whoreson's eyes before he died. The man was unruly and hated that this attack was Tormod's idea and not his. Not only that, but Macbeth's obsession with getting even with Jack put their mission at risk.

The idiot couldn't seem to focus on anything else.

Tormod wasn't so daft. He was looking forward to killing Rae—although not as much as he was Ross Macbeth—but he was too clever to let it consume him. To take Dounarwyse successfully, they all had to do their part. There could be no mistakes, or they'd be trapped inside the broch's walls and dead by the time the sun crested the hills to the east.

He itched to kill Macbeth too—and he would—but right now, they needed to focus on taking the fortress.

Casting murderous thoughts aside, and focusing instead on the task before him, Tormod turned and began wading right. Above, the moon was setting as it played hide-and-seek with the clouds. Unfortunately, the mist had cleared over the past few hours, something that made him a little nervous.

Maybe we should have come in earlier as Macbeth suggested.

Irritation sliced through him, and he pushed the errant thought aside. No, this was the right time. He'd planned every detail of what he'd do once he climbed up into the barmkin. While Macbeth stormed the guard house, he'd enter the tower house. He'd played the scene in his head, imagining himself running up the stairs to the first level, slamming open the door to the laird's bedchamber, and gutting Rae Maclean before he had the chance to reach for a weapon.

Tormod's skin prickled in anticipation. He hadn't forgotten the flogging the chieftain had given him—for it had left livid scars upon his back—or the vow he'd made himself that Maclean would pay. But more than that, he was about to get the thing he'd craved over all else: to have a broch of his own. Once he had it, the doors that had forever been closed to him would open. He'd be a laird—a man others would cower before. He'd build an army and make this corner of Mull his own. The Battle of Dounarwyse had shown that, aside from access through the storm drain that few knew about, the castle was difficult to take.

Loch Maclean would be incensed to hear of his cousins' deaths, but he wouldn't rid himself of Tormod. And when he was settled, he'd make a trip to Meggernie Castle and make Makenna MacGregor's father an offer he'd be a fool to refuse.

Tormod spied the tunnel opening ahead then, a couple of feet above the lapping water.

Knowing that the others were right behind him, he waded to it, grabbed the stone lip, and hauled himself over the edge. Then, on hands and knees, as he'd done a year earlier when he'd discovered where the drain exited, he moved inside.

A steady stream of water flowed through the tunnel, washing over his hands and knees as he crawled. It would make climbing up harder, but he'd expected this. It was a good sign too, for it meant the iron covering above was still open.

Tormod crawled for a while longer until the tunnel steepened, and he fumbled for handholds in the darkness. It wasn't long before the muscles in his upper arms started to burn. Behind him, he heard a dull thud followed by a muffled curse as one of the men likely hit his head on rock. Aye, it was a tight fit. This space was designed for water, not for large armed warriors.

A hard smile stretched Tormod's lips then. Maclean wouldn't expect an attack to come from a drain.

Cloak wrapped tightly about her, Kylie climbed the steps to the wall.

It was early. The first rays of light hadn't yet lightened the eastern sky, but after a sleepless night staring up at the rafters, she'd eventually risen from her bed and dressed for her journey. She'd even strapped on the slender blade Makenna had gifted her to her thigh. It felt odd wearing a weapon, but she'd be spending a few days on the road, and carrying a knife was prudent. It also brought her closer to Makenna, somehow, as if her sister were traveling with her. Two large leather satchels containing her belongings sat in the center of her bedchamber. Everything was packed. She was ready to leave.

But she'd been ready far too soon. Dawn hadn't yet broken, and the rest of the broch slumbered. After pacing the confines of her bedchamber, she'd eventually decided to burn off some of her restlessness on the walls instead. There, she could watch her last sunrise at Dounarwyse.

Reaching the top of the ramparts, Kylie moved slowly along it, past where a brazier burned low, on the verge of going out.

"Ye're up early, Lady Grant," one of the guards greeted her, turning from where he'd been looking south.

"Aye, Conan," she murmured. "I was hoping for a bonnie sunrise before I go."

The older man favored her with a tired smile. He'd likely been standing here for hours and looked as if he couldn't wait to crawl into his bed. "Ye might be in luck … for the mist is clearing."

Kylie forced a smile in return, even as her belly churned. "Well, I'd better wait for dawn on the eastern wall."

She walked on, her boots scuffing on stone, passing two other guards before she halted on the easternmost edge of the ramparts, near the terrace where Makenna had liked to train with that knave Tormod.

Thinking about her youngest sister made her throat constrict.

They'd soon be reunited. She hadn't heard from Makenna for a while now—something that niggled at Kylie. Her sister was usually reliable in her correspondence. She hoped the feud with the Campbells hadn't taken a turn for the worse. Had their father received a reply from Bran Mackinnon?

She'll be dreading Bealtunn.

Guilt speared Kylie then as she stood upon the shadowy wall, looking east. She hadn't exactly been sympathetic to Makenna's reluctance to wed the young clan-chief. However, she admitted to herself now that she resented her youngest sister's independence. Her bravery. Unlike Makenna, Kylie had behaved as a clan-chief's daughter should: she'd wedded young and forged a valuable alliance for their father. But for years, her sister had escaped that fate. Kylie hadn't seen why she should, but she regretted being so uncharitable now. Makenna loved serving in the Meggernie Guard, and she was fiercely protective of her home. Taking her from it would be a blow.

Kylie dragged in a deep breath.

After her brief exchange with Tara the eve before, she'd retreated to her bedchamber and cried until she felt like a wrung-out dish rag. She'd spent the rest of the night mulling over her choices.

She was fleeing Dounarwyse, and Rae, like a frightened fawn. The realization didn't make her feel particularly proud of herself. All the same, she'd thought her imminent departure might ease her panic, but it hadn't. Instead, an ache of loss had risen deep inside her chest, and as the moment of her departure approached, the sensation grew more insistent. She was steering her own ship once more, but she'd never been unhappier.

"Are ye really such a fazart, lass?" she asked herself softly. There were no guards nearby, so she didn't risk being overheard. Her chest started to ache piteously, and she raised a hand and rubbed at her breastbone with her knuckles. It seemed she was.

She imagined her life back at Meggernie Castle then. Makenna's concern. Her mother's panic. Her father's disappointment. So many questions she wouldn't, couldn't, answer. She'd feel like a burden to everyone: the widow who didn't fit in anywhere.

Of course, her mother—devoutly pious—would likely suggest Kylie become a nun. It was a good solution for high-born widows who didn't wish to remarry. She had no coin to pay the dowry, but her father would, if she asked. Nonetheless, the idea didn't appeal. The thought of locking herself away in a nunnery didn't thrill her. Such a life seemed like a punishment.

She squeezed her eyes shut then, silently cursing herself. She was a mess, her feelings in such a tangle that she felt as if she were losing her wits. Fresh tears burned behind her eyelids, and try as she may to stem them, they slid free.

Soon she was weeping, her head bowed, shoulders shaking.

It was too much.

She couldn't go on like this. Choking down her feelings was tearing her to pieces.

A sob clawed its way up her throat, and she slammed a hand over her mouth to muffle it.

I love him.

God's bones, she did. There was no denying it. The thought of leaving Rae behind, of never hearing the rumble of his voice, or seeing the boyish quirk of his smile that lifted years from his face, made her feel as if she were about to climb the steps to the hangman's noose. He was a part of her now, and pushing him away hurt too much.

Swallowing another sob, she opened her eyes.

A faint glow lightened the eastern horizon. Dawn was on its way.

And with the sunrise, something deep inside Kylie shifted. She was still terrified. Still a churning maelstrom of conflict. But she wouldn't ruin this one chance of happiness.

No, she'd go to Rae and tell him how she *really* felt.

She'd bare her soul and expose herself to ridicule and pain.

For the first time in her life, she'd risk her heart.

Pulse racing, she turned from the wall. She then swept her gaze over the broch, still shadowed by darkness, her attention shifting to the nearest set of stairs leading down to the barmkin.

However, she'd taken just one step toward it when movement below caught her eye.

25: A TREACHEROUS DAWN

KYLIE HALTED, HER gaze narrowing as she peered down at the shadowy barmkin. Like the braziers upon the walls, the torches hanging from chains below were starting to gutter—and some of them had gone out.

Visibility was poor, yet there was no mistaking the silhouettes of men who crept across the courtyard.

Instinctively, she dropped to a crouch. Standing up on the walls, outlined by the sky, made her far too easy to spot.

Breath held, she scrutinized the figures for a few moments. Since she'd been outdoors for a spell, her eyes had adjusted to the dim light. As such, she easily made out half a dozen of them. But as she looked on, more emerged, crawling like wasps from what appeared to be an open drain directly below her.

Her pulse started to thump in her ears.

She was the only one who'd seen them. The guards were all facing the wrong way, looking out to sea and land for any sign of trouble—not realizing that danger was right behind them.

I must raise the alarm!

There was a bell tower above the gates, yet that was too far away. She'd never reach it in time. She had to do something though—if she didn't, the broch would be overrun.

Her breath gusted out of her before she drew in another, deep, lungful of air. Fear clutched at her chest as the moments slid by—and then she mastered it.

Exhilaration swept over her. Fire ignited in her gut as fierce determination swelled under her breastbone. A door inside her gave way, and on the other side, she found her voice, her courage.

A moment later, she screamed, "To arms! Enemies within the walls!"

Her warning shattered the pregnant silence, ripping through it like a whetted blade. It boomed off stone and would likely have echoed deep within the broch. Even so, Kylie wasn't taking any chances. "To arms!" she bellowed once more, with such force that her throat hurt. "Enemies within the walls!"

Chaos broke loose.

The guards on the wall swiveled from their posts, drew their weapons, and dashed along the wall toward the nearest steps. Moments later, warriors, most of them half-clad yet bearing weapons, burst from the barracks.

The ring of steel and the grunts of fighting men then rose into the air.

Kylie remained crouched there, watching the Guard take on the men who now swarmed the barmkin. However, her pounding heart stuttered when she recognized one of the intruders. His long pale hair made him stand out amongst the others, as did the fluid way he fought.

And as she looked on, Tormod MacDougall thrust his dirk into a guard's chest and twisted viciously, before kicking him to the ground.

And then, as if feeling the weight of her stare, he glanced up at the wall.

Their gazes fused for one long moment—before Tormod smiled.

Kylie's already racing heart lurched into her throat. The expression was sinister, and the violence that bloomed in his pale eyes made her feel as if she'd just plunged headfirst into an icy loch.

Tormod tore his attention from her then, and she let out a relieved gasp. She rose to her feet and backed away from the edge of the walkway. Hades. She needed to get to safety.

Nonetheless, her gaze remained riveted on the man who'd once been part of the Dounarwyse Guard. Rage started to pulse in her gut. Here was the bastard who'd tried to rape her sister, who'd threatened her, even after Rae had flogged him. Someone needed to drive a dirk through his malicious heart.

Moments earlier, Tormod had been fighting his way through the press toward the tower house, but he now swiveled and headed toward the nearest set of steps. Men were fighting halfway up, but he shoved them aside, sending both friend and foe tumbling, and took the steps two at a time.

Kylie's breathing caught, her heart kicking hard against her breastbone.

Christ's blood, he was coming for her.

Rae raced down the steps of the tower house, dirk in hand. Upon hearing the woman's scream—a warning that had catapulted him from his bed—he'd yanked on his braies and boots, hauled on a lèine, and raced from his bedchamber, shutting Storm in behind him.

Fortunately, he hadn't been sleeping.

Instead, he'd been awake for hours, waiting for the treacherous dawn and Kylie's departure. After their last conversation, they'd barely spoken. He'd informed her of the ferry from Craignure to Oban, and that his men would accompany her, but apart from that, they'd avoided each other.

And now she was leaving.

But Rae's thoughts weren't on his lover now. Kylie would still be upstairs, as would his sons. Hopefully, they all had the wits to stay there, to lock themselves away in their bedchambers.

All he could think about was that intruders were in his broch. *How the devil did they get inside?* Over the past months, he'd been focused on keeping the people of the nearby village safe, as well as the crofters who lived on the hills around Dounarwyse. The Ghost Raiders had managed to get into Moy Castle, but his broch perched high with sheer grassy slopes and perilous rocks below. He'd never imagined anyone could scale these walls.

In the entrance hall below, he met two of his men who, like him, were heading toward the door. "Stay here!" he barked. "And prevent anyone from entering the tower house."

Not waiting for their response—for he knew they'd heed him—he shoved the heavy door open and burst outside.

Beyond, he found the barmkin filled with fighting men.

Growling a curse, Rae's gaze swept the melee. He couldn't see his brother amongst the guards. His attention shifted then to the guard tower, his breathing growing shallow when he saw that the door was open.

The enemy was within.

Without thinking, he skirted the edge of the fighting, heading toward the guard tower. Jack and his family lived on the top level. They were trapped. He had to get to them.

One of the intruders blocked his way then—a beast of a man with a bullish jaw. Rae engaged him, their dirks slashing as they tried to get under each other's guard. Rage caught fire in his blood. These shit-eaters were trying to take his broch—his home. He'd dedicated his life to protecting these walls, and he'd give it to keep them safe. He didn't know who these attackers were, or who'd sent them, but he was going to make each one of them pay.

His huge opponent tried to kick him then, attempting to knock him off balance before going in for the kill. But Rae sidestepped his heavy boot, rammed his dirk into the warrior's gut, and twisted.

The warrior's agonized scream ripped through the barmkin. He crumpled to his knees, bending double. Rae didn't bother to finish him off; someone else would surely do that. Instead, he yanked his dirk free and dove for the open door to the guard tower.

And as soon as he hit the first of the steep, narrow steps that coiled upward, he heard snarled curses and grunts echoing down the stairwell.

Jack had already engaged them.

Tightening his grip on his dirk, Rae raced up the stairs. However, halfway up, a large body collided with him, nearly sending him for a tumble. He slammed himself against the pitted stone wall, his boots digging into the step as a corpse slid past.

A big man with wild dark hair and beard, his brown eyes startled, as if his end had been a surprise, stared up at him. His throat was cut from ear to ear and blood pumped from the gaping wound, running like a stream down the steps now that he lay twitching on his back.

"Rae!" His chin kicked up then as Jack appeared above. His brother wore nothing but loosely tied braies. However, his green eyes gleamed and his expression was feral.

"Are Tara and the bairns safe?" Rae asked breathlessly, reassuring himself that his brother was uninjured.

"Aye." Jack descended the steps toward him, his lip curling as his gaze grazed the prone figure at Rae's feet. "They've barred the door from the inside."

"The barmkin is filled with intruders," Rae replied, fury thundering in his ears. "Let's deal with them."

Kylie whispered a curse. Heart galloping, she slammed the stairwell door closed. She'd been hoping to flee the walls down the stairs, yet when she'd opened the door, she heard fighting within: the clang of metal colliding and grunts.

She wouldn't be escaping that way.

Cornered, she backed across the wide terrace before the eastern walls.

Tormod had scaled the steps and was striding along the wall toward her. He wasn't smiling now. Instead, the look on his face made her bladder tingle.

"Good morning, little bird," he called out as he stepped onto the terrace. "How loudly ye sing."

Kylie clenched her jaw, the heat in her belly reigniting. She was afraid—sweat now trickled between her shoulder blades, and her pulse thumped in her ears—but she held onto her nerve.

Halting at the edge of the terrace, she glanced down. A tide of fighting men surged below her. If she jumped, she'd fall into their midst and surely be skewered by a blade or trampled underfoot.

But if she stayed up here, MacDougall intended to kill her.

There was no doubt.

Dropping to a crouch, she shifted to face him. "Get back, dog!"

Tormod halted, a cold smile tugging at his lips. "Ye are a haughty one, aren't ye … like yer bonnie sister." His smile twisted into a sneer then. "But I'm not yers to command." He lifted his dirk, its blade glinting in the sunlight that now cast him in a halo, for the sun was rising behind him. "Ye ruined our wee surprise though, and ye shall pay."

He advanced toward her, moving with terrifying, fluid grace.

Kylie didn't think.

Crouched as she was, it was easy to reach under her skirts and yank the slender blade from its sheath on her thigh. Over the years, Makenna had given her lessons on how to use a dagger, if needed. Like Liza, she'd humored their younger sister at the time. All the same, she remembered Makenna's tuition well.

Her sister had also told her she was quick. She hoped she was. Tormod was the best of the best. She'd get just one strike, and she had to make it count.

Of course, Tormod didn't expect the lady to spring from where she crouched and rush at him. He'd thought she'd cower there, while he slit her throat. As such, his step faltered when Kylie leaped.

His ice-blue eyes snapped wide as she stabbed at his groin, throwing all her weight behind the dagger. It sank deep into the softness of his flesh, and Tormod's roar of agony split the air.

Releasing her blade's hilt, she flung herself under his swiping blade and rolled across the terrace like a scattered marble.

Her knees skinned, the heels of her hands burning from where she'd saved herself as she fell, she scrambled to her feet, ready to flee. But before she did, she looked back at her attacker.

Face contorted into a rictus, Tormod was bent double, his hands clenched around the handle of the knife as he prepared to yank it free from his groin.

For a few blessed moments, he wasn't focused on her.

She then marked just how close he was standing to the edge.

In an instant, she made her decision. Seizing the moment, she rushed forward and shoved him hard in the back.

Tormod staggered, lurching sideways as the blade still embedded in his body twisted. And then he fell.

Her heartbeat drumming in her ears, she watched him land amongst the boiling sea of iron, steel, and ladders. An instant later, he was sucked under.

Kylie muttered an oath and backed away from the edge. Her breathing was ragged now. She'd come close to meeting her maker, but she wasn't out of danger yet. She'd also lost her only weapon and needed to find something else to defend herself with.

The fighting was still going on, and she had no idea who was winning. Men were fighting on all the steps leading up to the wall, and two of them were slashing at each other with dirks on the southern ramparts. It was much easier to see now, for the sun was creeping over the walls and illuminating the center of the barmkin.

She spied Rae then, fighting in the melee below, back-to-back with his brother. The pair were savage, bringing down each attacker that rushed them. Jack had been cut across his bare chest, but he barely seemed to notice. Meanwhile, Rae wielded two dirks, which he used with equal viciousness.

Kylie watched him with awe. She'd seen Rae wrestle with his men, and spar occasionally with a bound blade. But she had no idea just what a formidable warrior he was. She recognized the faces of other men fighting around them too.

It dawned on her then that the Dounarwyse Guard had turned the tide. They were besting the band of intruders.

Driving one of his dirks into a warrior's chest, while the other slashed across his throat, Rae watched as his opponent sagged and then toppled, blood gushing.

And then, just like that, the skirmish was over.

It had been so furious, so bloody, that the shock of it ending didn't seem real. Kylie stared down at the bodies littering the cobbled barmkin, a chill stealing over her. Her attention then returned to Rae's grim face as he stepped away from Jack and surveyed the ruin around him.

"Rae!"

His chin jerked up, his eyes narrowing as he swept his gaze around.

A heartbeat later, he found her. "Kylie!"

26: STEPPING OVER THE BRINK

KYLIE REMAINED WHERE she was while Rae raced up the steps to the wall. He then sprinted around the walkway, leaping over the prone body of one of the intruders, and approached her.

She rose to her feet when he drew near. She then staggered, nearly falling over. Cods. Her legs felt like congealed porridge. She'd kept her wits and courage throughout the attack, but now shock caught up with her.

Moments later, Rae reached Kylie and hauled her into his arms.

She clung to him, pressing her face to his chest. Beneath the thin material of his lèine, his skin was slick with sweat and his heart hammered. But he was uninjured. Alive. Relief splintered within her, and suddenly she was weeping. Loud, messy tears.

Lord, she'd never sobbed like this. It was as if a dyke had somehow burst, and years of pent-up emotion gushed forth. There was no holding it back now.

Rae didn't say a word. He merely held her tight and let her weep against his chest.

And when she was spent, she sagged, limp and exhausted, against him.

"Speak to me, lass," he murmured then, his breath feathering across her forehead. "What are ye doing out here? Ye aren't hurt?"

"No," she rasped, pulling back slightly and raising her gaze to meet his. Rae's eyes were shadowed with worry, yet achingly tender. "Tormod MacDougall tried to kill me … but I knifed him in the cods."

Rae's big body stiffened against hers, his eyes snapping wide.

"I then shoved him over the edge," Kylie added.

"Ye did?"

"Aye." She managed a tight smile. "Hopefully, he was trampled after he fell."

Rae's gaze glinted at this. He then shifted his attention to the barmkin below. "Tormod was behind this," he shouted down to where Jack was picking his way through the dead. Nearby, his men had cornered three of the attackers who were still alive. "Can ye see him?"

A pause followed before Jack eventually called back, "He's not here."

Kylie's breathing caught. She disentangled herself from Rae then and moved closer to the edge, scrutinizing the mess beneath her. Her gaze went from body to body, but there was no sign of Tormod. His distinctive long blond hair usually made him easy to spot. "He must have escaped," she said, even as bitterness filled her mouth. "The way they came in." She turned back to Rae, to find him watching her, confusion upon his face. "They climbed up through the storm drain … I saw them."

Rae's gaze held hers for a moment before he growled a low curse. "The bastard won't have gotten far … not after a blade to the balls."

Kylie's lips thinned. No, the warrior would be bleeding heavily and in pain.

"Send men out to where the storm drain exits," he called down to Jack. "Tormod can't be far away."

His brother gave a curt nod before turning and barking orders to those at the gate. Meanwhile, both Kylie and Rae had fallen silent, their attention taken up by the mess the rising sun now unveiled.

It looked as if at least ten of their own men had fallen during the skirmish. Below, a woman started to keen. One of the cook's assistants knelt on the cobbles next to her lover's prone body.

The harrowing sound made Kylie wrap her arms around herself. Suddenly, she couldn't stop shivering. "Come," Rae said roughly. "I need to question those we've taken captive … but let's get ye indoors first."

He moved close then and put a protective arm around her shoulders. Leaning into him, Kylie nodded numbly. Together, they turned, but they had only taken a couple of steps when Rae came to an abrupt halt. And when she followed his gaze east, to where the pale morning sunlight sparkled on the Sound of Mull, she saw what had caught his attention.

A large cog, its black sail billowing as it headed away from the coast.

Kylie's breathing caught, for she'd seen that cog before—the previous Bealtunn—at Moy Castle. It was *The Night Plunderer*.

"Those dog-humping bastards," Rae growled.

"The Ghost Raiders have cast aside their horned skulls it seems," she replied, even as a chill feathered down her spine.

"Aye," he muttered. "It's nigh impossible to climb a storm drain garbed like a demon." He turned then, waving to Jack and calling down to him, "Ye'd better get up here, brother."

Jack did as bid, taking the blood-splattered steps two at a time, and approaching the east wall. And when he spied the raider's cog sailing away, he also spat out a curse. "So, that's where Ramsay MacDonald ended up, is it?"

Kylie frowned. She didn't recognize the name.

Rae shot his brother a quizzical look. "Ramsay MacDonald … wasn't he the outlaw ye fell foul of years ago … the one who tried to rape Tara?"

"Aye … that's him," Jack growled back. He'd halted next to them, his gaze still trained east. The cut across his naked chest was oozing. It would need seeing to, but he paid it no mind. "He was also the warrior who tried to get into my quarters earlier."

Rae's brows drew together at this news. "Well, he won't be giving ye any more trouble." He paused then, his gaze flicking back to where the cog was quickly growing smaller in the distance. It sailed as if Satan's fiends were chasing it. "I wonder if he and Ross Macbeth are one and the same."

Kylie gave a soft gasp, and the brothers both glanced her way, surprised by her reaction. "I saw Ross Macbeth," she explained. "From a distance last spring near Moy Castle … when Liza and I were out walking. It was just before the attack at Bealtunn. Is the man ye speak of big with a permanent scowl and wild dark hair and beard."

"Aye," Jack replied, his jaw flexing. "Sounds like him … although he's now sprawled in the guard tower stairwell with a slit throat."

Rae's lips thinned. "MacDougall went looking for allies it seems," he muttered.

"Aye … and once Ramsay learned that I captain yer guard, he couldn't resist his chance for revenge."

"And he would have had it too," Rae said, his voice roughening, "if someone hadn't raised the alarm."

Both men looked at Kylie once more, and self-consciousness stole over her. "Well, luckily I was up early," she murmured. Her gaze shifted away then, for she marked the way Rae's eyes glinted. It was a reminder that she was supposed to be leaving this morning.

Kylie's pulse quickened. She needed to talk to him alone.

"Maclean!" A man called from below, intruding on their conversation. All three of them turned from the wall to see one of the Guard, out of breath, skid to a halt inside the gates. He'd clearly just sprinted up the hill outside and across the drawbridge. "There's no sign of Tormod … just two large abandoned rowboats. Three of us climbed up the tunnel to check, but it's empty."

Rae's curse was blistering, echoing off the surrounding stone. Likewise, Jack's expression was thunderous, while Kylie's stomach clenched.

How was it possible? She'd delivered the warrior a grievous wound before pushing him off a wall and into a crowd of fighting men. He shouldn't have been able to crawl to the storm drain let alone escape down it and disappear.

"Send more men north and south along the coast," Rae ordered. "He's not getting away."

"But he might have swum out to the cog," Kylie suggested. "We saw it set sail, but it was likely moored close to the coast earlier."

Both Rae and Jack's expressions pinched. It seemed unlikely, for Tormod was injured, but they couldn't discount the possibility that he'd made it to *The Night Plunderer* either.

Silence fell upon the wall, broken only by the soft sobbing of the grieving woman below. Her weeping rose and fell—like a lament for her dead lover, and for the others who'd fallen to defend Dounarwyse this morning.

"We wintered at Castle Coeffin!" The man's wail echoed across the barmkin.

Snarling, Rae leaned in close to the face of the warrior whose finger he'd just cut off. "Did Duncan MacDougall send ye?"

"No," the man panted, his eyes glazed with pain. "He merely sheltered us."

"MacDougall has no love for the Macleans," Jack muttered from behind Rae.

"Aye," Rae replied, never taking his gaze off the man he was questioning. "It would suit him to have a MacDougall take this broch."

Rae leaned in once more. "Was that Tormod's plan then?"

The warrior didn't reply, and Rae took hold of his hand once more. "I don't think ye need that thumb."

The man made a choking sound, his blue eyes bulging. "Aye ... he wanted Dounarwyse. We had more men onboard *The Plunderer* ... who were ready to help make the broch safe for us ... and enough supplies to see us through months. He spent all winter planning it."

This admission made Rae sit back on his heels. And all the while, fury pulsed under his breastbone.

Nearby, another of the men they'd taken captive lay dead in a pool of blood. Rae had taken off two of his fingers, but the Ghost Raider had merely spat at him. However, his companion had been much more forthcoming. A few feet away, the third of their captives glowered at him.

Christ's teeth, the bastards had nearly managed it. If Kylie hadn't warned them, the Raiders would have slaughtered them all in their beds. And they'd used the storm drain to get into the castle. No one outside the broch knew about it—but Tormod had, and he'd used the knowledge to plan an attack.

Rae's gaze shifted to the iron hatch, which had now been closed. He couldn't risk that ever happening again. He'd have the blacksmith make him an iron lattice covering to put over it. That way, the water could escape when they had heavy rain, but no one would ever be able to crawl up the drain and surprise them again.

Rising to his feet, Rae sheathed his dirk at his hip. He then turned to where Jack still looked on. His brother's face was set in hard lines, anger smoldering in his green eyes. He knew what the laird was about to say next.

"We're done here," Rae said, stepping away from their captives. "Hang these two from the walls."

"There ye go." Kylie finished wrapping the warrior's arm and secured the bandage tightly. "All yer injuries will need checking again tomorrow mind."

"Thank ye, Lady Grant," the young man replied with a brittle half-smile. Gareth Maclean had received a few deep gashes, two to his sword arm and one to his thigh. Kylie had just finished painstakingly sewing the wounds before dousing them with strong wine and wrapping them. The warrior's face was pale in the aftermath.

They were in the barracks, where two other warriors—who, like Gareth, had sustained wounds during the fight—had also been tended. Kylie and Tara had worked tirelessly all morning to help them. It was now noon, and Tara had gone up to look in on her daughters and relieve the maid who'd been looking after them for her.

Packing up bandages, ointments, and her bone needle and catgut into the healing basket she'd brought from the tower house, Kylie cast Gareth a reassuring smile. The lad's face was as pale as milk. He was a recent addition to the Guard, and this had been his first blooding. "Rest today," she ordered softly. "And make sure ye eat something."

He nodded, his boyish face creasing into another attempt at a smile.

Kylie left him then, stepping out into the barmkin with her basket hooked over one arm. To her relief, the dead had been carried out of the broch and the blood had been scrubbed away. Those of the Guard who'd fallen would be buried outside Dounarwsye kirk the following day, while the corpses of the attackers had been heaped upon the pyre, to be burned.

Above, the sky had cleared for the first time in days, and a crisp wind tugged at her hair and clothing. The rich aroma of roasting meat drifted across the barmkin then, for the laird had ordered Cadha and her assistants to put on a hearty meal for the broch's residents.

They'd lost men, but they'd also beaten those who'd tried to overrun the fortress.

It was a bittersweet day.

Looking at the cobbled expanse before her, Kylie could almost imagine the dawn skirmish had never taken place. But it had—and the corpses of the two captives now swung from the western wall. She hadn't gone out to see the grisly spectacle, but others had. Those men would likely hang there for a while, as their bodies bloated and crows pecked at them, as a warning to any who dared cross the Macleans.

Kylie suppressed a shiver. Of course, things could have gone very differently. It could be Rae and Jack strung up by their necks, while Tormod MacDougall took the laird's seat in the hall.

Trying not to think about such things, she walked across the cobbles and climbed the steps to the broch. She then made her way upstairs and found Storm sitting outside the door to the lady's solar. Tail wagging, he nudged at her until she put down her basket and gave him the affection he craved. "What are ye doing out here, lad?" she asked as a wet tongue swept across her cheek. "Why aren't ye with yer master?"

Her gaze shifted then, across the landing to the closed door to the other solar.

Instinctively, she knew Rae was inside.

She also knew she had to speak to him. There were words that had to be said.

Ducking into the lady's solar, she put away the healing basket before returning to the landing. She then crossed it, Storm padding after her, knocked on Rae's door, and waited.

27: IN EARNEST

"AYE," A GRUFF male voice answered.

"Rae … it's me … Kylie."

A heavy pause followed before he spoke once more. "Enter."

Pushing open the door, she slid inside and closed it behind her. Storm was eager to follow her, but she wouldn't let him in just yet. She needed to speak to Rae first and didn't wish to be interrupted by the needy collie.

The laird was standing by the window—his back to her, and his arms clasped behind him— hands resting in the small of his back. His stance, with his legs apart and his shoulders tense, made him appear as if he was bracing himself for something.

"I was expecting a visit from ye," he said softly.

Awkwardness filtered through Kylie then. She wanted him to turn and face her, so she might meet his eye, but he didn't. Earlier, on the wall, she'd felt close to him, but now there seemed a gulf between them. "I would have come to see ye earlier … but I've been busy helping Tara tend to the wounded."

"And how are the men faring?"

"Three have serious wounds, and will take time to recover … but with care, they'll all live."

He released a deep sigh. "Good." He paused then before clearing his throat. "I'm sorry ye missed the ferry."

Kylie snorted. "I don't care about that."

His strong body jerked at her response, and he finally turned to face her. "Ye don't?"

"No."

Across the room, their gazes fused. "There's another boat, the day after tomorrow," he said after a brief pause. His face was stern, his green eyes veiled. "I will take ye to Craignure myself, if ye wish?"

Kylie's pulse fluttered. Time rolled back then, and she was standing on the walls looking east, waiting for dawn. In the past hours, she hadn't had much time to think about the decision she'd made—she'd been too busy staying alive and then helping deal with the aftermath of the attack. But now, she let her choice settle.

It felt like stepping over the brink.

She was tumbling. She'd side-stepped fear and thrown herself into the unknown and strangely, she'd never felt freer.

"I don't want to leave, Rae," she said huskily, her gaze never leaving his. "Instead, I wish to remain here … to become yer wife." She broke off then, her confidence suddenly faltering. "If ye will still have me."

The laird's lips parted.

For a moment, he merely stared at her. And then his throat bobbed, and the grim expression that had etched itself upon his features dissolved, revealing the sensitive man beneath. Hope flared in his eyes, yet she sensed his wariness.

Kylie's breathing hitched, even as her chest started to ache. He didn't trust her words, so she would have to make herself plainer. "I *love* ye," she said, her voice catching. "I have for months now … but when ye were honest about how ye felt about me, I let foolish fears overrule my heart." Her voice faltered then. "And in doing so, I nearly lost ye."

A pause followed this admission. Rae's chest rose and fell sharply now, his gaze never leaving her face. He moved toward her then, drawing to an abrupt halt when they were around four feet apart. "Ye are in earnest?"

Kylie gave a soft laugh, which to her ears sounded more like a choked sob. "Aye … I've never been so sure about anything. I want to become yer wife. I want yer face to be the first thing I see every morning and the last thing I see every night. I want to grow old with ye, Rae Maclean … is that *earnest* enough for ye?"

Joy ignited in the depths of his eyes. An instant later, he bridged the final gap between them and hauled Kylie into his arms.

They clung together then, in a crushing hug that made it impossible to breathe.

She didn't care. All that mattered was that Rae understood how much she loved him.

And then suddenly, they weren't just hugging each other but kissing. Fierce, hot kisses that she felt right down to her toes. Desperate for him, she went up on tiptoe, her arms linking around his neck. She had to be closer to Rae. If she could, she'd have crawled inside him.

Even before the attack, she'd been certain, but now it was written in the marrow of her bones. Her place was here. With this man.

The rasp of his stubbled chin, the heat of his mouth as it devoured hers, just stoked the fire in her belly. Likewise, Rae couldn't get enough of her. Just hours before, both their lives had been at risk—and it made this moment even more poignant. Life was fragile. Neither of them could afford to waste a moment of it.

Still kissing her wildly, he walked her back.

An instant later, Kylie's spine hit the door, and his body crushed against hers. Moaning against his mouth, she slid her hands down his chest, to where his rod stiffened between them. She palmed it, rubbing him.

Rae cursed against her mouth. And then, before she knew it, he was lifting her skirts and nudging her knees apart.

Kylie's breathing was ragged now, hunger clenching low in her belly as she deftly unlaced his braies. "*Now*, Rae," she gasped. "*Hard.*" She needed him to plow her fiercely, for him to dominate her senses and chase away the shadow the brutal attack had cast over them.

Murmuring tender words, Rae pushed her thighs wide. He then lifted her up against the door—sheathing himself fully inside her in one deep thrust.

The shock of his shaft, as rigid as iron and hot, inside her, made her whimper. But she was already clawing at him, her quim tightening around his heft. No, she didn't want anything about this coupling to be gentle.

She wanted him to brand her as his. She wanted to ache afterward.

Sensing her desperation, and matching it with his own, he took her in slow, punishing thrusts, pinning her against the door as he did so. And all the while, his gaze burned into hers.

It was breathlessly intimate, to stare at each other like this during coupling—something that she'd avoided over the months they'd enjoyed their 'game'. She felt naked, not physically, but emotionally. Finally, there was nowhere left to hide. He saw all of her, including the parts she was ashamed of.

But he didn't shrink from it either.

Instead, he plowed her against the door, grinding into her each time he drove deep. This position was delicious—the friction of their bodies joining and the way his shaft stroked a place deep inside made her writhe upon him.

She was on fire for him, and the pulsing ache in her womb made her whimper once more. Their unions before now had been passionate and intense, for Rae had learned just what she liked and where to touch her, but this time was different. This time, there weren't any shields between them. This time, she was giving him her heart.

She shattered, hard, her ragged cry filling the solar. She didn't try and choke it back though; instead, she let the sound echo through the large chamber and out the open window.

"Kylie!" Rae's voice was strangled. "I love ye, lass!"

"Aye!" she cried, rolling her hips hard against his as he thrust wildly into her now. "I'm yers … I'm yers!"

He climaxed too then, his spine arching and his head falling back, a raw shout ripping from his throat.

Outside the door, Storm scratched and whined, but neither of them paid the poor dog any notice. Instead, they clung together, gasping for breath. Eventually, Kylie reached up, her hand tenderly cupping his cheek. "I think everyone in the broch heard that," she said huskily.

He snorted a laugh, his gaze meeting hers. "I couldn't care less … ye are my woman, and I'll shout it from the walls if I want to."

Her lips curved. How passionately this man loved. His emotions ran deep; he was someone who could appear serious, stern even, for the weight of responsibility had taken its toll on him over the years. But underneath, there was so much more to him.

She knew, instinctively, that he'd always guard her heart.

She was safe with him.

"Even so," she murmured. "I think Storm believes something terrible has befallen us."

Rae chuckled once more. "He'll soon learn we're both well." His hand lifted then, covering hers, for she still caressed his cheek. "Indeed, I've never been better."

She stared up at him, her chest tightening. "I'm sorry I made things so difficult," she whispered.

His expression sobered, yet his gaze remained gentle. "I understand."

"Aye … but I hurt ye all the same." She swallowed hard as her eyes grew hot and prickly. She'd wept more today than she had in years. "That was the last thing I wished for."

He favored her with a soft smile, his thumb stroking the back of her hand. "I'm glad ye changed yer mind." He paused then, his expression turning rueful. "Although, I don't think I could have let ye go without trying to persuade ye one last time … so ye saved me further humiliation."

She swallowed, tenderness swelling in her breast. "Ye wouldn't have been spurned," she admitted, her voice

roughening. "I was about to come to ye at dawn … right before
the attack. As I stood on the walls, watching my last
Dounarwyse sunrise, I understood that if I walked away from ye
… I'd regret it forever."

28: LIFE UNFOLDS AS IT'S MEANT TO

Four days later …

"KYLIE GRANT AND I shall wed."

Rae's voice carried over the hushed hall, and despite that Kylie had known he'd make this announcement, embarrassment flushed over her.

The hall of Dounarwyse was packed this evening—all eyes were upon her.

Murmurs followed Rae's words, and then, to Kylie's surprise, the men seated at the trestle tables heaved themselves to their feet and held their cups of ale and mead aloft.

"Well met, Maclean!"

The heat in Kylie's cheeks intensified. She felt as if she were glowing like the sun.

"Congratulations are in order!"

Rae smiled back at his retainers, his eyes darkening with emotion. Like Kylie, he likely hadn't expected such an enthusiastic response. Despite that they'd fended off their attackers, the casualties among the Guard had left a subdued mood over Dounarwyse in the days following.

Rae had wanted to announce their union immediately, although Kylie counseled him to wait a day or two—until they'd buried their dead and life had returned to normal within the broch.

All the same, the folk of Dounarwyse were still on edge.

Tormod MacDougall hadn't been found. Jack's men had scoured the coast both north and south of the broch, and some even traveled inland. But the warrior had disappeared. It seemed he'd somehow managed to swim to *The Night Plunderer*. Rae had been vexed that Tormod survived, and had sent word to the clan-chief, as well as the other Maclean chieftains, warning them to be on the lookout for the fugitive.

He'd resurface one day—and when he did, he'd be brought to justice.

Things hadn't been the same at Dounarwyse since the attack. However, the news of their laird's impending nuptials cleared the sadness away from the hall like spring sun on morning mist. A wedding represented hope. It was a reminder that although violence and treachery left a scar, they were no match for love.

It was the reminder all of them needed.

Nonetheless, across the table, Ailean and Lyle looked on, stunned. Likewise, Jack and Tara appeared poleaxed for a few moments before smiles split their faces. Passing Grace to her husband, Tara leaped up and skirted the table before throwing her arms around Rae.

He laughed at her exuberant response, but Tara wasn't done. Eyes sparkling, she moved to where Kylie rose from the bench seat to meet her. The two women clung together in a fierce hug. "I'm so relieved," Tara whispered to Kylie as the rest of the hall erupted in applause. "Ye both deserve happiness." Her friend drew back then, tears glittering in her eyes. "When ye stayed on after the attack … I dared hope something had changed."

"This is bonnie news indeed," Jack added with a grin from a few feet away. "And if I didn't have my hands full with these lassies, I'd congratulate ye both properly." Indeed, Rae's brother had two wriggling bairns upon his lap. Grace had just grabbed a piece of bread and was squashing it into her sister's hair.

"Ye will have yer chance, I'm sure," Rae replied, still smiling. "But for now, I wished everyone to know of our decision."

"When's the wedding, Maclean?" One of the men shouted.

"As soon as can be arranged," Rae called back without hesitation. He cast Kylie a soft look then, one that made her heart squeeze. "Prepare yerself for a glorious day of celebration and feasting!"

Cheers went up at this news, and the tightness in Kylie's chest intensified.

To think she'd been close to leaving this broch and the people who'd made her feel so welcome. She glanced over at the two lads who sat to their father's right. Ailean and Lyle still had wide confused gazes—as if they weren't sure what all the fuss was about.

"Won't ye teach us anymore?" Ailean asked, his green eyes shadowing. Both the brothers had been delighted when she'd lingered after the attack and resumed their lessons the following day. Although, she'd sensed their worry that she'd soon reschedule her departure.

"Of course, I will," she assured him, with a reassuring smile.

"But will I have to call ye 'Ma' now?" he asked, his expression still uncertain.

Her breathing hitched. Lyle also looked worried. She didn't blame him. Days earlier, they'd thought she was leaving, and now their father had just told them she was to be their stepmother. They needed to have the situation explained fully.

Stepping away from Tara, Kylie moved around the table and stopped before her two charges. Rae's sons had swiveled to face her, and she dropped to a crouch in front of them. Then, reaching out, she took their small hands in hers.

"I love yer Da," she murmured. "And I will be his wife … but I will also continue to teach ye as I do now. Nothing will change."

"Do ye promise not to leave us?" Ailean persisted.

"I promise." She favored him with a soft smile then. "My place is here … with ye all."

Ailean blinked rapidly at this admission, his eyes filling with tears, while Lyle started to sniff.

"Och, lads, don't fret." Rae joined them then, hunkering down and placing his hand over where Kylie still held theirs. "Everything will be well. We shall be a family."

They both nodded. Relief loosened Kylie's chest. They understood—and as she looked on, she marked the excitement that flickered to life in their eyes.

"Will ye still take us on walks?" Lyle asked Kylie, his apple-cheeked face hopeful. "Like ye used to?"

Her lips curved into a smile. "Aye … as long as ye behave yerself."

With a squeal, the lad surprised them all by lurching forward and throwing his arms around her neck.

Dusk settled over Dounarwyse in a rosy veil. Rae and Kylie went up onto the walls to watch it. Hand in hand, their fingers entwined, they mounted the steps and walked to the western ramparts. The sky in that direction glowed pink and gold.

"I never tire of the view from these walls," Kylie admitted with a sigh.

Rae cast her a sidelong glance, smiling. "So, ye like Dounarwyse then?"

Her full lips quirked. "Aye … isn't it obvious?"

Warmth suffused his chest. He hid his worries well, but they were still there. "Well, it isn't as grand as Meggernie Castle, I'd wager … and I'm no clan-chief."

She gave a soft snort. "My father's castle is a large one … but it's nestled amongst woodland and soft green hills. Ye certainly can't view the sea from its walls." She paused then. "Rae Baird Maclean … I do believe ye are looking for compliments."

He threw back his head and laughed, the deep sound echoing over the walls. "Guilty as charged." In truth, he was a little embarrassed she'd seen through him so easily. Kylie was a shrewd woman and missed little.

He slung an arm around her shoulders then, and they fell into companionable silence for a short while, watching as the sunset flared brighter still.

"Ye walked into my life at the right time," he admitted eventually. "I was becoming somewhat of a curmudgeon before ye came."

She snorted. "Aye, ye *were* intimidating. Ye have quite a temper when riled, Maclean."

He pulled a face. "That's what comes of pushing yer own needs aside, as if they don't matter … eventually, ye boil over," He paused then. "Not that it's an excuse, mind."

"Ye're allowed to have flaws, ye know?" she replied with a rueful shake of her head. "None of us are perfect … least of all me."

His mouth curved. "To me, ye are, lass."

A faint blush rose to her cheeks at this, and he tightened his hold on her. He wasn't a man given to empty words. It was the truth.

He cleared his throat then, as emotion swamped him. "It had all become too much … the responsibilities, the worry about the Ghost Raiders … the loneliness" —he paused before adding— "not to mention the tight balls." He broke off then, snorting a laugh as heat crept up his neck.

Christ's blood, he hoped his crudeness hadn't offended her. Despite all the intimacies they'd shared over the past months, things were still new between them.

He needn't have worried though, for Kylie's laughter drifted across the walls. Nonetheless, he noted the flush to her cheeks had deepened. "I was lonely too," she admitted softly, sobering. "I know how it leaves an ache, deep inside." She turned to him then, her hand splaying across his chest. "No one can see it … but it's always there."

"Aye," he agreed huskily. "We're alike in many ways, aren't we?"

Her lips tilted into a tender smile that made his chest tighten. "I noticed that from the first … maybe that's why we've always gotten on so well." She paused, her gaze gleaming. "I've always been able to be myself with ye."

He smiled back. "Why couldn't we have met years ago?"

She raised her hand to his face, her fingers tracing his jaw. "Because it wasn't yet time … life unfolds as it's meant to."

"I truly believed I'd never find love, ye know?" he said roughly, his throat thickening. "To my shame, Jack's good fortune turned me bitter for a time, as did my cousin Loch's." He lifted a hand and placed it gently over where hers now cupped his cheek. "But all this while, ye were waiting for me, weren't ye?"

Her sensual mouth tipped up into another smile that made his breathing grow shallow. The setting sun gilded her proud features and turned her eyes luminous. "Aye, love," she whispered. "I was."

EPILOGUE: THE INVITATION

One month later …

"A LETTER FOR *ye*, mo chridhe."

Looking up from where she was smearing a generous amount of heather honey onto her buttered wedge of bannock, Kylie watched her husband enter their bedchamber. "Me?"

Rae looked rumpled this morning, his lèine partially untucked, his hair—which he'd grown longer of late—spiky. It was how she liked him best; a vision she enjoyed every morning. Earlier, he'd been sitting in bed with her, breaking his fast on a leisurely Saturday morning, when a servant had announced a rider had arrived in the barmkin with a missive.

"Aye." He heeled off his boots, handed her a scroll of parchment, and climbed onto the bed, seating himself against the nest of pillows once more.

Glancing down at the wax seal, she noted the lion's head crest that had been pressed into it.

"It's from my father," she murmured.

"Open it then."

She did, although with a little trepidation. Bruce MacGregor wasn't one for writing missives. Unfurling the scroll, she cleared her throat.

"Dearest daughter, I hope this letter finds ye well," she read aloud. "Here at Meggernie Castle, we are preparing for the wedding of our youngest. Bran Mackinnon of Dùn Ara has finally confirmed that he shall arrive on the last day of April, and the union between him and Makenna will take place the day after Bealtunn." She paused there, glancing up at Rae.

Her husband was buttering himself some bannock as he listened, his brow furrowed. "Mackinnon is going through with it then."

"Aye … although he took a long while to answer my father's last missive. I'd say he left it as late as he could before responding."

Rae inclined his head. "Does he say anything else?"

Clearing her throat, Kylie lowered her gaze to the letter once more and continued reading. "As this marriage means all my daughters will be wedded, I wish to make it a true family affair. As such, I invite ye and yer husband to join us. I will also send invitations to Liza, Sonia, and Alma. I trust that ye are available to attend and look forward to welcoming ye and the laird of Dounarwyse to Meggernie … yer loving father. 'S Rioghal mo dhream."

Royal is my race. It was the MacGregor motto, and Bruce MacGregor ended all his missives with it.

Raising her gaze once more, she met Rae's. Swallowing a mouthful of bannock, his lips tugged into a wry smile. "That sounded more like a summons than an invitation."

She winced. "It did … that's my father's way, I'm afraid." She paused then, her gaze searching his face. Although they rarely spoke of it, she never forgot that the MacGregors had once sided with the Mackinnons and laid siege to this broch. Rae had assured her that it didn't bother him, although she wouldn't have blamed him if he secretly resented her father. However, she saw no anger in his eyes. "But if ye'd rather not attend, I can go alone."

He put down his bannock, his eyebrows knitting together. "Of course, I shall accompany ye."

"Are ye sure?" She paused then, choosing her words carefully. "After what he did?"

Rae gave a decisive nod. He then reached out and placed a hand over her forearm. "It's all done with now."

"That's fair-minded of ye." She pulled a face then. "I'm not sure my father would be in yer place."

He snorted. "Well then … that's another reason why I shall accompany ye to Meggernie. Relations between the Macleans and the MacGregors could do with repairing." He winked at her then. "And I do enjoy a wedding."

Her gaze roamed over his face, warmth blooming inside her like the daffodils on the hillside below the broch at present. She didn't think it was possible—but the longer she spent in Rae Maclean's company, the more she loved him. She adored his big heart. His kindness. He could be harsh when needed, deadly even, but he wasn't petty.

A smile curved her lips then as excitement fluttered in her belly. She'd get to see all her sisters again, and her parents. It had been nearly a decade since the whole family had been reunited. This would be a special occasion indeed. "Ye'll have to see Bran Mackinnon though," she warned him.

Rae shrugged. "As I said, this trip will be good for clan relations. After his father's defeat, I left him to nurse his bruises … but the time is coming for the Mackinnons and the Macleans to treat once more."

She must have looked doubtful, for he smiled then, his hand rising to stroke her cheek. "I'd prefer to conserve my energy in times of peace. Life can and will bring trials … but it's foolish to throw stones into yer own path unnecessarily."

Kylie smiled. "Well said."

He inclined his head. "Do ye mock me, wife?"

"Not at all." She caught his hand and brought it to her lips, kissing the back of it gently. "I'm madly in love with ye … and proud ye are my husband."

Their gazes drew out, and his lips tilted at the edges. His green eyes then darkened in a way she'd come to know well. "Are ye finished with yer bannock?"

"Aye."

"Good." He removed both the trays from the bed before dragging his lèine off, over his head, in a swift movement and kicking off his braies. "I think we'll stay abed for a little longer this morning."

"Is that so?" Her gaze slid hungrily over his nakedness. His body was one of a mature man; it bore the scars of over three decades. His chest was broad, his torso strong, and his legs and arms were heavily muscled. Her breathing quickened though when her attention moved down to his shaft: erect and hungry for her.

"Aye." His voice lowered to a sultry growl that made need clutch low in her belly.

Wriggling out of her thin night-rail, she tossed the garment aside. She marked how his chest now rose and fell sharply and swiftly.

Her gaze then flicked to the shelf behind him, where a familiar red leather-bound book sat. "It's been a while since we opened The Art of Coupling," she teased.

His eyes glinted. He glanced over his shoulder before reaching out and plucking the book off the shelf. "That's true … shall we let it fall open and see what it chooses for us?"

"Why not?" she replied huskily. She liked this side of Rae. His playfulness and sensuality thrilled her, as did the challenge in his gaze.

With a slow smile that made her feel dizzy with desire, he opened the volume, and let his fingers fan through the pages—and then, to her surprise, he tossed it into the air.

The book flipped and fell open, face down, upon the blankets.

Rae winked at her before his smile turned wicked. "Go on … take a peek."

The End

HISTORICAL NOTES

Most of this novel takes place at Dounarwyse Castle. Known today as Aros Castle, Dounarwyse is a ruined 13th-century castle near Salen on the Isle of Mull. The castle overlooks the Sound of Mull.

The castle was protected by a steep drop to the beach, and a ditch on the landward side, with a drawbridge. Built by the MacDougalls in the 13th century, the castle passed to the MacDonald Lords of the Isles at the beginning of the 14th century before being acquired by the MacLeans of Duart in 1493. In my series, I move the timeline a little so that the Macleans have possession of Dounarwyse a little earlier.

Today's ruins include a 13th-century hall-house and bailey with traces of other buildings, possibly of a later date, and a small stone-built galley landing east of the bailey.

In the novel, I refer to an 'oubliette' inside Dounarwyse broch. This is a basement room or dungeon in a Medieval castle—also known as a 'bottle dungeon'—that is only accessible through a small hole or hatch in a high ceiling. The name 'oubliette' comes from the French word *oublier*, which means 'to forget'.

During THE LAIRD'S WICKED GAME, we jump to Castle Coeffin on the Isle of Lismore for a couple of key scenes with Ramsay and Tormod. Located in Loch Linnhe, in Argyll, on the west coast of Scotland, the castle was built in the 13th century, probably by the MacDougalls of Lorn—but these days, it's a ruin. It's thought to have been built on the site of a Viking fortress. The name 'Coeffin' is believed to come from 'Caifen', who was a Danish prince. The story goes that his sister supposedly haunted the castle until her remains were taken back to be buried beside her lover in Norway.

Did you know that the Scottish Gaelic name for a resident of Mull is a *Muileach* (plural: *Muilich*)?

When Rae and Kylie get up to their shenanigans, they try out the '69' sexual position. There have been plenty of names used for this over the years, however, I used the French term for it: *soixante-neuf*. This was likely a little early for the usage, although in the 1790s, this term began to be more popular and it appeared in the 'Whore's Catechisms' in France.

DIVE INTO MY BACKLIST!

Check out my printable reading order list on my website:
https://www.jaynecastel.com/printable-reading-list

ABOUT THE AUTHOR

Multi-award-winning author Jayne Castel writes epic Historical and Fantasy Romance. Her vibrant characters, richly researched historical settings, and action-packed adventure romance transport readers to forgotten times and imaginary worlds.

Jayne is the author of a number of best-selling series. A hopeless romantic in love with all things Scottish, she writes romances set in both Dark Ages and Medieval Scotland, and Romantasy with a Celtic vibe.

When she's not writing, Jayne is reading (and re-reading) her favorite authors, cooking Italian feasts, and going on long walks with her husband. She's from New Zealand but now lives in Edinburgh, Scotland.

Connect with Jayne online:
www.jaynecastel.com
www.facebook.com/JayneCastelRomance
https://www.instagram.com/jaynecastelauthor/
Email: **contact@jaynecastel.com**